A VENETIAN ESCAPADE

The Continental Capers of Melody Chesterton Book 1

Sarah F. Noel

To my dear sort of cousin and loyal reader, Judi.

CONTENTS

FOREWORD

This book is written using British English spelling. e.g. dishonour instead of dishonor, realise instead of realize.

British spelling aside, while every effort has been made to proofread this thoroughly, typos do creep in. If you find any, I'd greatly appreciate a quick email to report them at sarahfnoelauthor@gmail.com

CHAPTER 1

May 1, 1911

"I do hope that I fare better than Miss Lucy Honeychurch on her first day in Florence."

"Who is Miss Lucy Honeychurch? One of your snooty friends, I presume," Rat said dismissively.

Dear Diary, is there anything more infuriating than an older brother? While I love Rat dearly, his lack of interest in anything that doesn't pertain to his work is infuriating. Though, I cannot argue with him about the young women in my social circle; they are snooty. Or at least they are towards him. I have been adopted as something of a curiosity thanks to Tabby Cat and Wolfie, to say nothing of Granny. She would accept nothing less than that I be treated as an equal, even if I am not, really. However, the way they all look down their nose at Rat just because he has a job is horrible. Nevertheless, I cannot believe that he does not know who Lucy Honeychurch is. Certainly, she is the perfect heroine for me to emulate during this trip. Even though I am going to Venice and not Florence, I can only hope to experience similar adventures and love. Yes, Dear Diary, I do know that A Room with a View *is only a book, but what a book! I consider it to be my Baedeker.*

Looking over at Mary sitting quietly in the corner of the carriage, Melody Chesterton considered whether Mary would be up to playing the role of spinster cousin and chaperone, Miss Charlotte Bartlett, like in *A Room with a View*. Mary had taken care of Melody since she first came to live at Chesterton House as a four-year-old. First nursery maid, then lady's maid, now more companion and confidante, Mary had been little more than sixteen when she had first met the charming and precocious little girl, and so was only just thirty years old. Still, as far as eighteen-year-old Melody was concerned, Mary qualified as a spinster. While there was no doubt that Mary was less fussy and absurd than Charlotte Bartlett, she was as beholden to the Chestertons as Miss Bartlett was to her cousin, Lucy Honeychurch, so the analogy worked well enough.

"Miss Lucy Honeychurch is my role model for a visit to Italy," Melody announced.

"Your role model?" Rat rolled his eyes. "What characteristics does someone need to be an appropriate role model for the headstrong, wilful Melody Chesterton?"

Melody screwed up her face and stuck her tongue out. Big brothers really were the worst.

"Is that how you intend to take Venetian society by storm? Making silly faces?"

"I have no more interest in taking Venetian society by storm than I had London society. I know what Tabby Cat wishes, and I am truly grateful for all the opportunities she has given to me. However, Granny agrees with me that there is so much more a young woman can achieve in 1911 than to marry well."

Rat chuckled. It was hard to envision the Dowager Countess of Pembroke as a champion for women's rights. Rat remembered all too well the woman's comments only the year before when the suffragettes clashed with police outside Parliament in the "Black Friday" incident. Her exact phrase was, "I cannot imagine why these women believe that behaviour such as that gives anyone confidence that they can be entrusted with the vote." There had then been a long debate, with Melody taking the side of the suffragettes in a full-throated endorsement of their methods and Tabitha trying to stake out the middle ground and keep the peace.

The dowager had been persuaded to move back into Chesterton House two years earlier when she suffered some health setbacks that worried the extended family. They had done their collective best to persuade the old woman that she wouldn't be giving up her independence even if she were no longer living alone. It was only once she was assured that her beloved butler, Manning, despite his advanced years, would be welcome to continue to care for her needs that she was finally convinced. Since then, Rat had noted that conversations at many of the family meals he attended seemed to come back around to women's rights in one way or another. It wasn't always his sister and the dowager at odds; it was as often Milady Tabby Cat, Lady Pembroke, who seemed uncomfortable with the changes the new century had brought.

Melody interrupted his wool-gathering. "I really would have imagined that Tabby Cat, of all people, would understand that there is more to a young woman's life than the Season and a good marriage. I have heard enough of her stories about how her mother pushed her into marrying the previous Earl of Pembroke, and Cousin Lily has told me how supportive Tabby Cat was when she wanted to skip her Season in favour of her studies."

Of course, that was a highly edited version of what had happened; the then Lady Lily had been obliged to marry a pliable viscount in order to persuade her family that having a Season was unnecessary. Nevertheless, Rat acknowledged that Melody's larger point was a good one: it was baffling that Tabitha, Lady Pembroke, a woman who had thumbed her nose at society with her involvement in murder investigations and had poked it in the eye with her refusal to leave Chesterton House when her deceased husband's cousin had ascended to the earldom, was now such an advocate of following the norms of aristocratic society.

Melody continued to bicker with Rat until Mary could no longer bear it and interjected, "Miss Melody, I believe that luncheon is now being served. Perhaps we should go through and eat. We will be arriving in Venice in two hours."

"Yes, Melly, go through with Mary. I have a few papers I need to read, and then I will join you. But don't wait for me," Rat said, catching Mary's eye in a moment of shared affection for the young woman but also exasperation. Apart from anything else, Rat needed time to reflect, and peace and tranquillity were rare when Melody was around.

Even though he was only four years older than his little sister, the young man had a maturity about him borne of his hardscrabble early life on the streets of Whitechapel. These hardships were exacerbated further when his parents died, and the then seven-year-old found himself responsible for his younger sister's wellbeing. It had been almost fourteen years since Rat had needed to worry about where Melody was going to sleep and where her next meal might come from, and yet he still carried the memory of the weight of the incessant anxiety of those early years on his shoulders. This early burden often surfaced as the world-weariness of a parent who shakes their head at the frivolity of the young.

"Boring papers. Boring work! Why are you always so boring these days, Rat? Come on, Mary, let us go. I am hungry and so bored of this carriage." The young woman pouted prettily. Of course, with her rich auburn hair, perfect porcelain skin, delicate features and bright blue eyes, it was easy for Melody to make most facial expressions prettily.

Finally, Rat was alone in the carriage. He had lied. There were no papers to read; he merely needed time to think. This was Rat's first official solo assignment as part of the Foreign Section of the British Secret Service Bureau. He had been studying under Lord Langley's tutelage to work in British Intelligence since he was eight years old. Langley had promised Tabitha that he would prepare the then-young boy for the safe, desk-bound work of cryptology. While Rat had shown a great aptitude for codebreaking, he had become restless recently and had yearned for the more adventurous fieldwork.

By the time that the Secret Service Bureau was formed in 1909 as a response to Britain's concerns about increasing foreign espionage, particularly from the increasingly warmongering Germany, Rat was old enough that Tabitha no longer had a say over his activities. When Lord Langley had been asked by the head of the Foreign Section himself, Sir Mansfield Cumming, to join the bureau, Rat felt ready to join him and move into a new phase of his career.

Of course, no one in his extended family besides Lord Langley had any idea about Rat's new assignment. As far as Tabitha, Wolf, the dowager, and Melody knew, he was merely accompanying his sister on her first tour of Europe. Langley, who adored Melody and had nurtured an avuncular relationship since she was a small child, was not initially persuaded that Rat should use this trip as a cover for his intelligence work. He was loathe to put Melody in potential danger in any way. It was only when the dowager had finally accepted that chaperoning Melody was beyond her physical capabilities these days and suggested that Rat go instead that Langley was finally convinced what a perfect cover it was for espionage. However, he also had to be convinced that Melody would be blithely unaware of Rat's role and, more to the point, perfectly safe.

Now that he had some peace and quiet, Rat considered the assignment ahead of him. Evidence of German espionage had grown exponentially in Britain over the past few years. Recently, Lord Langley had told him about one of Milady Tabby Cat and Wolf's first investigations together, which had been, at least in part, about stolen naval plans and German spies. Then, such incidents were relatively rare; these days, they were almost commonplace.

War was looming as an almost inevitable conclusion to the increasing German belligerence on display across Europe. While Germany was certainly not the only country jostling for dominance, there was little doubt that, under the leadership of Kaiser Wilhelm II, Germany had embarked on an aggressive military build-up, particularly of its navy. It was evident that the Kaiser sought to challenge Britain's imperial power and expand Germany's colonies and influence overseas.

Rat's assignment was simple in many ways: he had a variety of Italians, Germans, and even a few Englishmen with whom he was to ingratiate himself and watch closely. Prime

Minister Henry Asquith and his Liberal Party were increasingly worried about the relationship between Italy, Austria-Hungary and Germany. The Triple Alliance between the three countries, signed in 1882, was primarily defensive and often barely held together in the intervening years. Nevertheless, as war loomed over the continent, there were worries it might develop into something more threatening.

This assignment was vague, but Rat knew enough to realise that it was also potentially pivotal to Britain's understanding of the competing European powers. Given this, Rat couldn't help but be plagued by self-doubt. Despite his assurances to Lord Langley back in London that he was ready for such an assignment, was he? He was only twenty-one; was he really prepared to tangle with seasoned, Machiavellian foreign operatives?

Rat shook his head and said aloud, "I'm ready. I've been training for this since I was eight years old." Despite the self-assured words, the doubts continued to nag at him. Finally, deciding that he needed to stop himself from dwelling on all that could go wrong, Rat stood and went to find Melody and Mary in the dining car.

Entering the luxurious dining car, Rat saw Melody and Mary sitting at a table by the window in the middle of the carriage. Melody was writing in that infernal diary again!

Dear Diary, I cannot wait to arrive in Venice. I have read The Wings of a Dove *twice in order to prepare myself. Nevertheless, I am quite sure that no book can do justice to the beauty and majesty of the city. I have brought my paints and easel with me, but I doubt that my limited skills will suffice to capture Venice. I wish that Bear had come with us; his paintings always manage to capture the soul of a place so well.*

Mary is scowling at me for writing. Apparently, well-bred young women do not do such things at the dining table. Now, she can see me glancing at her and is scowling even more.

"Miss Melody, how many times do I have to tell you to put your diary away? You are a young woman now and should not need to be scolded about such things."

Melody smirked, "You know, Mary, now that I have come into my fortune from Granny, I can do whatever I want, including writing in my diary while I dine."

"Money, no matter how much, is not a license for poor manners."

"You sound like Granny now. That is precisely the kind of thing she would say."

"Then that should suffice to inform you that I am correct." Mary shook her head as she spoke and sighed. She loved the young woman as if she were her own child. However, as the years passed, their relationship had changed to the point where the older woman now felt she had lost any authority she might once have possessed. She was not a mother to the girl or even a maternal surrogate. The two Lady Pembrokes shared that role. She acted as a maid sometimes, a companion at others, but increasingly seemed to be relegated to the role of silly older spinster aunt who was loved but not respected. Indeed, if Mary had ever read *A Room with a View,* she might have recognised much of herself in the character of Charlotte Bartlett.

Turning back to her diary, Melody continued to write.

Diary, there is the most attractive man on this train. I have spotted him multiple times since we boarded it in Milan. Perhaps he is even thirty years old. Mary would say that he is too old for me, but I know for a fact that Tabby Cat's first husband was elderly when she married at my age, and even Wolfie is eight years older than she is. I am so sick of the men my age – at least the ones in society. Thank goodness I did not have to finish the Season out.

Melody would have kept writing, even once the food arrived if Rat hadn't approached the table. Despite all of her complaints about older brothers, Melody had the highest regard for hers. She knew enough of their history before moving to Mayfair to understand, at least somewhat, what her brother had done to ensure that she was safe. Melody also had a vague sense that he might not have chosen a life on the outskirts of aristocratic society if it hadn't been for a wish to see her raised as a lady.

She glanced up from her diary as he sat across from her, next to Mary. The disapproving look on his face sufficed for her to put down her pen and move her diary for the food that was being brought to the table.

CHAPTER 2

Approaching the Venezia Santa Lucia train station, Melody had caught glimpses of what she assumed was Venice. In fact, what she was really looking at were the many small islands, such as San Michele and Murano, that dotted the Venetian Lagoon. Just as the train was coming into the station, Melody was able to see the northern edge of the Cannaregio district, one of the city's six sestieri, as the Venetians called them.

Descending from the train, Melody was too impatient to wait for Mary and Rat or to worry about their luggage. Instead, she almost ran down the platform in a very unladylike way and burst out of the station. None of her reading about the city or studying paintings and even photographs of Venice had prepared her to exit the building and find herself confronted by the Grand Canal.

The first thing that struck Melody was how bustling the area surrounding the train station was. It was not so very different from the streets around King's Cross station, with Venetians hurrying about their business, street vendors hawking their wares, and gawking tourists clogging up the Fondamenta Santa Lucia that ran up each side of the Grand Canal.

As far as Melody could see, beautiful, colourful buildings with a distinctive, ornate architectural style lined the canal. Perhaps the most striking thing about the view was the myriad of long, thin boats. They were gondolas, with their gondoliers standing and using a single, long oar to steer and propel the boats. All the gondoliers were dressed in similar outfits: striped shirts, either black and white or blue and white, dark trousers and wide straw hats adorned with colourful ribbons.

Melody thought she could have stared at the view in front of her forever.

"It is glorious, is it not?" a suave, English-accented voice said from slightly behind her.

Startled out of her reverie, Melody turned to see the very handsome stranger from the train just slightly behind her. Up close, he was even more attractive than he had seemed from a distance. Despite his very cultured English accent, with the modulated lilt and rounded vowels that indicated an upper-class upbringing and education, the man had a distinctively foreign look about him. His olive skin tone and jet-black hair were far more indicative of the Mediterranean than of the home counties. Apart from perfectly even features marked by the most patrician of noses, the most striking thing about the man was his startling green eyes, whose colour seemed almost unnatural. In an unfair endowment of natural charms, those eyes were framed by thick, dark, curling lashes. Melody's first thought was what she would give to have similar eyes.

Melody realised that rather than staring at the man with her mouth agape, she should be answering him. "It is, sir," was all she could stammer out.

"The Conte Alessandro Foscari di Villa Foscari, at your service," the man said, executing a neat little bow.

Melody tried to remember what Granny had said about introductions by strange men. She had never paid much attention during the tedious etiquette and deportment lessons. Still, she vaguely remembered something about it being improper for a man to introduce himself directly to a woman without a formal introduction by a family member or close acquaintance. She also remembered thinking at the time how silly such a rule was.

Finally, deciding that any such social rules were from a different century and did not apply to a young, modern woman in 1911, Melody boldly held out her hand and said, "Miss Melody

Chesterton. It is very nice to meet you, Conte Foscari."

The man took the outstretched hand, raised it to his lips, then held it long past when it was socially acceptable to do so and said in a sultry voice, "Please, call me Alessandro." This was the sight that met Mary and Rat as they hurried out of the station, a porter in tow with their luggage, anxious to find where Melody had disappeared to.

"Melody!" Rat said sternly, "Why did you disappear like that? We had no idea where you had gone to." Then, realising the scene he had interrupted, he said in an almost paternal tone that was belied by his very youthful appearance, "And who is the gentleman holding your hand?"

Realising that Alessandro, as she was already thinking of him, still held her outstretched hand in his, Melody snatched it back and, in a flustered voice, said, "Conte Foscari, I would like to introduce you to my brother, Mr Matthew Sandworth, and my companion, Miss Mary Lark."

"I am sorry, I must have misheard you; I thought that you had introduced yourself as Miss Chesterton."

Rat sighed; he knew this was going to cause much confusion. He and Melody rarely went out in society together in London, so their different last names were seldom an issue.

Melody trilled some notes of laughter that sounded almost flirtatious to her older brother's ear and said, "Oh, that is because I am the ward of the Earl and Countess of Pembroke and my brother of the Earl of Langley."

"Melody, I hardly think that Conte Foscari needs or wants to hear our life stories," Rat snapped. Melody was entirely too open and trusting. How could they even be sure that this so-called conte was who he said he was? Rat thought there was something very cunning about the man, who he immediately distrusted. Rat was very conscious of his small stature, at a little over five foot seven. That this Foscari character was tall, broad-shouldered and exuded an air of great self-confidence did not endear him further to the younger man.

With an amused gleam in his eye, Alessandro Foscari gave

another neat little bow, "Miss Lark, Mr Sandworth, my pleasure. May I assist you in hiring a gondola?"

His voice now strained to the very edge of politeness, Rat said, "Thank you, sir. However, we do not need any assistance. We are being met."

"Then I will bid you all farewell." Turning back to Melody, Alessandro said, "It was a pleasure meeting you, Miss Chesterton. I am sure we will see more of each other; Venetian society is quite small."

As soon as Alessandro was out of earshot, Mary said in the exasperated voice that Melody knew all too well, "Miss Melody, you should know better than to talk to strange men. This may not be London, but the same standards apply, or should. It was not proper for him to introduce himself to you."

Melody laughed, "That is a stupid rule in England and just as stupid, no, maybe more stupid in Venice. I do not know a soul here; if I do not allow people to introduce themselves to me, how will I get to know anyone?"

"You will get to know people, the right sort of people, in the same way you do in England: in an appropriate social setting where Lady Bainbridge will make an introduction," Mary said primly. Melody sniffed contemptuously in reply.

Rat shared a look with Mary and tried a different approach. "Melody, no one wants to prevent you from getting to know people and having fun, but you know how reluctant Milady Tabby Cat was to let you come, particularly in the middle of the Season. We do not need to give her any more reason for concern, do we?"

"Tabby Cat will not know what I do unless you and Mary tattle on me, will she?" Melody pointed out.

It was clear that this argument was going nowhere and was entirely inappropriate for a public thoroughfare where anyone might overhear them. This was not the first impression that Rat wished his sister to make on Venetian society. Instead, he turned and looked around for the gondolas that Lady Bainbridge had promised to send. Unfortunately, all the gondolas and gondoliers looked the same to him.

Rat was saved when one of the many dark-haired men in straw hats waved and called out, "Signor Sandworth? Buongiorno."

Rat walked over and asked, "Inglese?"

"Sì I speak the English. I am having the name, Giovanni. Are you the Mr Sandworth?"

"Yes, I am Mr Sandworth." Lord Langley had legally made Rat his ward when the boy was ten, and he had now been using the name Sandworth long enough that it no longer felt jarring to him not to be using his father's family name, Berry. "I assume that Lady Bainbridge sent you to collect us?"

"Sì, sì. The Lady Bainbridge, she sent me and Pietro," at this, Giovanni pointed to the gondola next to his. "Pietro, he not speaks the Inglese so good as I do. He will took all the many, many bags you have, and I will take Mr Sandworth and la signorinas."

At this, Giovanni gestured to the porter and said something very quickly in the Venetian dialect. Rat had been studying Italian since the trip to Venice had first been proposed, but understanding the dialect was beyond his capabilities. The porter passed all the bags into Pietro's gondola and then gestured that he would help hand Rat, Mary and Melody down.

Rat hadn't been on many boats in his twenty-one years, and Mary had been on none. Of course, neither had Melody, but she approached the gondola as she did most new things, as an exciting adventure. Mary was less excited, and while she didn't say as such, her white-knuckled grip on the gondola's side made her fear clear enough.

The gondola was not large, and most of its length was not used for seating. There was a pair of comfortable, well-padded benches facing each other with barely three feet between them, where Mary, Rat and Melody settled themselves. Giovanni stood directly behind the bench that Melody and Mary sat on and used his long oar to push off from the side of the canal.

Melody's delight at Venice only increased as Giovanni rowed

them down the Grand Canal. She had never seen architecture like this before. The intricate stonework, ornate windows and numerous balconies were stunning. Even though many buildings had a slightly decrepit feel to them, that somehow only added to the charm. Melody thought it the most beautiful place she had ever been – even though the list of cities she had visited was limited.

Dear Diary, I am trying to write this while also not missing the view; Venice is the most beautiful city, and it is almost overwhelming trying to take it all in. It was a little scary getting into the gondola, but now that we are seated, it feels surprisingly stable. Though you might not be able to tell this by the look of terror on Mary's face. Meanwhile, Rat is sitting in front of me, glowering about that charming Conte Foscari. What was I supposed to do? Ignore the man when he introduced himself? I suppose that Granny might have put him down in the cutting manner she does so well, but that just is not who I am. Certainly, it is not who I wish to be on this trip."

"Oh Mary, look over there," Melody said, pointing to a building that added to its charms with beautiful Gothic windows and elegant pointed arches. "Is that not the most beautiful building?"

"Si, signorina, this is the home of the Lady Bainbridge. Palazzo Loredan dell'Ambasciatore. Where I bring you."

Melody clapped her hands together in glee. When their Venice plans had initially been discussed, Melody had not been particularly enthusiastic about being a guest of Lady Bainbridge's. The woman was an acquaintance of Lady Jameson, Tabitha's mother. The very few times that Melody had met Lady Jameson, she had found her cold and supercilious. It was hard to imagine that any friend of hers would be a pleasant person to be around. However, now that Lady Bainbridge's beautiful palazzo was in sight, Melody felt that there was much overbearing condescension she might tolerate to stay in such a home.

As Giovanni pulled the gondola close to the palazzo steps, a very handsome young man dressed as a footman might be in London opened a door above them. Standing just behind him slightly was an older man who, at least by his dress, seemed to be the butler.

The handsome footman held out his hand to help Melody from the gondola. "Grazie," she said shyly.

"Prego," the young man answered with a smile.

As Melody moved into the palazzo to allow Rat and Mary room to disembark, the butler said in excellent, if heavily accented English, "Welcome, Miss Chesterton. It is a pleasure to welcome you to Palazzo Loredan dell'Ambasciatore. I am the maggiordomo, what you would call the butler. My name is Rossi. Lady Bainbridge is in the salotto. I know that you have had a long trip. Would you prefer to freshen up first?"

Melody knew that the correct answer was that yes, she would prefer to freshen up. Granny would have been appalled at the idea of greeting one's host with the dust and grime of a trip on one's hands. However, Granny wasn't there, and Rat would hardly be a stickler for such niceties. While Mary might be, she was also too aware of her status as a servant to contradict her mistress in front of other servants. Comfortable in her ability to flout social norms and eager to meet their hostess, Melody indicated that she was happy to be shown through to the salotto immediately.

To Melody's eighteen-year-old eye, anyone older than Rat was old. Sometimes, she might even lump her brother into that group, though that had more to do with his seriousness than anything else. However, in Lady Bainbridge's case, it was a fair judgment; she was old. Very old. In fact, Lady Bainbridge was eighty-five and so almost as old as the dowager countess. The woman had led an interesting life and had moved to Venice forty years earlier. To the extent anyone still gossiped about her in London after so many decades away, they whispered that she became the lover of an Italian aristocrat who left her the palazzo on his death.

While Lady Bainbridge had been described to Melody as Lady Jameson's friend, the truth was that the two women had been introduced to each other many years before and had been only extremely casual correspondents over the years. In reality, Lady Bainbridge might more accurately be referred to as Tabitha's friend. She had only met Lady Bainbridge once as a very young woman, just before her coming out. The older woman visited London very infrequently and, on that occasion, had stayed with Tabitha's family at their estate for some weeks. The young girl and the eccentric, independent woman had formed an immediate and enduring bond which had been maintained through a twenty-year correspondence. When considering Melody's proposed stay in Venice, Tabitha knew that her older friend would appreciate the girl's curiosity and sense of adventure while enforcing suitable boundaries for the headstrong, young heiress.

Melody's first thought on entering the salotto was that it looked more like a museum. She had grown up in a grand house in Mayfair and had been in some beautifully furnished drawing rooms in her eighteen years but never seen anything as ornate as the room she now found herself in. There was a glorious fresco painted on the ceiling, and equally magnificent paintings hung on the walls. Much of the furniture was richly gilded, with intricate gold leaf embellishments that might have seemed excessive in another location. Perhaps the most spectacular part of the room was the view out onto the Grand Canal.

In the middle of this stately room sat an old woman dressed quite bizarrely, at least by the standards of elderly women in England's upper circles. While the dowager countess, Lady Pembroke, insisted on sticking with fashion from the previous century, Lady Bainbridge's dress had a very modern silhouette, from what Melody could tell. However, the dress was in a bright shade of blue that would have been considered quite outrageous, particularly for a woman of her age, in the drawing rooms of Mayfair. As if that were not shocking enough, she had a fuchsia turban sitting atop snow-white hair that was cut in a bob that sat just above her shoulders. The only woman Melody had ever seen who cut her hair into such a style was Granny's odd friend, Tuchinsky, and she also wore men's clothes.

Lady Bainbridge held out both hands to Melody, "Come child,

let me see you. I will not apologise for not standing; one of the few perks of old age is that one can remain seated." Melody approached the woman and allowed her to clasp her hands. "My my, but you are a beauty. There is something in your face that reminds me of Tabitha as a young woman." Lady Bainbridge paused, "Of course, I realise that any resemblance must be purely coincidental. Nevertheless, it is there."

This was not the first time that Melody had heard such a statement. Her similarity to Tabitha had been remarked on when Melody started coming out into society. There had been whispers that Melody was Tabitha's illegitimate daughter, given out to a foster mother at birth but then taken back a few years later. Of course, such a story conveniently overlooked the existence of Rat, a brother four years older. However, the most titillating of society gossip rarely needed to be logically defensible. It was only when such rumours first came to the dowager's attention that they were finally put to rest in the most definitive way possible.

Melody curtsied prettily. "It is lovely to meet you, Lady Bainbridge. Tabby Cat, I mean, Tabitha, speaks so highly of you."

"Tabby Cat? Is that your name for Tabitha?" Lady Bainbridge barked out, laughing in a rather unladylike manner. "How charming. I believe you are going to have to call me something similarly charming."

Then, turning towards Rat, who bowed, Lady Bainbridge said, "And you must be Melody's brother, Matthew."

"Indeed, Lady Bainbridge. Thank you so much for allowing us to stay with you in your beautiful home."

Lady Bainbridge waved her hand somewhat dismissively, "Yes, it is rather glorious, even if it is falling down around my ears. Marco was a dear to leave it to me. However, he was also a terror to leave me with such an obligation. Never mind; I will be dead soon enough, and then its upkeep will be someone else's problem."

They sat for a while, chatting with Lady Bainbridge, bringing her up to date on the comings and goings of London's finest.

Finally, with the help of an ornate, silver-topped cane, she stood. "You must wish to wash off the grime of your journey and get settled, and I have need of my afternoon nap. I must be at my best for the soiree this evening."

Melody and Rat exchanged looks. What soiree was this? Seeing their confusion, Lady Bainbridge said breezily, "Just a little dinner to welcome you both to Venice. In its way, Venetian society is as rigid as London's. I would like dear Melody here to meet some of the people who can help smooth her entry."

Melody tried her best not to sigh out loud. Had she escaped the Season in London only to be thrown into its equally boring and formal Italian cousin? She wanted to emulate Lucy Honeychurch and wander the city, experiencing the true Venice, not sit around in fancy houses making polite small talk. At home, Melody might have expressed such feelings, but she had been schooled well enough by Tabitha and the dowager that she inclined her head and expressed a forced delight at the evening ahead.

Mary had gone ahead to the large, sunlit bedroom assigned to Melody and had almost finished unpacking by the time the young woman entered. Mary knew Melody perhaps better than anyone did. She knew every pout, sigh, and sulky expression. "What has happened, Miss Melody? You look as if you have the weight of the world on your shoulders."

"There is to be a dinner party tonight in our honour."

Mary stopped arranging the brushes and hair accessories on the dressing table and turned to the young woman who was part mistress, part charge. "And isn't that a good thing? I'm sure that Lady Bainbridge only thought to introduce you into society."

"Exactly! Society! I do not wish to spend my days and evenings having the same boring conversations that I was forced to endure in London."

"Perhaps the conversations will be less boring with an Italian accent," Mary teased. "After all, you seemed quite taken with that handsome young man outside of the station, and wasn't he a count or something?"

Melody blushed. "Who says I was taken with him? He introduced himself, and I merely reciprocated. Nothing more." Mary didn't reply, but her raised eyebrows and pursed mouth clearly indicated, "If you say so."

CHAPTER 3

*D*ear Diary, I did manage to nap after all. We had an early start this morning from Milan, and travelling is quite tiring. Mary has chosen a lovely green silk dress for me to wear, and it will go beautifully with the pearl and emerald necklace that Granny gave me for my birthday.

Diary, I do hope that not everyone tonight is old. Lady Bainbridge seems like a dear; she even reminds me of Granny somewhat. However, the opportunities for adventure, to say nothing of romance, will be extremely limited if I cannot mingle with people closer to my age.

Comparing the elderly Lady Bainbridge to the dowager countess caused Melody to put down her pen and reflect on the even older woman left behind in London. As excited as Melody had been to travel to Europe, her one concern was leaving the older Lady Pembroke, "Granny." As much as her mind and wit were as rapier sharp as ever, there was no doubt that she was physically quite frail, and Melody worried that something might happen while she was gone.

For her part, the dowager's answer when Melody had cautiously mentioned her concerns was entirely predictable, "I have no plans to die anytime soon. Do not waste a moment of your young life worrying about my longevity. Go and see the world and have your adventures. There is an excellent chance that I will still be here when you return. I do not trust Asquith at all, and from what I hear, there is a movement afoot to take away power from the House of Lords. Whatever next? Now is not the time for someone as influential as I still am to up and die. "

Melody shook her head, determined not to dwell on what

might happen while she was gone. Granny was right; she had adventures ahead of her, and Melody intended to embrace them wholeheartedly.

Finally, dressed in her new Worth gown, wearing her new necklace and with her thick, wavy auburn hair expertly styled by Mary, Melody stood and looked at herself in the full-length mirror on the wall in her room.

"What do you think, Mary?" she asked, spinning around.

"You look beautiful, Miss Melody. You do the family proud." Mary paused and then said in a quieter, cautionary tone, "Just be sure that your behaviour tonight matches your outfit."

"What do you mean by that?" Melody challenged, though she already had a sense of what Mary meant.

"Just that you look like a sophisticated, young woman of society. Don't ruin the effect by being a hoyden."

Melody laughed, "Hoyden? Where on earth did you find that word? Was that something that Granny called me?" This had, in fact, been the case, so Mary said nothing. Melody continued, "Do not worry so, Mary. My behaviour will be all that it should be."

Mary's expression indicated scepticism, but she said kindly, "I know that you long for adventures, but that is not at odds with being accepted into the best circles in Venetian society. The dowager countess would be the first to lecture you on its value."

"Ha! Granny? All she ever talks about is how mind-numbingly dull the aristocracy is. Since she moved back into Chesterton House, she has used this as an excuse to refuse all society invitations, saying that if she is too infirm to live alone, she cannot then be expected to spend her last precious few months listening to the likes of Lady Willis drone on. Of course, she does somehow find the strength to continue to meet with her Ladies of KB."

Melody smirked as she said this last part; it had long been one of the dowager's many eccentricities that she dined monthly with a colourful group of madams she had met during an early solo investigation. One of her conditions for agreeing to move to Chesterton House had been that she would be allowed to host lunch there when her turn came around. While Tabitha had met the Ladies of KB and understood the charm they held for the old woman, nevertheless, the prospect of the Earl of Pembroke hosting such a group had given her serious pause. Of course, the dowager had her way in the end.

A few minutes later, Melody entered the palazzo's sala, the main formal receiving room on the first floor. Rat had been the first one down that evening and was standing with a glass of prosecco in his hand by the room's floor-to-ceiling windows that looked out onto the Grand Canal. This room was even grander than the salotto, if that were possible. It was also longer, stretching most of the length of the palazzo. Rat had no idea how many guests were expected that evening, but certainly, the room could accommodate a large group easily.

Intellectually, Rat knew that his little sister was a grown woman now. However, memories of those early years of caring for and protecting Melody were still firmly lodged in the deepest parts of his heart and soul. It was hard to see her as an independent woman, ready and eager to take on the world. Despite all this, when Melody first entered the room, Rat was taken aback; when had she transformed from a gangly little girl in pinafore dresses into this beautiful, radiant, and sophisticated young woman?

In her new Worth gown, with her hair gathered up high and just a few tendrils artfully loose around her neck, for the first time, Rat saw the woman Melody was becoming instead of Melly, the child. Rat's heart was bursting with pride, even as it clenched at the realisation that his sister was ready for her adventures and that his role as protector was unwanted and probably no longer needed. The weight of this realisation sat heavily with him. Melody caught him looking at her and smiled shyly, eager for her brother's approval.

Melody came further into the room and joined Rat by the windows. "You look beautiful, Melody," Rat said, holding out his hands. His sister noticed that he didn't use her nickname. Melody was both happy at this evidence of Rat's acceptance that she was no longer a child and a little sad at this inevitable change in their relationship. Even though they had lived in different houses for the past fourteen years, Rat and Melody had seen each other almost daily. As much as he could be an annoying, bossy, overly protective older brother, Melody loved him more than anyone else in the world. She barely remembered their time living on the streets of Whitechapel, but what she did remember was how safe her brother had managed to make her feel.

Putting her hands into Rat's outstretched ones, Melody said, "And you look very handsome and debonair, Matthew." They were not Rat and Melly anymore, at least to the rest of the world.

The next thirty minutes were a whirlwind of introductions and handshaking. While Lady Bainbridge seemed to have invited many of the great and good of Venetian high society, some foreigners were also in attendance. Italian was being spoken all around Rat, though he would hear some occasional smatterings of English and, in one instance, French. Rat could understand very little of the Italian being spoken and he suspected that many of those present were speaking in the Venetian dialect.

"Hard to understand what they're all saying, is it not?" A cultured, English voice said. Looking towards the source of the words, Rat saw a young man, perhaps a few years older than himself, who couldn't look more English; a fair complexion with floppy, reddish blonde hair that the man had made an effort to oil back, but which still fell into his eyes. The face was open, and the pale blue eyes, framed by reddish lashes, crinkled as the man smiled.

"Xander Ashby," the man said, holding out a hand. "I work at the British consulate."

"Matthew Sandworth," Rat said, shaking the hand. "I am chaperoning my sister." As he said this, Rat pointed towards Melody, who was deep in conversation with Lady Bainbridge and a patrician-looking man with silver hair and an impressive Roman nose.

"That is your sister?" Xander asked eagerly. "I noticed her

as soon as I entered the room and have been waiting for an opportunity to be introduced. She is quite the most beautiful woman here."

Rat wasn't sure how he felt about this stranger discussing his sister in such a manner. On the other hand, Rat's overall impression of Xander was of a friendly, overly excited puppy. It was hard to imagine the young man taking liberties with Melody.

"Then let me introduce you," Rat said.

He took his new friend over to Melody and made the introduction. "Mr Xander Ashby, let me introduce my sister, Miss Melody Chesterton." Xander looked momentarily confused by the different surname to the one Rat had used to introduce himself, but then seemed to shake himself out of it and took Melody's outstretched hand.

"Miss Chesterton, what a great pleasure," the young man gushed. He so reminded Rat of a friendly, over-eager dog, perhaps a Labrador Retriever, that he half expected Xander's tongue to loll out of his mouth and for him to start panting in anticipation.

For her part, Melody observed the young man with amusement. She knew that she was pretty, perhaps even very pretty, and was used to the attention of young men charmed by her bright blue eyes, rosebud lips, and abundant wavy, auburn hair. Even so, Xander Ashby's eagerness stood out.

Retrieving her hand, Melody tried to control the twitching of her lips and said, "Likewise, Mr Ashby. Do you live in Venice?"

"I have been here for a year," Xander explained. "I work for Mr Burrows, His Majesty's Consul in Venice." Melody looked at the young man, who couldn't have been more than twenty-five and certainly seemed to lack a certain gravitas. It was hard to imagine such a man helping with important diplomatic work. Though, she reflected, it was likely that a consul had a large team of people helping him, and it was doubtful that this particular man was entrusted with the most important missions of The British Empire.

Xander continued, "Is this your first visit to Venice, Miss Chesterton?"

"It is my first overseas trip," Melody admitted.

"Well, you chose the right place to begin your travels. Venice is the most beautiful of cities." Xander paused, then added shyly, "It would be my honour to be your tour guide."

Xander Ashby was quite attractive if one looked past the overeagerness. There were certainly worse things than being escorted around Venice by a handsome young admirer. "That would be delightful, Mr Ashby," Melody replied. As she answered, Melody glanced over at Rat; would he object to this stranger squiring his sister around Venice? Had he envisioned this role for himself?

As it happened, Xander Ashby had done Rat an enormous favour; he had a job to do, and one of his concerns had been how he might balance this with chaperoning Melody. As protective as Rat was towards his sister, he seriously doubted that Ashby would take any liberties. If Mary accompanied the pair, then Xander Ashby seemed to be as benign a male companion as Rat was likely to find. Certainly, as a guest of Lady Bainbridge's, it was reasonable to assume Ashby was a good sort. Rat made a mental note to double-check this assumption with their hostess later. Nevertheless, he saw no reason for concern and graced Melody with an approving smile.

"Then, perhaps I might be so bold as to suggest that we begin with the St Mark's Square and its Basilica tomorrow?"

Melody knew that there was no real reason to rush; she would have more than enough time to see all of Venice's glories. Nevertheless, she was naturally impatient and found it hard to resist such an offer.

Melody's back was towards the door, and she couldn't see any late arrivals. Just as she was about to accept Xander's offer, Melody saw his expression change. In a moment, it went from an eager-to-please Labrador Retriever to an alert, ready-to-attack German Shepherd. Melody was sure she was imagining it, but it even seemed as if his ears had perked up. Turning to see what on earth could account for such an extreme change, Melody found herself face-to-face with Conte Alessandro Foscari. My my, but she had forgotten just how mesmerising those green eyes were. He was also taller than she remembered.

"Miss Chesterton, what a delightful surprise to run into you so soon and looking so ravishing," Alessandro murmured in a voice that was sultry enough to make Melody blush and Rat glare.

"Conte Foscari," Melody stammered. She had never dealt with the flirtations of such a suave, older man.

"Alessandro. I insist that you call me Alessandro."

Rat stepped in immediately, "Conte Foscari, I am not sure what the etiquette is in Italy, but in Britain, a young lady of good character and family does not address a gentleman she does not know by his given name."

Not taking his eyes off Melody, Alessandro took her hand and said, "Then we shall just have to ensure that Miss Chesterton gets to know me. Well." With that, he lifted her hand to his mouth, bowed over it, and kissed it. Xander had taken her hand mere minutes before, but this felt entirely different. Even though the conte had performed a similar gesture when they had first met, that had been quite formal and perfunctory. This time, his lips lingered on her skin while he looked up into her eyes, almost hypnotising her with his gaze. Melody gave a little shiver. Alessandro noticed and stood, keeping hold of her hand and smiling with almost feline satisfaction.

Melody had forgotten that she had been in the middle of a conversation, forgotten even that she was at a party, in Venice. All she knew was that the most handsome, charming man she had ever met was holding her hand. Her reverie was interrupted abruptly, "Foscari, I should have known you'd worm your way into an invitation," Xander Ashby spat.

Finally, breaking his eye contact with Melody and releasing her hand, Alessandro looked up at the belligerent Englishman and replied, "Ashby. Burrows could not come and sent his lapdog in his place?"

The fact that Xander really did remind her of a puppy dog caused Melody to almost giggle at this put-down. As if to confirm the similarity, Xander growled, "Lady Bainbridge is an Englishwoman, and I am a countryman of hers, unlike some mongrel half-breed."

Alessandro laughed, "If you believe that you will wound me with your pathetic attempts at insults, you are sorely mistaken. Such slurs are no more than I heard throughout my years at Eton from other jumped-up sons of men with titles but no fortune to maintain them. You remind me of them. Though, from what I understand, Ashby, your father has neither fortune nor title these days. It was unfortunate that his uncle remarried and now has a new heir."

This airing of dirty laundry, while entertaining to a degree, was also far from appropriate at such a gathering and in front of strangers; Melody could only imagine what Granny would say about such an uncouth display. As if this suddenly occurred to Xander and Alessandro simultaneously, they turned towards Melody, almost at the same time, and began apologising.

"My dear Miss Chesterton, I am mortified that you had to witness this," Xander began.

"Indeed, my dear Miss Chesterton, I am ashamed that I allowed myself to be goaded in such a way, and by such a man," Alessandro proclaimed, holding his hands over his heart to emphasise how heartfelt such shame was.

Rat couldn't remember when he had last witnessed such a juvenile display by two grown men and was appalled by them both. Taking his sister's elbow firmly in his hand, he nodded at both men and said, "I believe there is someone Lady Bainbridge wishes to introduce Melody to."

As he led her towards the fireplace where Lady Bainbridge was now ensconced in a comfortable armchair, deep in discussion with another very old woman, Melody asked, "Who does Lady Bainbridge wish me to meet?"

"No one, but I could not allow you to stand there while those two – well, I was going to say gentlemen, but I don't think either one deserves that title – those two men preened their feathers and strutted around each other."

Melody laughed, "I found it quite amusing. Although, they are both lucky that Granny was not here to witness that."

"Indeed!" Rat agreed.

CHAPTER 4

*D*ear Diary, Mary said I should go to sleep, but I have far too much energy to even think of slumber. Why were none of the London parties I was ever forced to attend even half as much fun as this was? Perhaps it was because I did not have men vying for my attention there. Well, it was not that attention was not paid, but tonight, I worried that Xander might call Alessandro out. To be fair, while it is flattering to believe that I was the cause of their bickering, I believe that there is a deep-seated hatred between them. I wonder why.

It was quite delightful to have Alessandro flirt with me, even if he might only have been doing so to rile Xander up. And what of Mr Ashby? He really is quite handsome, in a very English way. He certainly seems eager for my company. A charming, attractive young man to escort me around Venice could be a delightful way to get to know the city.

Of course, Xander pales into consideration next to Alessandro. However, I suspect that he is one of those men who flirts as easily as he breathes. I have no illusions that there is any substance behind his words. I imagine that he has some dark, sultry Italian mistress with shiny, ebony ringlets and sparkling, heavily lashed eyes. Tabby Cat would be appalled if she heard me say such a thing – well-brought-up young women are not supposed to know about mistresses.

Rat dragged me away from the men, but Alessandro ended up sitting next to me at dinner – was that by design? I could see Xander shooting darts at him with his eyes through the entire meal. If Alessandro noticed, he certainly did not mention anything. He was a charming dinner companion, witty, intelligent and erudite. He *offered to show me some of the sights of Venice. Did I agree to go to St Mark's tomorrow with Xander? I cannot remember exactly where we left that plan now. I do not think that I agreed. However, it would be considered something of a social faux pas to take Alessandro up on his offer when Xander has the prior claim on my time. What do I do? Granny would know exactly the right way of solving this dilemma.*

Finally, Melody put away her diary and went to sleep. Her dreams were full of dark-haired men with roguish smiles.

The following morning, Melody woke late. The trip to Venice had been more exhausting than she was willing to acknowledge; it was hard to sleep deeply on trains. Lady Bainbridge's guest room was comfortable and its bed soft and pillowy. Once sleep came for Melody, it was many hours before it relinquished its hold.

Descending the next morning, Melody was led by Rossi to a small dining room where Lady Bainbridge was drinking coffee and breakfasting on a delicious-looking pastry. Rat was seated next to her, eating some cheese and cold meats. As Melody entered the room, they both looked up.

"Did you sleep well, my dear?" Lady Bainbridge asked. Melody nodded. Her hostess continued, "For myself, I am thrilled if I can get four hours of sleep these days. A heavy meal does not help. I should have shown more self-control; I know what those rich sauces do to me. However, I am unable to resist mushroom risotto and the way Venetians cook liver is sublime. In England, liver is rather looked down on as peasant food, but Fegato alla Veneziana has been elevated to the food of the gods. I do wonder if they get terrible heartburn as well."

While Lady Bainbridge spoke, Melody sat across from her and took a pastry from the plate in the middle of the table. While they all looked delicious, one that was shaped almost like a shell caught her eye. It had thin, flaky layers of dough and was filled with a light green cream. Melody had wondered what flavour it was, but biting into it didn't illuminate her – though it was delicious.

Seeing a look of surprise and then confusion cross Melody's

face, Lady Bainbridge said, "Pistachio cream. It is heavenly."
Melody had to agree. "The pastry itself is called a Sfogliatelle,"
she explained.

It seemed that coffee was all that was on offer for breakfast.
At home, Melody usually drank hot chocolate. Given the choice
between a small cup of dark, strong-smelling coffee, apparently
called espresso, and a lighter, milkier drink that she was told
was caffè latte, she opted for the latter. It was still stronger than
Melody would have chosen to drink in England, but with enough
sugar and paired with the pastry, it began to grow on her.

Breakfast was a languorous affair. Everyone was tired from
the evening before, and there were no firm plans for how to
spend their day that needed attending to. Rat attempted to read
the local newspaper, hoping to improve his Italian, while Melody
and Lady Bainbridge chitchatted about the various guests at the
dinner party.

Finally, hoping to introduce the topic of Alessandro casually,
Melody mentioned his name. "Ah, yes, the delicious and
charming Conte Foscari. If I were twenty years younger... maybe
thirty years younger, oh, what I would do." Melody wasn't
entirely clear what Lady Bainbridge was intimating she would
do but was too polite to ask. The woman continued, "The
Foscaris are an old Venetian family, as so many are. However,
also like so many, they fell on hard times during the last century.
Again, like so many, they accumulated debts, borrowed money
from other aristocrats, then failed to pay that back and ended up
forfeiting property. Alessandro's father, another very handsome
man, had been educated in England and decided to return to
London in order to find himself a rich wife."

Melody was on the edge of her seat; she couldn't wait to hear
how this story ended. If she were writing it, the man would
marry for money, only to fall in love with his wife after all. She
hoped that this was how this story would continue.

"Paolo Foscari was the catch of that Season. While his title
wasn't English, his dashing looks more than made up for it.
Young women and their scheming mamas threw themselves at

him. I personally witnessed some very unseemly behaviour. "

Lady Bainbridge paused, called for another espresso, and selected a Sfogliatelle for herself, sighing as she took her first bite. "Anyway, the lucky maiden who caught Paolo's eye was a Madeleine Grove. She was a rather plain young woman whose father had made a fortune in steel. The father hailed from Newcastle, and so the stench of trade that wafted around the young woman was compounded by a papa who sounded as if he had just walked out of the coal mines. However, there was money. So much money."

The story that Lady Bainbridge told felt very familiar to Melody; not only was she not born of a noble family, but she had begun her life in Whitechapel as an orphaned street waif. She knew that this was often whispered behind hands when she entered the grand salons of London. It was not a secret that Tabby Cat had taken her in when she was a child. The fortune bequeathed to her by the dowager countess certainly mitigated some of her own stench, but never enough to shield her from the low murmur of gossip and condescension.

"Did Paolo Foscari marry Madeleine?" Melody asked, still caught up in the hope of a happy ending.

"He did. He used her money to build back up the fortunes of the title; he even bought back the palazzo, not far from here, that his father had been forced to sell. Madeleine moved to Venice and, by most accounts, was miserable. She gave birth to a daughter and then came an heir, Alessandro. With the title and the family fortune intact, Paolo allowed his wife to return to England to live with her family. Alessandro was then raised as an Englishman, attended Eton and Oxford, and returned to Venice for summers with his father."

"That was quite gracious of Conte Foscari to allow his children to remain with their mother," Rat observed. Such behaviour was not the norm amongst English aristocrats. "Was the law more favourable to mothers in Italy than it was in England then?"

"Not at all. If anything, Italy may be a more patriarchal

society. But Paolo Foscari was a good man. He had married Madeleine for her money and had no illusions that she felt any more for him than he did for her. While he did not beat her, he did neglect her, and he felt the guilt of that and let her go."

This was not the heartwarming love story that Melody had been hoping for, and her disappointment showed on her face. "For someone who proclaims herself uninterested in marriage, you become very invested in the romance of other people's unions," Rat said teasingly.

Melody pouted, "Is it so wrong to wish for happy endings even if I believe that mine is unlikely to be found through matrimony?"

"You are young, dear, and it is 1911. A young woman, particularly one with an independent fortune, has options, and that is a wonderful thing. If and when you fall in love, you will make the choice to marry. Again, that you have that choice, unlike so many women before you, is something for which we should all give praise." Lady Bainbridge said these words with a knowing tone to her voice, continuing, "Never discount the power of falling in love, young lady. You will be surprised what you are prepared to do for the right man."

"At this point, I think the right man is whoever is willing to put up with her," Rat joked. Melody stuck her tongue out.

"Children, children," Lady Bainbridge said with an indulgent smile. "I…"

Whatever Lady Bainbridge had been about to say was interrupted by her butler's entrance, his arms full of red roses.

Seeing his employer's raised eyebrows, Rossi explained, "These were delivered for Miss Chesterton. There is a card."

Melody jumped up. "Roses? For me? How romantic. I do wonder who they are from?" Rossi brought over the notecard that had accompanied the flowers, and Melody read it.

"Do not keep us in suspense, dear. Who is your admirer?"

"They are from Xander Ashby, Lady Bainbridge. He writes that it was delightful to meet me last night and he hopes that our tour of St Mark's and the Basilica can go ahead this afternoon."

Lady Bainbridge did not respond immediately. Instead, she lifted her serviette and dabbed at her mouth. Replacing it in her lap, she said in a tone that seemed to have an undercurrent of caution, "Xander Ashby is a delightful young man."

"I am sensing there is a 'but'," Rat observed.

"Indeed."

"Foscari made a jab last night about Ashby having neither fortune nor title. Is that your concern?"

"As I said, a delightful young man. My understanding is that his father pulled whatever strings he's still connected enough to pull to get Xander assigned to the consulate here. It is never easy being raised to a lifestyle that one is unable to maintain. Mr Ashby's father was heir to an earldom, and he spent and gambled whatever independent resources he had freely under the assumption that he was to inherit a fortune. Unfortunately for him, his elderly uncle, the current earl, remarried late in life and finally produced an heir and a spare. By this time, Mr Ashby senior's resources were almost entirely depleted, and all the sons have had to find themselves careers."

"I still do not understand what your concern is, Lady Bainbridge," Melody said. "Do you believe he is a fortune hunter?"

"That is certainly one possibility," Lady Bainbridge acknowledged. She added quickly, "Not that you are not charming, my dear. Of course, a young man would desire to know you better. How can I say this delicately? Perhaps it is better to be blunt: despite the circumstances of your own birth, you have been raised in the household of an earl and are now a very wealthy woman. I would hope that, if you choose to marry, you might aim higher than Xander Ashby. There, I've said it."

Melody laughed, "I can assure you that I have no intention of marrying Xander Ashby. Or, indeed, anyone. It is just a tour of St Mark's, nothing more."

"Yes, well, in my experience, these things always start as no matter and often develop into something more. However, I have done my duty and warned you."

Dear Diary, whatever should I make of Xander's invitation and Lady Bainbridge's warning? Having finished breakfast, I returned to my bedroom to consider what to do. I would very much like to have a tour of St Mark's by someone who is familiar with Venice. It is not like Rat knows any more than I do, and Lady Bainbridge does not seem as if she is up to wandering Venice for hours. Of course, there is Alessandro's invitation to show me Venice. However, that was rather vague and he was not the one who sent me a dozen red roses this morning.

As Melody wrote this, she looked up at the roses now in a vase on her dressing table. It really was a wonderfully romantic thing to do. It wasn't her fault if she secretly wished a different man had sent them.

Diary, I have made a decision: I will accept Xander Ashby's offer. It is 1911, and I am an independent woman. Mary will accompany us, of course, for propriety's sake. However, accepting this offer means nothing more than that. If Mr Ashby harbours any romantic illusions, then that is not my problem. Anyway, there is nothing wrong with a little light flirtation. After all, I could do with the practice. I have no intention of being overwhelmed by the romance of Venice and accepting an offer essentially to use my fortune to prop up the Ashby estate.

Satisfied with her decision, Melody wrote a pretty little note of acceptance and asked Mary to ensure it was delivered to Xander Ashby.

Raising her eyebrows, Mary said tartly, "I hope you know what you're doing, Miss Melody."

"Oh, Mary, you are such a worrywart. Mr Ashby is charming. He has graciously offered to be a tour guide. Why would I not accept?"

"Because he sent the invitation with a dozen red roses, and I think you know that the offer has more to it."

Melody pouted. Wasn't the whole point of this European trip to escape the strictures of London's aristocratic society? Finally, to spread her wings and learn to fly away from Tabby Cat's worrying eye and Wolfie's stern one? Even Granny, who understood her better than anyone, nevertheless was unable to shrug off fully the norms of the society she had spent ninety years being formed by – as much as she would vehemently deny such a sentiment, claiming that she formed it, rather than the other way around. Perhaps in London, Melody would not have accepted such an overtly romantic gesture from a man she had no interest in, but this was not London.

Reforming the pout into the stubborn, wilful stare that Mary knew all too well, Melody replied, "And what if it does? Of course, you will be accompanying us." Melody paused, then said evilly, "Unless that is, your qualms about the outing mean that you refuse to be part of it. In which case, I will go alone with Xander."

Mary just shook her head. Her charge was perfectly aware that she would never refuse her anything, out of love, duty and an abiding sense of responsibility.

"Now, we must go through all the clothes that you have unpacked. If this is to be my first foray into Venice, I must be sure to look my best." Even as she said these words, Melody tried to ignore the thought that she was concerned about her outfit just in case they ran into Alessandro. She hated to think that she might be the kind of young woman who made eyes at one man while on the arm of another. Hating to think it didn't lessen the reality of her most secret desires.

CHAPTER 5

Rat's instructions from Lord Langley hadn't been as detailed as he might have wished. In truth, that was because the Secret Service Bureau's information was not as detailed as they wished. As tensions had been ratcheting up across Europe, the levels of distrust between the various countries had soared. The European powers had always spied on each other, but the level of espionage had never been higher than it was now. There was little doubt that war was imminent. Battlelines were being drawn across the continent, and the major antagonists wished to ensure that the odds were stacked in their favour before the first shot was fired. Military, and especially naval, innovation would help determine dominance. Even the most well-guarded designs and plans had somehow been stolen on occasion, on all sides.

Rat had the names of a few people he was to keep under observation, most suspected spies and agitators. However, Langley's feeling was that the real danger was not from the Germans and Austro-Hungarians that the British Government had long kept a nervous eye on. Instead, it was from less likely characters, perhaps even traitors within their ranks. Britain's own espionage efforts had uncovered evidence of a new German warship that bore a suspicious resemblance to one that was being built secretly in Southampton.

While Rat had enjoyed the puzzle-solving aspects of cryptology, it had been almost too prescribed; there was a code, a cypher, and a solution. Once he became adept at cracking the codes, the challenge was over. While there were always increasingly complex codes, which should have ensured his continued interest, it did not.

Rat often thought back wistfully to his days working for Wolf on the streets of Whitechapel and then those first few months in Mayfair helping with investigations. That was before Milady Tabby Cat insisted that Wolf stop putting the young boy in harm's way. This expedition was an opportunity to return to the life of adventure he had secretly been missing since he was a child.

Even as he thought this, Rat felt guilty; he would always be grateful to Lady Pembroke for taking Melody in and making the little girl her ward. And Rat knew that his life was also immeasurably better than it might have been. Nevertheless, there was a part of him that had chafed at the constraints of life amongst the British upper classes. Now, he was away from all that on his first secret mission and he should be thrilled. Yet, all he felt on that first day in Venice was self-doubt and fear that he would fail, disappoint Lord Langley, and let down his country.

As Rat had listened to Melody and Lady Bainbridge at breakfast discussing the invitation from Xander Ashby, it occurred to him that Ashby was the perfect person to help Rat break into the diplomatic circles in Venice. The two men had hit it off the prior evening, and it was clear that the eager Englishman was quite smitten with Melody. Surely, he would do whatever he could to ingratiate himself with her brother. Melody had to be chaperoned on this proposed tour of St Mark's. Who was more appropriate to be that chaperone than her brother?

Making up his mind, Rat rose from his seat in the palazzo's library, where he had been pretending to read as he wool-gathered and went in search of Melody's room. After asking a young maid, whose command of the English language was minimal, and receiving an answer that he had little confidence in, Rat finally knocked on a door that he hoped was correct. When Mary opened the door, Rat breathed a sigh of relief.

"Rat, is that you?" Melody called out, hearing his voice. "Come in, I'm just trying to choose an outfit. You can help."

Rat doubted that his sister had any true faith in his ideas on fashion, such as they were, but he entered the room and told her his suggestion about her afternoon tour. Of course, he omitted the part where he hoped to get close to Xander Ashby to gather information on possible spies. Instead, he said that he was also interested in seeing St Mark's Basilica and that he'd found Ashby a good sort.

Melody wasn't sure how she felt about her brother's suggestion. On the one hand, Rat was not nearly as malleable as Mary and was likely to play the big brother and try to spoil all her fun. On the other hand, Rat's presence was far more likely to deter any romantic overtures from Xander. Finally, this consideration won out over any other.

"That would be lovely, Rat. Mary, do you still wish to accompany us, or would you prefer to stay behind?"

Mary had not been as excited to leave British shores for the first time as her young mistress. She had a deep distrust of foreigners, their exotic food and their funny ways. It had never occurred to her that she might not accompany Melody on the trip, but she was also far from enthusiastic at the opportunity to explore Europe. On top of that, she did not enjoy boats and had been in a state of abject terror for most of the gondola ride the day before. If she could postpone repeating the experience, then she would leap at the chance. She indicated her preference for remaining at the palazzo.

"Rat, I told Mr Ashby to collect me at two o'clock," Melody announced. "Do you think he has his own gondola?"

"I have no idea. I assume that just as with carriages in London, they are mostly owned by the upper echelons of society."

"Is it possible to get around without going by water?" Mary asked, suddenly wondering if it would be possible to spend the rest of their stay in Venice without ever setting foot in another gondola.

"I believe that it is quite a walkable city. Certainly, Venice is far smaller than London," Rat observed. "But having looked at a map, I can see how it would be easy to get lost," he cautioned. "However, if one were determined not to travel by boat, I think that would be feasible."

Melody had thoroughly enjoyed the gondola ride the previous day and had no intention of having that be the only one of their stay. While she had noticed Mary's fear in the gondola, it had been a casual observation and quickly forgotten. "Anyway, why would one want only to walk around Venice, Mary? It is not as if we do so in London." Given the dowager's many pronouncements over the years about the inappropriateness of members of the Chesterton family perambulating for anything other than a healthful stroll through Hyde Park, this statement was hardly surprising.

Whatever brief hope Rat had given Mary was shattered by her realisation that her young charge would not only be undeterred from future gondola rides, but she would likely enthusiastically seek them out. Given this likelihood, Mary was even more determined to bow out of any outings when she had the option to do so.

The issue of how they would be travelling to St Mark's was put to rest over an early luncheon when Lady Bainbridge remarked that, while they were more than welcome to make use of one of her gondolas whenever they chose, she believed that the consulate had various ones at its disposal. She imagined that Xander would call for Melody in one of those. Hearing that Rat would be joining the party, Lady Bainbridge nodded her approval and exchanged a knowing look with the young man; given the circumstances, she believed he was a far more appropriate chaperone.

Melody had changed her outfit three times before settling on a light grey walking dress with a pale pink bolero jacket. The temperature in Venice was significantly hotter than London and Mary insisted that she accessorise her outfit with a pink parasol that complemented the jacket nicely. Looking at herself in the mirror, Melody felt that the outfit conveyed youthful sophistication and that she would not be embarrassed on the off chance that they did run into Alessandro.

At the stroke of two o'clock, Rossi announced that Mr Xander Ashby awaited Miss Chesterton in the vestibule. As Rat and Melody exited the salotto, they saw Xander waiting eagerly, a straw boater in hand. His enthusiasm waned noticeably when he realised Rat would be joining their party.

Noticing Xander's crestfallen face, Rat said, "I hope that you do not mind me tagging along, Ashby. My sister's companion is not fond of boats, and I would like to see the Basilica."

Schooling his face in an attempt not to show his disappointment, Xander replied, "Of course not, Sandworth. The more the merrier." He followed these words with an insincere chuckle and a forced smile.

As the host, it was incumbent upon Xander to allow Melody and Rat to board the gondola first. So, he was denied the opportunity of sitting next to the delightful Miss Chesterton as Rat made a point of sitting by his sister. However, Xander decided to make the best of the situation; at least he could now sit opposite her and gaze upon that angelic face, watching the delight dance across her features as she turned her head back and forth, trying to take in all the views along the Grand Canal.

Melody was quite grateful to Rat for saving her from the discomfort of having to sit next to Xander. However, he now was sitting opposite her with a soppy grin on his face, watching her every move. Even before they had reached St Mark's she was wondering how long good manners demanded that the outing must be before she could escape. Remembering one of Granny's lessons on how to extricate oneself from boring social events, Melody considered that a terrible headache was a tried and trusted possible solution. In truth, if Xander Ashby kept looking at her with those puppy dog eyes, she might develop an actual headache.

Luckily, the gondola ride to St Mark's Square was not long. Melody was fascinated by all the boat traffic on the canal. Seeing her interest, Xander explained that everything that horse and cart might deliver in London had to be transported by boat within Venice. "Why, even the police force, such as it is, usually arrives in such a manner."

After disembarking from the gondola, Xander led them on a short walk on the fondamenta running alongside the canal. Xander pointed ahead, drawing their attention to a beautiful building with cream-coloured bricks and all manner of ornamentation. "This is the Doge's Palace," he explained. "We should return another day to tour this if we are to do it justice."

Neither Melody nor Rat missed his use of the word 'we'. Clearly, Xander considered this outing the first of many. Turning left before the Doge's Palace into St Mark's Square, or Piazza San Marco, as the Venetians called it, Melody caught her breath. Ahead was a building so exquisite and highly decorated that it could only be the Basilica San Marco with its four magnificent enormous bronze horses guarding the entrance. Its Gothic and Byzantine-influenced exterior was a riot of gorgeous mosaics, lavish marble columns and intricate arches. The building was topped with five great domes.

Melody was so entranced by its stunning facade that she didn't even notice the imposing, red-brick clock tower on her other side. Wrenching her eyes from the basilica, she took in the rest of St Mark's Square, which was full of people but even more full of pigeons. Interspersed with shops selling lace and glass, lively cafes and restaurants lined the square. Tables, full of patrons drinking wine and espressos and eating large bowls of pasta, spilt out into San Marco.

As Xander led the way into the basilica, Melody gasped at the opulence that greeted her; it seemed as if shimmering gold mosaics covered almost every surface, depicting biblical scenes intended to inspire religious awe and fervour. Xander led them through the marble-floored nave of the basilica to the highly ornate gold altar, which he explained was called the Pala d'Oro. Xander was certainly a knowledgeable tour guide, with an endless supply of trivial details that Melody quickly found quite annoying.

"The altarpiece is studded with 1,300 pearls, 300 emeralds,

300 sapphires, 400 garnets, and 100 amethysts, rubies, and topazes," Xander explained.

Melody couldn't imagine why anyone would bother remembering such details. She whispered to Rat, "It would have been sufficient to say, a lot of jewels."

Rat smiled at the comment. He didn't disagree but was impressed with the amount of information that Xander Ashby had bothered to acquire. This was a detail-oriented person, which was likely a very useful skill for someone working for the consul. Certainly, he would always have even the smallest details to hand about the local political situation.

Picking up on Rat and Melody's reaction, Xander said in an almost apologetic tone, "I have a photographic memory. I know that I can sometimes sound a bit like a walking encyclopaedia."

"Well, at the very least, a walking Baedeker," Melody said teasingly.

At her words, Xander asked, "I do not see a Baedeker guide in your hand, Miss Chesterton. Are you not as much a devotee as seemingly every other British tourist to Europe is?"

"I do not wish to fall into the Baedeker trap that Lucy Honeychurch does," Melody explained.

Rat rolled his eyes, "Why would Mr Ashby know what you are talking about, Melody?"

Before Melody could explain, Xander said eagerly, "Oh, are you a Forster fan, Miss Chesterton?"

"You know *A Room with a View*?" Melody exclaimed. Suddenly, Xander Ashby seemed far less a tiresome obligation and far more a rather handsome and charming potential beau.

"Indeed! I find Forster's illuminations on the hypocrisy that underpins so much of British society to be a revelation."

Melody was far less taken with any political and social themes in the writer's work than she was with the very relatable story of a young woman taking her first steps out of the confines of her family's and society's expectations for her. Nevertheless, their differing reasons for enjoying the novels did not diminish Melody's thrill at finding someone with whom she could discuss her favourite book. After this revelation, Melody found that Xander's detailed knowledge about the basilica was far more interesting than she had first thought. She also decided that if she squinted, the young man might be a reasonable likeness to George Emerson, Lucy Honeychurch's eventual love interest. George had opened Forster's heroine's eyes to the world around her, and perhaps Xander might do likewise for Melody.

Emerging from the gloom of the basilica, it took a few moments for Melody's eyes to adjust to the bright sunshine. She put her parasol up, grateful for Mary's insistence that she carry one. Granny was quite a stickler about staying out of the sun, particularly given Melody's predisposition to freckles. Personally, Melody had no problem with the light spray of freckles that would emerge across her nose during summer, but the dowager insisted that well-brought-up young ladies did not succumb to freckles; only farm girls were so afflicted. The dowager had impressed upon Mary the vital importance of Melody using a parasol whenever she was outside, and the maid, sometimes companion, was far too intimated to do anything but take that counsel as canon.

From what Melody could see, there were exits out of each of the three sides of the piazza, in addition to the way they had entered. Deciding on the spur of the moment that she did not feel like another gondola ride just yet, Melody said, "I believe that I would like to walk back. Is that possible from here?"

"Well, I..." Xander stammered.

"You do not have to accompany us if you would prefer not to," Rat said. "I am sure we can find our own way back." Actually, he was not sure that was true but sensed Melody's eagerness to get caught up in the bustle of the city.

"I would not dream of abandoning you," Xander exclaimed, finding his voice at this outrageous suggestion. He considered himself far too much of a gentleman to consider deserting Miss Chesterton to find her way through the maze of calles that wound their way back to the palazzo. "Please wait in the shade for me for a few minutes while I return and tell the gondolier that we will not need his services."

Five minutes later, Xander returned and indicated that they should follow him through the north exit.

CHAPTER 6

Seeing Venice from a gondola on the Grand Canal was very different from walking its narrow and winding streets, which were interspersed with bridges spanning small canals. Even where the buildings were crumbling a little, paint flaking, there was a charm to the city that similar building conditions in London did not engender.

Holding tight to Rat's arm, Melody followed Xander, sure that, without him, they would have quickly become totally lost. She was reminded of Lucy Honeychurch's first day exploring Florence with Miss Lavish and getting lost. Miss Lavish had pronounced it a true adventure. Melody wondered if she were brave enough to venture out alone to follow in the footsteps of her heroine.

As they walked, Xander continued to spout facts and figures. Many of these were details of Venetian history, some of which were interesting. Others were mundane minutiae. Xander seemed unable to differentiate between all the information that his photographic memory had stored. Eventually, Melody found she could not be bothered to listen to the boring facts in the hope that the next item would be more interesting, and she tuned it all out and instead looked in the shop windows they passed.

Suddenly, she stopped and announced, "I would like to go into this bookshop for a few minutes."

Xander turned with a look of irritation on his face. He had been mid-sentence, explaining Venice's rise to power as a centre of commerce in the early 13th century, exemplified by one of its most famous merchants, Marco Polo. This apparent irritability was wiped away quickly and replaced with a look of slavish devotion; if Miss Chesterton wanted to look at books, of course, that was what they would do.

Melody would have been quite content to continue rereading *A Room with a View.* Still, it occurred to her that if she wished to have an adventure exploring Venice, she needed to have a bilingual dictionary in hand. Melody had learned Italian, German, and French but wasn't fluent in any of the three languages. She should have thought to buy such a book before she left London. Having failed to do so, this seemed like the perfect opportunity to rectify the situation and perhaps buy a novel in Italian to help her practice.

"If you do not mind, I will wait for you outside and smoke a cigarette," Xander said apologetically. Rat decided to take the opportunity to befriend the young man and indicated that he would also stay outside and smoke. He wasn't much of a smoker, but it seemed like the kind of bonding experience that might encourage confidences to be shared. He accepted a cigarette out of a colourful package with what looked like Egyptian imagery and deities on it. Taking his first puff, he did his best not to choke on it.

"They're not for everyone," Xander conceded. "A blend of Turkish and Egyptian tobacco, they're called Egyptian Deities."

Well, that explained the packaging, Rat thought.

"It took me a few tries to get used to them."

"If you didn't like them, why did you continue to smoke them?" Rat asked.

"Because they are the best. Did you know that the late king enjoyed these?"

Privately, Rat thought that the recently deceased King Edward VII's endorsement should be taken with a pinch of salt, given the man's well-known proclivities towards debauchery of all kinds. He took another couple of puffs before conceding defeat; they were just too vile.

Rat made good use of his time outside with Xander. He asked him some general questions about the consulate's activities. As he might have expected, much of it was the mundane work of supporting British nationals abroad with everything from medical to legal emergencies. There were also the diplomatic activities that all consuls routinely engaged in.

Finally, realising that he might not get what he was looking for unless he was more direct, Rat asked, "And what of intelligence work? Does that fall within the consulate's domain?"

"Spying and that sort of thing?" Xander had asked a little too loudly.

Indicating that he should lower his voice, Rat said, "Well, given how the situation is in Italy, it would only make sense if British diplomats who are already so embedded in local communities were a good source of information gathering." Rat had tried to make the comment as nonchalant as possible. He certainly didn't want to alert anyone to his role with the Secret Service Bureau.

Xander had looked at Rat with a rather confused look on his face, almost as if it was news to him that the continent was on the brink of war. Finally, he'd said, "Well, if anyone is spying, I certainly know nothing about it." Then he continued, "Why not come to the consulate one afternoon this week and see for yourself? I'm sure Mr Burrows would like to meet you. He's always interested in new dignitaries who visit Venice."

Rat laughed, "I would hardly call myself a dignitary."

"Are you not the ward of the Earl of Langley and your sister of the Earl of Pembroke? Two very powerful and well-respected men."

That was interesting, Rat thought. He was quite certain he had never mentioned his relationship to Lord Langley when he had met Xander Ashby the previous evening. Clearly, the man had done his homework. Perhaps he wasn't quite as sweetly naive as he appeared.

Melody was more than happy to leave the men outside and peruse the store alone. The shop wasn't large, but every square inch was crammed with bookshelves that were stuffed with books. As she'd entered, a little bell had rung over the door. Nevertheless, if the bell was supposed to alert someone that there was a customer, it seemed ineffectual; there was no one around to help her. The stacks of books seemed organised with little rhyme or reason, and Melody wished there was someone to give her assistance.

Finally, after looking in vain through the bookshelves, she called out, "Scusi. Excuse me. Is there anyone here who could help me?"

There was no answer. Melody was about to give up and leave when she heard a noise coming from the back of the shop. A moment longer, and a gravelly voice called out, "Aspetta. Sto arrivando."

An old man came into view. He might have been quite tall once, but he was now stooped over and walked with a cane. Behind thick-lensed glasses, bright blue eyes twinkled as he peered at Melody and asked, "Sei inglese?"

"Yes, I am English."

"Bueno, bueno," the old man said, coming closer.

Melody hoped his English was better than her Italian because she wasn't sure how to say dictionary. In fact, she wasn't comfortable saying much in Italian, and she now wished she'd paid more attention to the Italian tutor Granny had insisted on. "While the Italians cannot be credited with much, many of the great operas and poetry are in their language, and it behoves an educated young woman of fortune to be able to enjoy these without the interference of translation," Granny had said on more than one occasion.

"How may I help you?" the old man asked, to Melody's great relief. She quickly explained what she was looking for.

"Sì, I have what you want. Un dizionario; how do you call it?"

"A dictionary."

"Sì, a dictionary." The old man went to another bookshelf and, without even having to search, somehow pulled a book from the chaotic jumble which, when he handed it to Melody, was indeed a dictionary.

Remembering that she also wanted a novel, Melody considered whether she was better off getting an Italian book she didn't know or an Italian translation of a book with which she was familiar. She indicated to the old man that she would browse for a little while. He nodded his head, then went and sat at a rickety little desk by the window.

Melody was used to bookshops that sorted their books by clearly displayed genre. It was evident this was no such bookshop. That the old man had so quickly located the dictionary wasn't because there was any rational order to the shelves. Nevertheless, there was something delightful about perusing the shelves and being surprised by the literary gems she stumbled across. Melody could have happily spent all afternoon in the bookshop. As it was, she got so caught up in looking through the books that she lost track of time.

"Melody, will you please hurry up. Xander and I are cooling our heels out there, and there are only so many of his disgusting cigarettes I can smoke," Rat said from behind her.

"I still have not found a book," she explained.

Noting the book in her hand, he asked, "Then what is that you have?"

"Well, I found a dictionary but not a novel."

"Then let us come back another day. Xander has a job, you know. I'm sure he cannot spend the entire afternoon entertaining us."

Reluctantly, Melody pulled herself away from the books and went over to the old man to pay.

"Va tutto bene?" he asked.

"Sì. Grazie."

When Rat and Melody finally exited the bookshop, Xander stubbed out his latest cigarette. Melody found smoking to be a disgusting habit, which somewhat offset the progress Xander had made with his surprising affinity for Forster's books.

The rest of the walk back was uneventful and only took about ten minutes. Luckily, Xander seemed to have run out of facts to spout. Either that or he had finally picked up on his audience's

50

lack of interest in hearing them. Melody was excited that they got to walk over the Academia Bridge. Having crossed it, Xander led them through the streets of the Dorsoduro sestieri, or district, until they turned right down the Calle dei Cerchieri and approached the palazzo from the rear.

Arriving back at the palazzo, Xander bent over Melody's hand and said, "The consulate is throwing its annual ball a week on Saturday. Is there any chance I could prevail upon you to join us, Miss Chesterton? And, of course, Mr Sandworth, as well," he hastily added.

Whatever potential romantic interest had flickered briefly in Melody's heart had been snuffed out by the time she had spent three full hours in Xander's company. As much as she wanted to attend the ball, she was worried that Xander's invitation would mean attending on his arm. The very last thing she wanted was to announce to Venetian society that she and Mr Ashby had any kind of understanding.

Conflicted over what she wanted to answer, Melody paused long enough before answering that perhaps Xander intuited something of her hesitation, even if he perhaps falsely put it down to an overly well-developed sense of propriety.

"Of course, I hope it goes without saying that you and Mr Sandworth would be guests of Mr Burrows and the consulate. I am extending an invitation on his behalf, which I am sure he would thoroughly endorse," Xander stammered.

Rat almost felt sorry for the awkward young man. He glanced at his sister, who gave a nearly imperceptible nod. Correctly identifying this as her assent, he answered for them both, "We would be honoured to attend, Mr Ashby. Please relay our gratitude to His Majesty's Consul." This piece of absurd polite pantomime over, they bid Xander farewell.

On entering the palazzo, Rossi informed them that Lady Bainbridge was taking her afternoon nap but that she had asked him to inform them that a guest would join them for dinner.

Melody's heart leapt; was it possible it was Alessandro? These hopes were quickly dashed when Rossi continued, "It is the

Marchesa Luisa Casati." Neither Rat nor Melody had any clue who this marchesa was, and Rossi did not seem inclined to illuminate them any further. They retired to their rooms to wash the city's grime off them and to dress for dinner.

Melody found Mary in her room finishing up the last of the unpacking.

"How was the basilica?"

"It is quite beautiful, Mary. You must make sure that you go and see it one day." She then added in a teasing tone, "It is quite possible to walk there. In fact, we walked home."

Mary was shocked to her core. "You walked through the city? And your brother allowed that? What would your grandmother say?"

Mary had absorbed more of the dowager's dictates than just the importance of using a parasol when out in the sun. Mary had been an impressionable young woman when she had been plucked from her life as a housemaid and given charge of four-year-old Melody. The sixteen-year-old Mary couldn't quite believe her luck at the time and spent the first two years sure that she would make a mistake and be demoted. She then spent the next few years equally sure that she was not educated or sophisticated enough to raise the highly intelligent ward of a countess and an earl. To mitigate these fears, Mary became the dowager's most ardent pupil, sure that if she could learn all that the old woman cared to share on social etiquette, she might prove herself worthy of caring for the little girl she quickly came to love.

Melody laughed. "You are so silly sometimes, Mary. This is not London. There are no carriages. I am sure that there are plenty of places that cannot be reached by gondola."

"And I am equally sure that well-bred young ladies don't visit wherever such places might be."

Despite her censorious tone, Mary had no real expectations that Melody would pay any attention. It had been many years since the young woman had paid her much mind. Not that Melody didn't care for Mary. Quite the opposite; she considered the older woman more a beloved aunt than a servant. Still, her affection for Mary did not extend to respect for the woman's opinions about much more than which evening dress she should wear.

Indeed, sometimes Melody didn't even heed Mary's advice on that topic, and this evening was one such time. Looking at the blue silk dress that was laid out on the bed for that evening, Melody shook her head and said, "That dress will never do. There is to be a guest for dinner, and I must look my best."

"As you do in the blue silk," Mary said, defending her choice.

"I look adequate in that dress," Melody insisted. "In fact, I am not even sure why we brought it with us. Adequate might do for dinner with Wolfie and Tabby Cat, but it hardly suffices for Venice. I will wear the pale green."

Mary shook her head, but any argument she might have with the choice was kept to herself. Instead, she returned the blue silk dress to the wardrobe and pulled out the requested pale green dress. Mary's real issue with this dress was that it made Miss Melody look too grown-up. She wasn't ready for her to be out in the world, flirting, maybe marrying soon enough. To Mary, Melody was still the delightful little girl with red-gold ringlets who stole her heart from the first moment she entered Chesterton House.

CHAPTER 7

Whatever Melody and Rat had anticipated about their surprise dinner companion, the Marchesa Luisa Casati confounded all expectations. In fact, Melody had never met anyone quite like her. The marchesa was not beautiful, quite the opposite. Objectively, she might be considered almost ugly. She was too tall, taller than Rat, in fact, too thin, and her face was long and angular with chiselled cheekbones. However, somehow, between the woman's beautifully made, if rather unusual dress, flaming red hair that was styled almost as a halo, and large, mournful eyes accentuated by the kohl lining them, she was the most striking woman that either sibling had ever seen.

The marchesa seemed quite shy, almost awkward in her conversation. Nevertheless, there was a gentle kindness about her that immediately endeared her to Melody.

"Thank you for not bringing the leopard, Luisa, dear," Lady Bainbridge said as nonchalantly as if she were talking about a poodle.

"Non, non, ma chérie. It is not a leopard; it is a cheetah. Si?" the marchesa replied, seamlessly mixing French, English, and Italian.

"Is there a difference?" Lady Bainbridge asked with genuine curiosity.

"Sì. Many. The cheetah he is the fastest of the animals."

Luisa then proceeded to explain a variety of differences between the two big cats. Melody listened in fascination. The idea that someone would choose to have such an animal as a pet was astounding. Melody's beloved Cavalier King Charles Spaniel, Dodo, had died the year before. The loss was devastating, and Melody missed her enormously. Any thought she had entertained about a replacement pet had remained firmly in the category of another domesticated dog. Now, she wondered if she was being too conventional in her thinking. Anyone could have a dog as a pet. Of course, she was quite sure that Tabby Cat would not be happy to have a wild animal living in Chesterton House; it had taken her long enough even to warm up to Dodo.

"Do you live in Venice, marchesa?" Melody asked.

"For the most part now. And chérie, por favor, call me Luisa and I will call you Melody."

Luisa told them that the year before, she had moved into an unfinished palazzo on the Grand Canal, the Palazzo Venier dei Leoni. She explained that the Venier family had commissioned the building in the 18th century. Originally planned as a five-storey structure, work had stopped not long after starting in 1751. Between the fading fortunes of the family and then Napoleon's occupation of Venice, nothing beyond the first storey was ever completed.

"When I moved into my palazzo, it was in a terrible state. There was, how do you call it, the plant that climbs…"

"Ivy?" Rat suggested.

"Sì. The ivy she was all over. The roof was falling in, the walls, they were crumbling."

Melody couldn't help but ask, "Then why did you buy it?"

"Ah, that is what all of Venice exclaimed. They said, this Luisa Casati she is a crazy one. I was all anyone could talk about. Oh, the fantastico melodrama; it was everything."

"Luisa had made great strides with the inside of the palazzo; it's barely recognisable from the derelict, abandoned building she bought last year. When will you begin work on the exterior?" Lady Bainbridge asked.

Luisa threw back her head, exposing her graceful, porcelain-white, long neck and laughed. It was not the dainty laugh that women in society were taught to use, but instead, a throaty, hearty chuckle. "I am leaving the outside as it is. With its overgrown, crumbling walls my palazzo, is magnifico. I would not have fixed inside, except that I was told it would collapse on me if I did not. This palazzo is to be the stage on which I will perform the next act in the life of Luisa Casati."

The rest of dinner was filled with one outrageous story after another. There were tales of extravagant, outlandish parties, intimations of love affairs or, at the very least, very intense flirtations, and an overall narrative of a woman who lived life as she chose to with no reference to the norms of society or its judgement. It seemed there was a husband and even a young daughter living somewhere else, but neither were spoken of except as brief asides.

Melody was fascinated with Luisa Casati. Was it really possible to live life so entirely on one's own terms? It was evident that an enormous fortune fuelled the independence and freedom that Luisa enjoyed to the fullest. Melody wasn't sure that she wished her life to be quite the performance that her new friend relished. However, she believed there was much she might learn from the outrageous marchesa.

During a lull in Luisa's stories, Lady Bainbridge asked Melody and Rat about their afternoon excursion. They described their visit to the Basilica and their walk home. Melody talked about the bookshop with its odd proprietor.

"Ah yes, Signor Antonio Graziano," Luisa said knowingly. "His shop is a favourite of mine. Every shelf is a mystery; one never knows what will be discovered."

"It sounds quite messy to me," Lady Bainbridge said dismissively.

However, Melody clapped her hands together and exclaimed, "Yes, Luisa! That is exactly how I felt about Signor Graziano's shop; it was an adventure." She then said in a more measured tone, "Except that I did not have time to explore properly. I wished to buy a novel to help me with my Italian. While the prospect of roaming amongst the bookshelves for hours was very tempting, my brother made me hurry and pay for the dictionary and then dragged me out of the shop."

"Melody, that isn't fair. Mr Ashby was waiting for us. I am sure you can return another day," Rat protested.

"Sì," Luisa said vehemently. "I will take you tomorrow. It has been far too long since I visited Signor Graziano."

A plan was made, which Melody was delighted with and Rat apprehensive of. He found the marchesa rather overwhelming and shocking. More to the point, he wasn't sure she was an entirely appropriate friend for the impressionable Melody. However, he realised that there was no way to deter his sister now that the invitation had been given and enthusiastically accepted.

The following morning, Melody woke up early, excited for her outing with the marchesa. Would she bring the cheetah? Having walked through the narrow streets of Venice, Melody couldn't even imagine how one might take such a beast around the city without causing consternation. Of course, it was hard to imagine how one might walk such an animal anywhere.

One thing she was sure of: Luisa was the most fascinating person Melody had ever met. Everything about the woman was wonderful, curious and inspirational. That she had seemingly abandoned her husband and child to live alone in Venice in a decrepit, unfinished palazzo was not even the most outrageous thing about the marchesa. Her clothes, her makeup, the cheetah, it was all almost too eccentric. Melody couldn't wait to take Luisa up on her offer to visit the palazzo for one of her infamous parties. Meanwhile, their proposed outing to the bookshop was enough to have the normally morning-averse Melody positively leaping out of bed.

"You're very eager this morning," Mary observed.

"I have plans to visit a bookshop."

Mary narrowed her eyes suspiciously. "And why are you this excited about such an outing? Is that handsome Mr Ashby involved?"

"Oh, Mary, he's not handsome. Well, not all that handsome, anyway. And even if he is reasonably attractive, he does drone on about all sorts of boring things."

"So he is not who you are going with? I hope you don't think you're going alone."

"No, I am going with the Marchesa Casati. She is coming to get me in her gondola. Apparently, it is possible to get quite close to the shop on the smaller canals. She said it is one of her favourite shops in Venice. Oh, Mary, she is quite amazing. To live independently as she does would be quite wonderful."

Even as Melody said these words, the image of a handsome, olive-skinned face popped into her mind. Melody quickly banished such thoughts; she would not let the gorgeous conte distract her. She had come to Venice to escape the expectations that she would achieve nothing more in her life than to marry well. She did not intend to let a man, however handsome, upset her plans. Whatever Melody's ambitions for her trip were before she met the enigmatic marchesa, now she felt as if she had never truly understood what it meant to be a worldly woman before.

After bathing, Melody proceeded to torture Mary by going through every dress she had brought with her to Venice and judging each one as too childish, too boring, or too conventional.

"You do not understand, Mary. Luisa, that is Marchesa Casati, has a sense of style and fashion that is so unique. She told me that she sometimes drugs live snakes and wears them as necklaces. I do not want her to be embarrassed to be seen out in public with me," Melody said melodramatically before throwing herself on the bed next to her pile of dresses in a fit of pique at the state of her wardrobe.

Mary sat on the bed beside her and stroked Melody's hair as she had when she was upset as a child. "There, there, Miss Melody. I am sure that the marchesa likes you for who you are, not your clothes."

Melody sat up at this, her temper now turning to exasperation, "Mary, you do not understand. It is not enough for Luisa to like me; I wish to emulate her in every way. All my clothes are the prim, proper dresses of a young, wealthy debutante who knows nothing of life."

Mary knew enough about her mistress's moods that she didn't point out that this description quite aptly fitted Melody. Instead, she kept her own counsel and made soothing sounds.

"I wish my wardrobe to be an expression of something more than that my family can afford to shop at the House of Worth!"

Finally, Mary persuaded Melody that this was not a problem that could be solved that morning and that if she wished to go on her outing with the marchesa, she would have to choose something to wear from the mound of clothes on the bed. Eventually, after trying on and rejecting at least four more outfits, Melody was persuaded to settle on a forest green dress that Tabitha had initially refused to buy for her because she thought it was too mature for an eighteen-year-old girl. Its neckline was more daring than Melody's other day dresses, and its cut was slimmer and very modern.

Thirty minutes later, Melody was satisfied that she looked as sophisticated as she was likely to, given what she had to work with. She had made Mary redo her hair three times, sure each time that the look was too childish. Now, it was coiled simply at her neck, with just a few ringlets framing her face.

By the time Melody descended the stairs, the marchesa had already arrived and was being entertained by Lady Bainbridge in the salotto. When Melody entered the room, Luisa appraised her outfit approvingly and announced, "Charming, charming. You are molto bella, Melody."

While Melody appreciated the marchese's kind words, she did wonder how genuine they really were. Luisa's outfit that morning was so outrageous that it might almost have been a costume if they were attending a masquerade ball. Her tulle skirt resembled one that a ballerina might wear, while on top, she had a bolero fur jacket that seemed as if it would be much too warm for a sunny June day in Venice. Luisa wore a long strand of pearls that she had wound around her neck many times, and to top off the outfit, she was wearing a hat with an enormous brim that was covered in pink feathers. How was it possible that someone who could put together such an outfit could really believe that Melody's Worth dress was anything other than boringly pedestrian?

Luisa's gondola was far more ornate and opulent than either of the ones that Melody had travelled in so far. Settling back into the ruby red, plush velvet cushions, Luisa told her, "Signor Graziano is not as spry as he once was. He has aged visibly even since I first met him last year." Melody thought back to the stooped old man she had met yesterday and reflected that "not spry" was an understatement.

Luisa continued, "He has two sons, but neither of them has ever been interested in taking over the business. One, he tries to make his fortune as an artist – not a very good one, from what I have seen. The other has left Venezia altogether and is living in Vienna now. Maybe the son, he works in a library, or something like that. Every time I see Antonio, he says the shop is getting too much for him and that if he can't persuade his artist son to join him, he will just sell the store. Il poveretto, he rarely opens before mid-morning and normally closes early."

Melody thought about the old man with the twinkly blue eyes and his marvellous shop and was deeply saddened to think of him abandoned by his sons and forced to sell up. As Luisa promised, her gondola was able to navigate the maze of small canals that wound their way off the Grand Canal and through Venice to bring them within sight of the shop. Luisa's gondolier helped them both out of the boat, and they then walked the short distance to the bookshop.

Just as the day before, the ringing bell above the door failed to summon Signor Graziano. It was evident that Luisa knew her way around the shop's labyrinth of overcrowded shelves. Melody trailed the marchesa as she drifted from one shelf to another. In the gondola, Melody told Luisa about her dilemma of a well-known book in translation versus a totally new book. While she hadn't commented on the choice in that moment, now Luisa picked books that were Italian translations of British classics.

"If you want to improve your Italian, then you should read a book whose story you already know," she decided. "It is how I improved my Inglese."

As Luisa perused the shelves, she picked up books and showed them to Melody, who would indicate her familiarity with the English originals. They had been in the bookshop more than twenty minutes and Signor Graziano hadn't appeared. Luisa didn't seem either surprised or concerned. "Antonio is probably in the back taking a nap," she confided. "It really is all becoming too much for him. We will call for him when we are ready to pay."

CHAPTER 8

After another ten minutes, they had a small pile of books: *Pride and Prejudice*, *Bleak House*, and *Vanity Fair*. Melody knew all three books well enough to be able to follow the story in Italian if she had her new dictionary at hand.

Putting the books on the rickety desk that Signor Graziano had sat at previously, Luisa called out, "Signor Graziano, Antonio, sono io, Luisa Casati." There was no answer. She waited for a few seconds, then called out again, "Antonio, va tutto bene?" Melody's Italian was good enough that she knew that Luisa was calling out to the old man to see if he was alright. Still, there was no answer.

"This is not like Antonio," Luisa said in a worried voice.

"Might he have stepped out briefly?" Melody wondered.

"And leave the store unlocked? Never," Luisa asserted. "Something must have happened. He may have fallen in the back. Let us go and make the investigation."

With Luisa leading the way, the two women wound their way through the shop to the back, where a dark blue curtain was drawn to separate the shop front from its back. Luisa pulled back the curtain and walked through the doorway, continuing to call out. There was no answer. They found themselves in a small stockroom that was even more overstuffed than the front of the shop. Piles of books lay on every surface and stacked up on the floor. If Signor Graziano had a system of organisation, it was a very unusual one that was likely impenetrable to anyone else.

Luisa expressed a fear that the bookshop owner might have

hit his head during a fall and be unable to call out. They looked in every corner of the stockroom, though even with the books lying everywhere, it quickly became clear to Melody that there was no one there. There was a door leading off the stockroom, which Melody assumed led to an office. Luisa made her way over to there, opened the door and screamed. Melody was behind Luisa, whose tall frame blocked the doorway, cutting off the view into the room.

"Antonio! Oh, mio Dio!"

Following Luisa into the room, Melody was confronted with the gruesome sight of the elderly bookseller slumped over his desk. The distinctive smell of a gunshot was still evident in the air, even though the lack of smoke in the poorly ventilated room indicated the use of smokeless powder.

"Oh my!" Melody exclaimed. Her first impulse was to ask if the man might be still alive, but a second look at the body negated the need for such a question. Signor Graziano's face was turned towards them, and his glassy eyes indicated that his soul had left his body. Melody wasn't sure what propelled her forwards, but she moved towards the body and lightly touched the hand that was stretched out across the desk; it was warm to the touch.

Melody also considered the still-lingering smell of the gunpowder. "He has not been dead long," she informed her new friend. Luisa didn't ask how Melody might know that and instead looked around the room rather melodramatically as if the killer might be hiding there in a corner and about to jump out at them.

The office had a window that, while not large, was certainly large enough for a medium-sized man to get through. Had the murderer heard them in the shop and escaped out this way? Melody got chills just thinking about it; while she was busy debating whether she wanted to read Jane Austen or George Elliot, poor Signor Graziano was being brutally murdered.

Moving over to the window, she saw that not only was it open, but there was a small piece of fabric caught on the metal of the frame. Plucking the material, she inspected it. Melody didn't know much about men's tailoring, but she believed that it was a piece of grey gaberdine of the kind that expensive suits were often made from. She considered the material. It was soft and of a tight weave, not the sort of material she expected working-class men to be able to afford. She wasn't sure what to make of such a deduction except that it perhaps implied that whoever had escaped out of this window was a man of some means. Why would such a man murder an elderly bookseller?

Melody strained to lean out of the window and saw that it led to a narrow calle. "How would I get onto this street?" she asked Luisa. While it had briefly occurred to her to follow the killer out through the window, she knew that if he had struggled to get through it in trousers, she would never manage it in a dress.

Luisa seemed quite undone by their discovery and was standing next to the body, her hands over her mouth in shock. Now, looking at Melody, the older woman asked the young girl, "What should we do?"

Melody had grown up in a household where murder investigations were routine. When Melody was younger, even Granny had been an active member of Tabby Cat and Wolfie's investigative team. Over the past few years, the dowager had reluctantly reduced her participation to that of a wise advisor, as she liked to describe her role. However, Tabitha and Wolf, with Bear's help, still took on cases, even if not as frequently as they once had.

While Tabitha had insisted that Melody not be drawn into their investigations in any way, the young woman had been on the peripheries many times and had listened to enough murder-related dinner conversations to have a good sense of how to proceed. "How might one summon the police in Venice?" she asked, noticing that there was no telephone in the office.

"Sì, sì. La polizia." Luisa was not from Venice and had lived there only a little more than a year. She had no more idea how to summon the authorities than Melody. "I will go out and ask my gondolier, Giuseppe. He will know what to do. Antonio, he did not believe in the telephono."

"Tell him that there is a dead body and that we suspect foul play. If Italy is anything like London, the police will need to bring a medical examiner with them."

Luisa looked at the young English girl in surprise, but she didn't question why Melody was able to assert this with such cool confidence. Instead, she said, "If you go out of the front, turn right towards the canal and then walk along the fondamenta away from where we left the gondola, then make the first right, you will come onto the calle you can see from that window." With that, she turned and left to request that her gondolier summon the police.

Melody decided to use the time it took Luisa to call for help to examine the crime scene more closely. The desk was situated to the left of the door to the small office and the window straight ahead. The door had been closed when they entered. Would a murderer, surprising his victim, have bothered to close the door behind him before shooting? He certainly wouldn't have taken the time to close it after shooting, but before escaping through the window. Considering this and the fact that Antonio was seated when he was shot, Melody wondered if the murderer didn't surprise the old man but had, in fact, been expected, or at least was known to him.

Looking again at Antonio's slumped form, she considered whether he might have been standing when the killer entered the room and then fallen into this position when he was shot. No, that wasn't likely. If he had stood, he would have pushed the chair back more than it was, and if he had then fallen back, it wouldn't have been into a seated position; in fact, it was far more likely that they would have found the body lying on the floor. There seemed little doubt that the victim had been seated and probably not surprised by his murderer bursting through the door.

Looking at the chair sitting in front of the desk, Melody noticed an ashtray on the desk that was closer to that chair than Antonio's. Was it possible that the murderer had sat before his victim, casually smoking a cigarette before pulling a gun and shooting him?

Melody went and sat in the chair and looked across the desk at the dead body. Assuming that the killer had heard them come into the shop and fled out the window, then was Antonio shot while they were perusing the bookshelves? That was a chilling thought. But if that had been the case, why hadn't they heard the gunshot? Melody thought about the layout of the bookshop and the enormous number of shelves stacked high with books; would they have muffled the sound? Perhaps they would have.

Then, Melody thought back on the timeline since they first entered the bookshop: they had come in, not found Signor Graziano, but Luisa, not finding it unusual, hadn't called out. Assuming the killer had entered through the front of the shop, then he must have already been with Antonio in the office. Melody tried to remember if she had noticed anyone entering as they disembarked from the gondola, but she hadn't been paying attention to anything save trying to exit the boat.

Luisa hadn't called out to the bookseller until they had been in the shop for about twenty minutes. The murderer must have heard them; why else not leave the store through the front entrance and instead escape out of the window? So, if he had entered before they had and not escaped until Luisa had called out, then he must have been with Antonio for more than twenty minutes. This and the fact that he seemed to have sat and smoked a cigarette indicated that his sole purpose hadn't been to kill the elderly man. Instead, Melody deduced, he had come to talk. Was the murder a last resort because he hadn't received the answers he'd wanted? What had the old man become mixed up in?

Melody considered whether it was worth seeing where the calle outside of the window led to. She was sure the murderer was long gone. Someone might have seen him, but she wasn't sure her Italian was up to having such a conversation. Surely, this was something that the police would pursue. Instead, she decided to wait for them to arrive. No sooner had she made this decision than Luisa returned.

"La polizia will be here soon," she assured Melody. "Poor Antonio. Who could have done this to him, and why?"

Melody considered sharing her deductions with Luisa, but the woman still seemed very flustered. It appeared that the marchesa's love of the dramatic did not extend to finding dead bodies. Instead, Melody asked, "How well did you know Signor Graziano? You spoke about his sons, but is there anything else you can tell me?"

Luisa considered the question. "Well, he was from the ghetto."

"The ghetto?" Melody asked in a horrified voice. Her knowledge of the usage of the word was limited, but in England, it was often used by the more sensational newspaper reporters to refer to some of the grittier, overpopulated urban areas.

"Sì. The ghetto in the Cannaregio sestieri is where many of il Ebrei, you say Jews, of Venezia still live, even though they are no longer compelled to," Luisa explained. "Antonio once told me that when he was a child, his mother would use stories of the life she had led during her childhood, before most of the restrictions were lifted, to try to make him appreciate the freedoms he had." Luisa paused, then added thoughtfully, "Though, perhaps the feeling of being free is relative; I know that when Antonio was a young man and Venezia, she was under Austrian control, the Jews of Italy still were not considered equal under the law."

Melody considered the other woman's words. Throughout her life, living at Chesterton House, her family had maintained relationships, even friendships, with an unusual variety of people in London. Not the least of these unconventional friendships were with some of the Jews in London's poverty-stricken East End and amongst some of Britain's more prominent Jewish members. She had not considered these friendships particularly noteworthy until she had come out into society and had observed for herself the prejudices rampant in aristocratic circles.

Was Antonio Graziano's murder somehow related to his Judaism? She couldn't imagine many reasons why a kindly old bookseller would be killed. It occurred to Melody that perhaps this was a robbery gone wrong. That didn't really sit comfortably with the well-outfitted killer sitting and smoking a leisurely cigarette with his victim, but it was possible. Looking around the office, she saw a small safe in the corner of the room. It seemed to be closed. Perhaps the killer had come upon Antonio in his office, forced him at gunpoint to open the safe and remove any money in there. Then, out of habit, Antonio had closed the safe before handing the money over.

Melody considered this scenario: If this were the case, why would Antonio then sit back at the desk, and why would the killer not just immediately leave the scene of the crime? Why bother to stay and chat? No, this narrative made no sense. She was sure that if the safe were to be opened, they would find its contents intact.

CHAPTER 9

I spettore Paolo Moretti was exhausted, something he seemed to be a lot these days. His wife had recently given birth to their fifth child, a girl, and the baby kept them up most nights. They shared a house near the university, Ca' Foscari, with his wife's family. While Paolo had been grateful to his father-in-law for the offer when he was first starting out in the Regia Guardia di Pubblica Sicurezza as a guardia, now, all he could focus on was how overcrowded and noisy the house had become.

Paolo had suggested to his wife, Gianna, quite a few times that it might be time to move out of her family's house, but each time, the conversation had ended with recriminations and tears. So, for now, he was resigned to sleepless nights and days without the possibility of even a moment of peace and solitude. In fact, he looked forward to going to the Questura in the mornings; at least he could get some time alone in his small, cramped, windowless office.

The gondolier had reported the murder at the Questura and demanded that an inspector be dispatched immediately. The standard protocol would be for lower-ranking members of the police force to be the first at a crime scene, with the inspector coming once the scene had been secured. However, once the gondolier mentioned his employer, the infamous Marchesa Luisa Casati, Ispettore Moretti realised that he needed to take charge of the situation personally.

Moretti had heard the tales of the marchesa and her cheetah, outrageous outfits and decadent parties. He was a simple man who led a simple life; he provided for his family and kept his city safe, and if he secretly aspired to promotion to commissario, he was nevertheless clear-eyed enough to keep his ambition in check. Of average height, weight, looks, and abilities, Moretti nevertheless was comfortable with who he was and his status in life and could not understand those who felt the need to turn their life into a public performance. He wasn't sure he had the energy that morning to deal with a murder and a notorious aristocrat.

Turning to the sergeant, Sovrintendente Vinditti, he had brought along, Moretti asked, "Did the gondolier tell you anything more than that there had been a murder?"

Murders were not particularly common in Venice. Unlike the south of Italy, where organised crime in the form of the Cosa Nostra and Camorra made murder prevalent, Venetians tended to contain their criminal activities to smuggling and pickpocketing.

Vinditti shook his head, "It seemed that he didn't know much more than that. His mistress came out to the gondola in a panic, and all she said was that he was to fetch the police and tell them that a man had been murdered in the bookshop."

Moretti walked home past the bookshop every day. He wasn't much of a reader and so had never had cause to go in, but he knew the owner, Antonio Graziano, by sight in the way that so many Venetians knew their fellow citizens. The last time he had seen the old man, he had been shutting up the shop for the day. They had exchanged friendly "good evenings", "Bono sera" in the Venetian dialect that was so natural when Venetians spoke to each other. Even though Venice had been part of a unified Italy since 1866, its people's dialect still helped set them proudly apart from the rest of the country.

At the time, Moretti had a passing thought that the elderly bookseller seemed particularly old and worn down. Now, he found himself hoping that whoever the murder victim was, it wasn't the kindly-looking Graziano.

It didn't take long to get to the shop from the Questura. It was a lovely early summer's day, and Moretti would have enjoyed the walk if he hadn't been on his way to view a dead body. Arriving at the shop, he and Vinditti found no one in the front so they walked through to the back. They followed the sound of voices into the office.

Like all Venetians, Moretti knew who Luisa Casati was. Crowds would often gather to watch as she paraded about the city with her cheetah and enormous, dark-skinned manservant. If he was surprised at her outlandish outfit that morning, he did his best not to let this show. Who was the pretty young woman with the marchesa? While Venetians were not as olive-skinned as their more southern brethren, there was something in the young woman's porcelain complexion and auburn hair that suggested she was not a local.

"Buongiorno," he said respectfully, dipping his head.

The pretty young woman was the first to come forward and said in English, "Thank you for coming."

Moretti's command of English was minimal. His confusion must have been apparent, for the marchesa said in Italian, "Thank you for coming so quickly. I am the Marchesa Luisa Casati, and this is Miss Melody Chesterton." Moretti introduced himself and Vinditti quickly.

As soon as he entered the office, Moretti realised with sadness that the dead man was Antonio Graziano. He asked the marchesa how they had happened to come across the victim, and she had given him a rather melodramatic response. It was clear that the young Englishwoman understood some Italian because she nodded along.

The basics of the story out of the way, the pretty young girl said something in English to the crazy marchesa, who said in Italian, "Miss Chesterton has a theory that she'd like me to translate. While she does speak some Italian, she is not comfortable enough to relay her thoughts."

With that, Melody, translated by Luisa, explained about the piece of gaberdine she had found caught on the window frame, her observations about the cigarette ash, and when Antonio

Graziano must have been killed. As Luisa translated Melody's deductions about the likelihood that the victim had welcomed his killer into his office and sat talking with him, Moretti raised his eyebrows slightly but didn't interrupt. Compared to some of his colleagues in the Questura, his ego was contained. If this young woman had something to contribute that might help solve this murder, he was more than happy to listen to her thoughts. When the medico legale, Dottore Leone, arrived, he would confirm or deny her guess as to how recent the murder had been.

When Melody got to her hypothesis about why this hadn't been a robbery and pointed out the closed safe, Moretti nodded, increasingly impressed at the woman's intelligence and observations. She ended with her supposition that the murderer had heard them calling out to the bookseller and had escaped out of the window.

Moretti nodded again and said to Vinditti, "Make sure that your men walk the calle and see if anyone saw anything. A man climbing out of the window isn't an everyday occurrence, after all." Sovrintendente Vinditti wasn't as inclined as the ispettore to take the word of a slip of a girl, or indeed any female, but he knew enough just to nod his head in agreement. Moretti had been particularly short-tempered ever since the birth of the latest baby, and Vinditti had no desire to be on the receiving end of his boss's ire.

By the time Melody had got to the end of her conclusions, the medical examiner, Dottore Leone, had arrived with men who could remove the body. The white-haired medico legale probably should have handed the job over to a younger man many years before. However, Pasquale Leone had no wife or children. He lived alone with only a cat for company and couldn't imagine how he would fill his days without the work that had sustained him for more than forty years. His hearing and sight were not what they once were, but his intellect was as sharp as ever, and so no one was inclined to force the issue of retirement with him.

Unlike Moretti, Dottore Leone spoke excellent English, and

once it became clear that Melody's Italian was insufficient, the medical examiner happily switched languages.

Melody explained that the body was still warm to the touch when they discovered it, which couldn't have been more than thirty minutes before.

"Sì," Dottore Leone agreed, "La rigidità cadaverica, in English you say, rigor mortis, it has not set in at all yet. In the warmer weather we are having now, I would expect it to start in one to two hours. If you found him half an hour ago, I think it is very likely that the murder was not much before that."

Melody was gratified to have her conclusions validated, and she appreciated that neither the police inspector nor the elderly medical examiner condescended to her but instead took her observations seriously. The other policeman, the more junior one, had a bit of a sour look on his face, but Melody was more than used to men discounting her intelligence. The only woman she had ever known who immediately commanded the respect of men of any rank was Granny, who, even in her advanced years, would never stand for anything less than total deference.

Despite the men's willingness to consider her theories, it was clear that her continued presence would not be tolerated. Melody didn't need Luisa to translate to understand that the inspector was thanking them for their help and inviting them to leave. Luisa told him only where Melody was staying; most of Venice knew where the marchesa could be found.

It had been evident that her friend's death had very much shaken Luisa, but once they were back in her gondola and making their way back to the Grand Canal, she began to recover her composure.

"Melody, I would not have known what to do if you had not been with me," Luisa confessed.

Melody guessed that her friend must have been in her late twenties, perhaps even thirty, and yet, despite her bizarre outfits and lifestyle, in many ways, she had an almost childish naivety about her. There was so much about her appearance that was artifice; even her pupils seemed abnormally large as if she used something to dilate them. And yes, despite the performative nature of so much in her life, Luisa seemed to have a fragility about her that intrigued the self-assured Melody Chesterton.

"I am having a party tomorrow night." It seemed not to occur to Luisa that continuing with her planned festivities, having just discovered a so-called friend murdered, might be in poor taste. Instead, she became more animated just at the thought of her soiree. "You must attend, sì? And, of course, bring your brother."

Melody was delighted to receive the invitation, but she wasn't sure what Rat would think about accompanying her. She knew that he took his role as her guardian during this trip very seriously and was as concerned for her moral well-being as he was for her physical. The previous evening, she had sensed his apprehensiveness when the plan was formed to visit the bookshop with the intriguing marchesa. She could only imagine how much more concerned he would be about his sister attending one of her notorious parties. Nevertheless, Melody was determined to attend, one way or another, and eagerly accepted the invitation.

As excited as she was, even Melody was somewhat taken aback by her new friend's next statement, "My parties, they always have the themes. Tomorrow night, we will be ancient gods and goddesses. I will be Aphrodite!"

Melody had never been to a masquerade ball, and the thought of attending one thrown by the outlandish Marchesa Casati was thrilling, except that she and Rat didn't have any costumes to wear. With not much more than twenty-four hours until the party, she couldn't imagine how they would acquire some.

Intuiting her young friend's dilemma, Luisa said, "I have a dressmaker who is dedicated to my costumes. I will have her come to Lady Bainbridge's palazzo this afternoon, and it is Luisa's promise that she will have costumes ready before the party."

Of course, Melody thought, this still didn't resolve the issue of how she would persuade Rat to let her attend. He would never countenance the thought of her attending alone, but now that she knew it was to be a costume party, it seemed even less likely that her strait-laced brother would agree to escort her.

CHAPTER 10

*D*ear *Diary, where do I even begin? When I arrived back at the palazzo after my morning's adventure with Luisa, I knew that I would have to tell Rat about Signor Graziano's murder. I also knew that he'd immediately become overprotective, and I was correct. He seemed more concerned that I had seen a dead body than about the poor man's death. Even when I told him about my deductions, he seemed unable to focus on anything more than that the police questioned me. One thing was very clear: he believes that my involvement with this murder investigation is at an end. What would Tabby Cat and Wolfie do in this situation, to say nothing of Granny? I know what they'd do: they'd investigate, and that is what I intend to do. I will show my big brother that I am more than a pea-brained, silly debutante.*

As if that wasn't enough, I then had to tell him about Luisa's invitation. I assumed that Rat's first instinct would be to forbid me from attending. So, imagine my surprise when he agreed to chaperone me. Of course, that was before he knew it was to be a masquerade ball. Nevertheless, even then, he seemed more interested in going than I would have expected. There is something going on that he's not telling me; I just know it.

Anyway, whatever the reason, he only sulked a little when Luisa's dressmaker, Signora Bianchi, came to measure us and discuss costumes. I have no idea how she will create two outfits in so short a period, but she assures me that they will both be ready by tomorrow afternoon.

Melody would have been very surprised to learn why her brother was willing, perhaps even eager, to attend the marchesa's party. The truth was that Rat was frustrated with his lack of progress. Forget progress; he didn't even have a plan. Was this what espionage was always like? He didn't know who he was supposed to be watching or what he should be looking for. This party might be just what he needed to meet a broader swath of Venetian society. And more important than Venetians, he hoped that the marchesa's guest list would include some of the foreigners he was most interested in.

As it happened, Rat knew something of Marchesa Luisa Casati before meeting her the previous evening. While Lord Langley had given him few instructions, he had given him some information on some of the people he might meet in society. While Melody had been out on her excursion with the marchesa, Rat had been rereading some of the information that had been provided.

Luisa Casati, born in Milan in 1881, was the daughter of a wealthy cotton manufacturer. Orphaned at thirteen when her parents died in an accident while travelling, she, along with her sister, inherited a substantial fortune. In 1900, she married the Marquis Camillo Casati Stampa di Soncino. By all accounts, a loveless marriage of convenience, they had one daughter, Cristina, a year later. When her daughter was still young, Luisa began living between Venice and Paris while her husband and daughter moved between the family estate in Milan and a home in Rome.

Rat considered the woman he had met two days earlier. He had spent the last fourteen years on the peripheries of British aristocratic society, sometimes scorned by it, mostly barely tolerated or ignored. Was the Italian aristocracy much different? Unless it was, he couldn't imagine a character as colourful and eccentric as Luisa being easily accepted. And, for all her seeming outlandishness, Rat sensed an underlying fragility to the woman. Did she long to be embraced by society, or was she happy to be an outcast?

As he continued to read, Rat's instincts were corroborated; Luisa's antics had caused her to be shunned by the Italian aristocracy in Rome and Venice, and her social circle now consisted of bohemians, artists and foreigners. This validated his decision to accompany Melody to the marchesa's party. It also raised the question: was Marchesa Luisa Casati herself someone he should be keeping a watchful eye on?

Based on his brief time with her, it was hard to envision Luisa as a devious, hardened political operative. However, perhaps she had merely adopted the persona of a flighty, hedonistic dilettante as a disguise. Considering such potential machinations made Rat's head spin. Still, he knew that such serpentine behaviour underpinned much international espionage.

Certainly, Melody's burgeoning friendship with the woman was proving useful if only as a way to gain access to Venice's more unconventional social circle. Even as he had this thought, Rat felt guilty at the realisation that he was not only using his sister but potentially putting her in harm's way. He knew that Lord Langley would disapprove, but, at least for the moment, this seemed the only avenue the neophyte intelligence officer felt he had at his disposal. Even if Luisa Casati wasn't an enemy operative, it was certainly possible that a hostile power might be using her soirees as a way to gain influence.

After the adventure-filled morning she'd had with Luisa, Melody was quite content to have a quiet afternoon and evening with Lady Bainbridge. As much as she did appreciate a little less excitement, at least for a few hours, Melody's brain could not switch off from dissecting Antonio Graziano's murder. Through an early, delicious dinner of pasta in what Lady Bainbridge called a pesto sauce, followed by slow-braised lamb shanks, Melody couldn't stop thinking about what the motive for the murder might be.

She had watched Tabby Cat and Wolfie far more closely over the years than either of them realised. Always an observant, astute child, Melody had sat quietly when investigations were being discussed, listening and digesting. One thing that Wolfie had said many times over the years was that one of the first steps in investigating a murder was to discover a motive: Who benefited? Who wanted revenge? Who had a reason to hate the victim?

While Tabitha and Wolf had undoubtedly come across some random acts of violence in their years investigating crimes, it was noteworthy how rare such a situation was. Even when the victims seemed random, as they had many years ago when someone seemed to be mimicking the notorious Jack the Ripper, there was often a method to the murderer's madness. While Melody had only been four when they had solved those murders, Tabitha and Wolf had frequently referred to that case over the years when the choice of victims had appeared to be arbitrary.

Why would someone kill a seemingly harmless old man? One thing that she hadn't even thought to point out to the police inspector was that the killer had to be relatively young and nimble to escape through the window. There had been no chair by it, so the murderer had been able to jump up onto the ledge and escape unaided. A youngish, male, relatively well-heeled killer; it wasn't a lot to go on, but it was a start.

Based on her observations over the years, Melody knew that her first step had to be to learn more about the murder victim. Was he, in fact, a kindly old man, or was there a darker side to the bookseller? She considered the little Luisa had shared about the man. He lived in the Jewish Ghetto and had two sons, but only one, an artist, was still living in Venice. That wasn't a lot. She thought about Granny's rather unconventional friendship with the Jewish East End gangster, Tuchinsky. From what Melody had seen and heard over the years, that community was close-knit. Was the Venice Jewish community similar? Certainly, the city itself was much smaller than London, so it would make sense that people would be more likely to know of each other.

This led to a new dilemma: could she walk the streets of Venice alone? Certainly, this wasn't something Melody would ever think to do in London. Perhaps walking through Mayfair from Chesterton House to Granny's or Lord Langley's, but it would never occur to her to go further afield alone. Perhaps it should have occurred to her, Melody mused. However, that didn't solve her immediate conundrum; she didn't know her way around the labyrinth that Venice appeared to be, and she had no idea what dangers might lurk, particularly in the ominously named Ghetto.

Over a delicious, light chocolate mousse, Melody reflected on her options for companions. Luisa had a gondola at her disposal and clearly knew the city well. However, the woman had not struck Melody as a level-headed companion during the crisis. While she certainly hoped that her questions about Signor Graziano wouldn't be accompanied by any drama, what if they were? Could Luisa be relied upon to help? And then there was her notoriety in Venice. Was that a help or a hindrance? During all these musings, it never occurred to Melody that one of her impediments might be Luisa's willingness to participate. The woman clearly lived her life as if it was one long theatrical production; it seemed likely that a murder mystery would be just the kind of performance she'd enjoy starring in.

Putting Luisa aside as an option, for the time being, Melody considered Xander Ashby. There was no doubt that the infatuated young man would be a willing, even eager companion, but perhaps too eager? The thought of possibly encouraging Xander and putting herself under an obligation to the young Englishman was not appealing. Perhaps he might be a last resort, but definitely not a first choice. That left her with Rat. Was it possible to have her brother accompany her to the Ghetto without telling him why?

Melody had a first-rate mind and certainly was no stranger to manipulating those around her on occasion. Nevertheless, it was hard to imagine how she might persuade her brother to escort her, let her ask the questions she needed to ask, and yet have him none the wiser about why. Perhaps the most obvious answer was to confide in her brother about her plans to investigate. Yet this was the one option that never occurred to Melody.

Rat could see that his sister's attention was not on their

dinner conversation, but he put her wool-gathering down to shock from her morning's discovery. Despite her insistence to the contrary, Rat knew that she was an impressionable, sheltered young woman, and it was only to be expected that discovering a dead body and then having to deal with the police had left her subdued. It never occurred to Rat that his sister's inattentiveness was caused by quite a different response to the murder.

Signora Bianchi was as good as her word, even better, in fact. Not only were the costumes for the ball delivered the next afternoon, but they arrived not long after luncheon. Rat had gone out for a stroll, curious to explore their Dorsoduro neighbourhood further. Melody was far too excited to see her outfit to wait for his return. Rossi had delivered the large box to Melody's bedroom, and she bounced on her toes with anticipation as Mary undid the pretty ribbon tied around the elaborately decorated gold and black box.

As Mary lifted the layers of tissue paper, the outfit was revealed. The first thing that Melody saw was an almost shimmering pearl-grey, or maybe more like silver, chiffon. Without even seeing the rest of the gown, Melody could imagine the ethereal effect such a fabric would lend her costume. Melody pulled the dress out of the box and held it up. The bodice was crafted from delicate, silvery lace encrusted with pearls. Filigreed silver chains would loop over her shoulders with lightly gathered silk attached to skim her upper arms. The high-waisted chiffon skirt was all elegant folds and soft draping.

Melody caught her breath. "Oh, Mary, it's beautiful!"

For her part, Mary's first thought was that it was far too revealing and not at all appropriate for an innocent young girl. However, she knew her charge too well to say such a comment out loud. Now that the dress had been admired so ardently, no force in heaven or hell would dissuade Melody from wearing it to the party. At the bottom of the box lay a delicate silver laurel wreath-shaped headpiece to finish the ensemble. Without even trying the outfit on, Melody could see how beautifully it would suggest a Greek goddess without feeling like a costume. She wondered if Rat's outfit had been designed to complement hers and couldn't wait for the pair of them to cause heads to turn as they entered the party that evening.

Impatient for her brother's return, Melody was tempted to unwrap his outfit and take a quick peek. However, while she didn't know why he so readily agreed to escort her that night, she did know that he was not happy that it was a masquerade party, and she didn't want to give him any excuse to change his mind.

After leaving the palazzo, Rat headed to Campo Santa Margherita. He chose a cafe with tables arranged outside where people were sitting and drinking coffee and wine. Joining them, he sat facing the campo so he could watch the children playing and the locals going about their day.

The campo led up to the university, and there were crowds of young men who looked as if they might be students. Lord Langley had generously offered Rat the opportunity to attend Oxford or Cambridge. While Rat was not at all worried about the educational side of taking up the offer, he had no desire to play the working-class charity case alongside the sons of Britain's wealthy and well-born.

There were other, lesser universities he might have chosen to attend, but even then, he knew he would feel like an interloper. Now, watching the young men engaging in playful banter, Rat had a moment's regret. He had no friends, or at least friends his own age. He had always been close with Bear, Wolf's dearest friend and putative private secretary, but he was more than twenty years older than Rat. If he'd gone to university, would he have found the kind of friendship that Wolf and Bear had shared for almost twenty-five years?

Was Xander Ashby someone he might build that kind of friendship with? Rat wondered. He had often pondered what made Wolf and Bear's friendship so solid and long-lasting. He suspected that many people, in society and beyond, wondered the same thing. One thing he knew for sure and understood better than the people who hadn't known them back in their thief-taking days was that what underpinned their friendship more than anything else was trust and loyalty. There were other things that they each brought to the relationship for sure – Bear's taciturn, yet sensible, nature made him the perfect sounding board – but these were not what had kept this friendship going so long.

So far, Xander seemed friendly, well-informed to be sure, the sort of thoroughly decent chap that Britain's top public schools, like Eton and Harrow, excelled at turning out. Rat did not doubt that Xander was just the kind of man one would want on your cricket team or when crewing a boat down the Thames. So far, Rat liked Xander Ashby well enough. But was 'well enough' what a lifelong friendship was based on?

Perhaps not every man was destined to have the kind of trusted confidant, and second that Wolf and Bear were to each other, Rat thought with a shrug before paying for his coffee and rising to return to the palazzo.

CHAPTER 11

*D*ear Diary, my dress is sublime. I cannot wait to put it on. I could hardly wait for Rat to return and unpack his outfit to see what he will be wearing. I am glad I did wait; he was grumpy enough once he saw it without the added insult of me taking a secret look at it before him. I think it is a perfect costume in which to accompany my Greek goddess, but Rat did not see it that way. The rich and soft fabric of his tunic with intricate silver and gold embroidery at the edges is divine. Over the tunic, he is to wear a bronze breastplate with matching arm pieces. I have no idea how Signora Bianchi managed to find such things at short notice, but I am sure they will look very regal. A decorative belt is to cinch the tunic, and she even provided sandals to wear that lace up around his calves.

As soon as he saw his costume, he adamantly refused to wear it, saying that he would wear evening kit instead. It was only when Lady Bainbridge, the voice of reason, pointed out that at a masquerade party, he would stand out more for not wearing a costume that, much to my surprise, he gave in. Rat has an absolute fear of standing out in a crowd and I expected his response to be that we would then not attend. What on earth could have caused his immediate capitulation?

Melody could barely contain her excitement for the rest of the day. Luisa had sent a formal invitation in the early afternoon when they were gathered with Lady Bainbridge for tea. The invitation made clear that the party would not begin until ten o'clock that evening. Even by society's standards, that was quite late, and Rat started grumbling almost immediately.

"Take a nap if you need to," Melody snapped at him. The thick, creamy, gold-embossed invitation was too entrancing to have the moment ruined by her brother's sulkiness. She silently read the invitation.

Honour, riches, marriage-blessing,
Long continuance, and increasing,
Hourly joys be still upon you!
Juno sings her blessings upon you.

After reading it once more to herself, Melody read it out loud. "Is that not delightful?" she asked rhetorically.

"It is Shakespeare, my dear," Lady Bainbridge informed her after taking her first sip of tea. "*The Tempest*, in fact. Juno, who was a Roman goddess rather than a Greek one, gives this blessing to Ferdinand and Miranda on their marriage at the end of the play."

Melody had little interest in the theatre and ignored the literary commentary, asking instead, "Is this usual, Lady Bainbridge? The invitation says that we must arrive by gondola. Is there another way to arrive?"

"Indeed. Just as with all palazzi, including this one, it is possible to enter from the streets. The marchesa has a particularly large, though quite wild, garden that abuts the calle. If memory serves me correctly, the Calle San Cristoforo, to be exact."

"Why would anyone dictate how their guests travel to their party?" Rat asked irritably. So far, there was little about their evening's plans that he looked forward to. He only hoped that the gathering would prove fruitful in other ways.

"Oh, my dear boy, you have no idea what is in store for you?" Lady Bainbridge chuckled. "From all I have heard, each party that Luisa throws is a performance, stage managed down to the finest detail."

"Were you not invited?" Melody asked.

Lady Bainbridge smiled, perhaps a little sadly. "Dear Luisa

always makes it a point to invite me, but my days of gadding about at such hours are long behind me, I fear."

As beautiful as Melody's dress for the party was in its box, it was even more glorious when worn. Melody was not vain, quite the opposite in fact. She was usually quite oblivious to the attention she garnered when she entered a room. However, in this gown, she felt mysterious, sultry and beautiful. This was a dress for a grown woman, not a young girl. Even as she looked at herself in the mirror, Melody had a good idea what Tabby Cat and Wolfie would have said about her attending a soiree in such a gown. For a start, it showed far more décolletage than anything Melody had ever owned, and there was a lightness to the diaphanous overdress that seemed suggestive in some way that Melody could feel rather than articulate.

That the dress was risqué, almost Dionysian was not lost on Mary, who battled with herself internally while she fixed Melody's hair. She knew that it was impossible to suggest that Melody not attend the party and that, if she attended, this dress was the only option. Would it be possible to make some last-minute adjustments to the neckline at least? Melody wanted her hair to be pinned up quite loosely, with one thick ringlet left hanging over her left shoulder. Mary's hands worked quickly even as she silently berated herself for not countering her charge's choice of coiffure, which she was sure would only add to the outfit's lasciviousness.

Melody had chosen a very simple pearl necklace from which hung an elegant diamond pendant. It had been a gift from Granny but had always seemed a little too ostentatious previously. Now, it perfectly suited the outrageous dress. Pearl hair pins complemented the necklace, and elegant diamond teardrop earrings finished the outfit beautifully.

Whatever Mary had considered saying flew out of her mind as she stood back and looked at the young woman in front of her. How could she deny Melody the chance to enchant Venetian society with her beauty and charm?

When Luisa had sent the invitation, she had included two

elegantly wrapped, small boxes. Opening them, Melody had been delighted to find masks for the masquerade. Rat had been less enthused. Now, as the finishing touch to her outfit, Melody put on her pearl-encrusted half mask. Rat's was bronzed to match his breastplate, and Melody only hoped that he could be persuaded eventually to wear it by the sight of all the other guests wearing theirs.

The evening was warm, and Melody rebuffed Mary's efforts to have her take a shawl to wear over her shoulders, at least for the gondola ride. Finally, descending the stairs and making her way to the salotto, Melody found Rat standing by the window, looking very stiff and uncomfortable in his robes and breastplate.

As it happened, Melody thought, he looked extremely handsome in his costume. Rat had been a slight boy for his age, mostly caused by malnutrition for most of his early years, and he was not a large man now. However, his slim frame suited his fine features, and his gentle kindness shone in his blue eyes. However, he wasn't radiating gentle kindness at that precise moment, more like irritable discomfort.

"I can't believe you talked me into this," Rat snapped, fiddling with his breastplate.

"You look very regal, dear," Lady Bainbridge assured him.

"I look ridiculous. I can't believe that all the other men will be wearing such getups."

Melody was glad that it was almost time to leave for the marchesa's palazzo because Rat's whining was putting a dampener on what otherwise looked to be a wonderful evening.

Twenty minutes later, they were seated in Lady Bainbridge's gondola, gliding down the Grand Canal. A large, full moon cast a silvery glow over the water as Giovanni steered them towards the Palazzo Venier dei Leoni. The ride was brief, and almost as soon as they went under the Academia Bridge, Melody could see flickering lanterns and hear music. Other gondolas were transporting party guests who were met by a string quartet playing on the palazzo's terrace. Melody's breath caught in her throat at the magical scene.

"Oh, Rat, look how wonderful it is."

Wonderful wasn't quite the word Rat would have used. While marble columns and other decorative features hinted at the grandeur that had been planned for the palazzo, its unfinished, overgrown facade, only one storey high, looked a little sad to him. Even strewn with garlands and replete with lanterns, Rat thought that the palazzo couldn't escape the impression of dereliction.

Melody saw what Rat did, but her more creative imagination saw the unfinished, overgrown palazzo as breathtakingly romantic rather than run-down and sad. Servants handed out champagne flutes to guests as they disembarked from their gondolas. The air was thick with the almost overwhelmingly sweet smell of flowers intermingled with incense. People in extravagant costumes milled about the large marble terrace, sipping their champagne as they greeted each other with air kisses and handshakes.

At the centre of this stood a figure that could only be Luisa Casati. Her tall, lithe figure was draped in an extraordinary gown that seemed as much feathers as fabric with a billowing, silk taffeta skirt. Melody wasn't sure what bird had such long, black and white dappled plumage, and she wondered if the exotic marchesa had ordered her couturier to paint them for her costume. Unlike her guests, Luisa hadn't put on a mask but had instead made up her face to be one; her skin was painted snow white, and her eyes were covered in a thick, black and dark blue makeup that was painted to appear as if it were dripping down her cheeks. Luisa's lips were painted a dark, dark purple. She was wearing a dark, curly wig that gave the illusion that snakes were woven into it. More dramatic feathers had been crafted into a tall, dramatic headdress to top off the ensemble.

Melody couldn't decide if the marchesa looked beautiful or terrifying, perhaps both. As she pondered this thought, she saw something move in Luisa's hair. Wait, were those actual snakes and not pretend ones?

As she wondered if she were seeing things, a smooth voice behind her said, "Only Luisa would so completely commit to playing Medusa as actually to wear live snakes."

Melody started; that seductive voice could only belong to one person. She turned towards Alessandro Foscari. The conte was dressed not dissimilarly to Rat, indeed to most of the men at the party. It seemed that even the more bohemian men of Venice were limited in their imaginations when it came to costume parties. Rather like the masquerade balls in London, it was mostly left to the female guests to push the creative boundaries.

Like Rat, Alessandro wore a tunic with a breastplate, sandals and a mask. However, unlike Rat, whose discomfort in his outfit was evident, somehow, the handsome conte managed to look positively dashing in his costume. The tunic and sandals showed his long, lean, yet well-defined calves off in a manner that kept drawing back Melody's eye, as much as she tried not to stare. The red, gold-edged cape that he wore was thrown back enough that averting her eyes from his legs merely drew them towards his muscular arms.

Melody was so taken with Alessandro's outfit, or more to the point, the parts of his body that it revealed, that she still hadn't responded to his comment.

If Alessandro had noticed her ogling, he was too much of a gentleman to comment. However, he could not prevent a knowing smile, which quickly brought Melody to her senses.

"Conte Foscari," she stuttered. "I had no idea that you and the marchesa were friends." Of course, she had only met Luisa three days ago, so this was quite an inane comment to make, Melody immediately realised.

Alessandro took her hand, bowed, then kissed it. "You look quite ravishing, Miss Chesterton; at least I assume that you are Miss Chesterton. I believe that a masquerade becomes you."

As flustered as Melody was by her reaction to the dashing Alessandro Foscari, she was not so distracted that she was unaware of the very genuine appreciation in the man's eyes. She would have been even more pleased if she had been able to read his thoughts. When Alessandro had first met Melody Chesterton, he had thought that she was a very pretty, sweetly innocent young woman of the sort that the British upper classes were so adept at turning out. However, in this dress, she seemed anything other than a naive, virginal debutante.

There was something altogether delicious about the young Miss Chesterton in this costume that caused Alessandro to hold her hand for just a moment longer than was socially acceptable as he said in a low, seductive voice, "You must be Aphrodite, the goddess of love."

Melody's cheeks warmed over with nervous embarrassment; was she excited by the conte's outrageous flirting or appalled? She had a good idea what she was supposed to feel. Yet she had trouble summoning the righteous indignation that she believed the situation probably demanded.

Luckily, Melody was saved from having to decide on an appropriately modulated response by Rat's appearance. He had been just a little behind Melody as she had disembarked from the gondola. Rat had received a glass of champagne and begun to make his way through the crowds, which he had got caught up in, slowing his progress. Like his sister, Rat was captivated by the sights, sounds and aromas that the Marchesa Casati had conjured up to intoxicate her guests and his progress was further slowed by the need to take in everything. Rat's sense of appreciative awe quickly dissipated as he came through the crowds of guests and saw his sister's hand being pawed by that oily Foscari fellow.

CHAPTER 12

"To the garden, my lovelies!" Luisa exclaimed in English, which perhaps said more than anything else about the diverse nationalities of her friends. As she said this, servants gently shepherded the guests through a pair of highly ornate, wrought iron gates, up stone steps, and into the palazzo's marble-floor vestibule. Melody had barely a moment to glance around before being swept through glass doors covered with more wrought iron that had been thrown open onto the garden.

Melody stood on the steps, looking into the garden in wonder.

"It is quite something, isn't it?" Alessandro said. Melody turned; she had almost forgotten about his presence in the frantic push of the crowd into and then out of the palazzo. He continued, "Luisa calls this her sanctuary. Despite her flair for the dramatic, she is quite a shy, awkward person, and the peace and tranquillity of this space are where she withdraws to when she feels overwhelmed."

Peaceful and tranquil were not two words Melody would have used to describe the setting that evening. A band was playing in one corner, and laughter and talking rang out over the melodic clinking of champagne flutes and popping of corks throughout the expansive garden.

Melody wasn't sure what the region's native plants might be. Nevertheless, she guessed that at least some of the more exotic-looking blooms reflected Luisa's penchant for the unusual. Colourful flowers with long, trailing vines were wound around tree trunks, giving an almost jungle-like feeling - or what Melody at least imagined a jungle must be like. Statues and sculptures were scattered throughout the garden, lining meandering pathways that seemed laid out to encourage wandering and contemplation. Lanterns were placed strategically throughout the garden to illuminate some areas while throwing others into mysterious gloom.

The entire effect was one of enchantment and alluring possibility, as if the garden itself was beckoning young lovers to get lost within it. As if sensing Melody's thoughts, Alessandro whispered in her ear, "Perhaps we will find a dark corner later, Miss Chesterton."

The suggestion was so outrageous and yet so tempting that Melody didn't know how to answer. Instead, she used Rat's emergence from the vestibule to dip her head and say, "A presto, Conte Foscari."

"Oh, you will indeed see me soon," he chuckled.

Rat wasn't sure what he had interrupted, but he didn't like Foscari's tone, and his sister's demeanour discombobulated him. Unwilling to show the conte how much he disturbed him, Rat took Melody's arm and said, "I see a refreshment table over by the wall."

Melody let herself be led away, unsure if she was irritated at Rat's presumption or grateful for the rescue.

"Why do you allow that man to importune you?" he asked petulantly.

"I would hardly say that the Conte Foscari was importuning me," Melody answered with a smile. "He is a little flirtatious, I will admit. However, I am sure that is just how he is with women."

"Well, that's not how I expect him to be with my sister!"

Melody's natural inclination to stand up for herself and not let her brother try to swaddle her in cotton was tempered by a realisation that he was merely being protective. Rather than snapping a reply, she felt grateful for the genuine love from which the impulse stemmed. Instead, she turned her attention to the refreshment tables weighed down with savoury and sweet treats.

Even after only a partial London season, Melody had become bored by the comestibles that seemed so similar, whether she was attending the Duchess of Cambridgeshire's ball or the Viscountess Wilslow's violin quartet recital. By contrast, there was something so intriguing about the food that Luisa had provided for her guests. Platters of cured meats abutted boards of soft and hard cheeses. There were bowls of marinated olives, artichokes, and sundried tomatoes and plates of little round toasts with various appetising-looking toppings. Selecting a toast with a white, creamy-looking spread on it, Melody bit into it tentatively at first and then with gusto.

"This is delicious, though I am not sure what it is."

Behind her, a heavily German-accented reply came: "It is Baccalà Mantecato: whipped salt cod. A reminder of Venice's storied naval and mercantile past."

Melody turned towards the owner of the voice, who turned out to be a small, round man, perhaps in his mid-sixties. What was left of the white hair surrounding his bald, shiny pate stood up and out and gave the impression that he had a halo of puffy, white clouds. A beaked nose and small, beady eyes that were a little too close together gave the man an unfortunately devious air. Unfortunate because, at least so far, his words were benign and his demeanour almost avuncular.

However friendly his tone, all that Rat heard was the Teutonic accent. Should he be even more suspicious of Luisa Casati, knowing that she invited Germans to her parties? Of course, Europe was not at war, at least officially, and there were plenty of Germans and Austro-Hungarians mixing in the best circles in London. So why not in Italy? Nevertheless, given Rat's mission, he felt it would be foolish to ignore the first German he encountered.

Realising that he would catch more flies with honey than with vinegar, he forced himself to smile, put out his hand and said, "Mr Matthew Sandworth and this is my sister, Miss Melody Chesterton." There was usually a moment's confusion at their different last names, and this time was no exception.

Their new German friend pushed whatever questions he might have aside and returned the handshake accompanied by a very Germanic heel click and bow, "I am Herr Dieter Peetz. Are you new to Venice? I do not believe I have seen you before at one of mein Engel Luisa's soirées."

Now, wasn't that interesting? Rat thought. This German was not merely a guest but apparently a close friend. Rat's German was minimal, but it was sufficient to realise that Herr Peetz was using the affectionate term, my angel, to refer to their host. If Rat's suspicions about the marchesa had been insubstantial previously, suddenly, they had real heft to them.

Rat was so caught up in his suspicions that he had failed to answer Herr Peetz, and it was left to Melody to reply, "We have been here less than a week. I wished to tour Europe, and my brother was kind enough to offer to chaperone."

"Jawohl! The Grand Tour, so beloved of the British. And where else have you seen so far?"

"Our first stop was Venice. My mother, Lady Pembroke, has an old friend here who we are staying with, Lady Bainbridge." Melody commonly referred to Tabby Cat as her mother and Wolfie as her father, if only because the terms guardians felt far too cold and formal for the couple who had never treated her as anything less than their natural daughter.

"Ja, Lady Bainbridge, I have heard of the lady but have not had the pleasure of meeting her."

Rat thought about this answer. Despite her absence that evening, his impression of Lady Bainbridge was that she was hardly a hermit, and Venice's society was tiny compared to London's. It seemed unlikely that a man of any standing would have been in the city long without their paths crossing. So, either Herr Peetz was new to Venice, or he was not a man of standing.

As if intuiting Rat's thoughts, Herr Peetz continued, "I was first here in 1863, and it has been many years since I was last in Venice. I have only been back here for a short time. I travelled here with my daughter." The man pointed to a young woman, perhaps a year or so older than Melody, standing under a tree, deep in conversation. He continued, "Luckily, Venice, she never changes."

Picking up on the significance of the date, Rat asked, "When Venice was still under Austrian rule. Are you Austrian, Herr Peetz, or German?"

"Very observant, Mr Sandworth. I am indeed Austrian, from Vienna in fact. My father was a merchant, and much of his trade came in and out of Venice. He had great hopes that I would join him in his work and brought me with him on one of his trips to introduce me to the business."

"So, you are a merchant?" Melody asked.

"Sadly, at least for my father, no. I never had any interest in the family business and only wanted to read books and to dream of one day writing one."

"And did you?" Melody asked.

"I wrote one, but it was not very good. However, I did become a publisher of books; quite a successful one, some might say. I also publish a popular newspaper in Vienna."

Rat never enjoyed small talk at the best of times. Now, he was impatient to discover whether the old Austrian man might have a hidden agenda for his trip to Venice. "What brings you back here now, Herr Peetz?" Rat asked in what he hoped was a casual, disinterested voice.

"I think the better question, young man, is why did I stay away so long? And now, I can even have an Austrian home away from home at the Hotel Bauer-Grünwald." And with that evasive answer, Herr Peetz repeated his bow, made his excuses, and moved away to sample some of the pasta and risottos laid out further up the table.

"You were rather rude to that lovely old man, you know, Rat?" Melody said critically.

"No, I wasn't," he countered. "What did I say that was rude?"

"It was less what you said and rather the accusatory tone in which you said it. It was almost as if you believed that he was not telling us the truth about who he is and why he is here."

Given that was exactly what Rat suspected, he wasn't sure how to counter the charge. He was irritated that he had been so transparent. Perhaps only Melody, who knew him so well, had sensed an underlying tone to his words. Even then, he would not go far in the world of espionage if he couldn't do a better job of masking his feelings, whatever they were.

Over the years, Rat had witnessed Lord Langley handle situations with cold detachment. Indeed, Wolf had once confessed that this coolness had led him and Tabitha, particularly Tabitha, to view Lord Langley as quite reptilian when they had first met him. Their relationship with his mentor had eventually become warm and trusting, which spoke to how effective a mask Lord Langley could wear until he chose to drop it.

Irritated by his sister's comment, Rat wanted to observe the Austrian man alone. Just as he wondered how he might shake his sister off without arousing even more suspicions, he was saved by Marchesa Casati swooping in, feathers gently fluttering as she moved.

"Melody, have you seen my bambinos yet?" Luisa asked.

For a moment, Melody wondered if Luisa's daughter, Cristina, had joined her in Venice. However, it quickly became apparent who her babies were as Luisa swept Melody away from Rat and towards a part of the garden dominated by a small, pretty marble ivy-covered rotunda with built-in seats. Strutting around the rotunda, occasionally pecking at the grass, were two glorious peacocks.

It seemed these were not the only birds who inhabited the garden. As Luisa approached the rotunda, she called out, "Chicci, la mamma sta arrivando."

In response, a loud, squawking voice replied, "La mamma sta arrivando."

Looking in the direction of the voice, Melody saw a large, multi-coloured bird on a wooden perch, one leg attached to a thin chain.

"This is my baby, Chicci. He is a macaw," Luisa explained, going up to the bird and stroking its head lovingly.

Looking at Luisa's birds, Melody said, "Is what you said to Lady Bainbridge true? Do you have a cheetah?"

"Sì. Shaitan is my great love." Anticipating Melody's next question, Luisa said, "He is a very good boy and behaves himself very well in public, but people, they are often silly, are they not? So, to be a good hostess and not subject my bambino to the absurd performance that so many feel they must go through in his presence, he is resting in my bedroom, away from the crowds."

Melody was a little disappointed that she wouldn't get to see the infamous feline, but also thought that his absence from such a crowded party was probably a good thing.

With his sister opportunely escorted off by the marchesa, Rat considered how to watch Herr Peetz stealthily. He decided to follow the other man's actions and make his way up the table that was overloaded with nibbles, heavier dishes like pasta, succulent-looking and smelling roast meats, and ended with an abundance of sinfully good-looking desserts.

Rat attempted to keep a sufficient distance from the other man while not losing sight of him in the crowd. At least filling his plate with food gave him a good reason not to be in a group socialising. From what Rat could see, the portly Herr Peetz had filled his plate with a little bit of almost every savoury dish on offer. While many people daintily picked at small portions of food that could be held in one hand, there were tables and chairs scattered around the garden for those who were looking to enjoy a more substantial meal. Herr Peetz made his way to one of these tables and sat down.

As he followed at a discreet distance, Rat wondered how he could observe the man while he ate. Having just introduced himself, it would be odd for Rat then to choose to sit at another table, particularly as Herr Peetz was sitting alone. He was considering this dilemma when the choice was taken out of his hands; Conte Foscari sidled up to the table, whispered something to Herr Peetz, who looked sorrowfully at his plate of mostly uneaten food, then rose and followed the other man into a dark corner of the garden.

There was an unholy alliance if there ever was one, Rat thought. The two men he found most suspicious in Venice had disappeared together for an illicit meeting. Of course, Rat reminded himself, he didn't know for sure that the meeting was about anything illicit. However, if the conversation was entirely innocent, why did Foscari not just sit at the table to talk to Herr Peetz? No, the entire exchange had all the marks of some kind of conspiracy.

Rat thought about what he had witnessed; he certainly didn't want to act like Melody and jump to all sorts of fanciful conclusions. What had he seen? It was evident that Foscari wanted to talk to the Austrian and that, whatever it was, it was urgent enough that Dieter Peetz left the plate of food he had so eagerly amassed. He replayed how their interaction seemed when the conte had first approached the table; they hadn't greeted each other in any visible way. It was clear that they knew each other already, and it also appeared as if this wasn't their first time running into each other that evening or that, if it was, they had been expecting to meet.

Whatever Foscari wished to discuss needed privacy, but even then, why choose a party? If they knew each other and had something to discuss, why not do so another time? There was clearly an urgency to this conversation; whatever it was, it couldn't wait.

As Rat considered all this, he watched the two men disappear into the shadows of one of the few unlit corners of the garden. How close could he get to them without being discovered? He decided to find out. After all, this was a party; if they realised they were not alone, surely they would merely assume their company was an amorous couple seeking the privacy of a dark nook.

While it was hard to see much in this part of the garden, as Rat's eyes became accustomed to the sudden gloom, he saw two figures sitting on a bench. Not far from where they sat, there was a large statue of a horse, its base surrounded by shrubs. If he went around and then stayed low as he approached, he thought that he could come upon them and hide behind the statue while being close enough to hear their conversation.

Rat's plan had not taken his costume into consideration. While it might have been easy enough to slither silently wearing trousers, the tunic and breastplate made the endeavour twice as hard and significantly slower than it would have been. Rat considered taking the breastplate off and discarding it but then realised he would have to explain why he had done so when he met up with Melody. Instead, he crawled along as best he could. While the two men had found the quietest part of the garden, there was still enough noise emanating from the rest of the guests that whatever noise Rat made didn't alert the conspirators. Or at least, that was his hope.

Rat also hoped that he didn't miss the main thrust of their conversation because of his snail's pace. When he finally was close enough to hear their conversation, Rat stopped, lying in the grass and trying to catch the whispered words.

"Graziano is a huge loss for us," Herr Peetz said.

"Indeed," Foscari answered. "And more than that, it indicates that our plan may have been discovered."

Plan? Rat thought, feeling thoroughly vindicated in his mistrust of Herr Peetz and dislike of Conte Foscari.

CHAPTER 13

*D*ear Diary, Luisa's party was everything I had hoped for, *and more. Can you believe that she had live snakes intertwined in her hair? I have no idea how she stopped them just slithering away. The food, the music, the costumes, the romance of it all! What a wonderful evening it was. I am a little disappointed that I did not get a chance for the rendezvous that Alessandro promised. Or perhaps I am relieved? Why does the man leave me so confused whenever I am in his company?*

Rat behaved quite oddly for much of the night. In fact, he's been behaving oddly ever since we left London. Perhaps the most surprising thing he did all evening was to raise the topic of Signor Graziano's death with me! I had been wracking my brain to come up with a way to persuade him to accompany me to the Ghetto, and then, in the end, he was the one who brought it up.

As we watched the sun rise over the Grand Canal in the gondola on the way back to Lady Bainbridge's palazzo, he asked me to tell him everything I knew about Antonio Graziano and to go back over my observations around his murder. I ended by saying that I thought it important to go to the Ghetto and talk to his son, if possible. Rather than focusing on the fact that I was involving myself further in the murder investigation, Rat was quite distracted and said that going to the Ghetto was a good idea and that he would accompany me. As much as that was the outcome I was hoping to achieve, I do wonder what on earth has got into my brother.

Despite the party having carried on until the wee hours, Rat still had a hard time falling asleep. While he was concerned about what he had overheard, he was also excited at having stumbled across two of Britain's enemies discussing their nefarious scheme, whatever it was. Perhaps he also felt guilty at having dragged Melody into the investigation. He hadn't intended to, of course, but she had been the one to find Antonio Graziano's body and to talk with the police. And, while he would never admit it out loud, his sister had made some interesting observations and deductions about the scene of the crime.

If he were truly honest with himself, Rat welcomed Melody's help asking questions in the Jewish Ghetto. Melody was a genial, likeable person who made friends easily. People opened up to her in a way that always amazed Rat, who found casual interactions far more difficult.

After their very late night into early morning, neither Rat nor Melody stirred from their beds until long past the time when Lady Bainbridge had eaten and then retired for her post-luncheon nap. After eating a light repast, they left word with Rossi and asked Giovanni to take them to the Ghetto. The ride was almost the mirror of their first gondola ride from the station, except that, at some point, the gondolier branched off to a smaller canal. Finally, pulling up at the side of a fondamenta, he pointed to a low, old, wooden door frame that, rather than being the entryway to a building, seemed to lead down a calle.

Giovanni pointed towards the wooden entrance, "This is the Sotoportego Ghetto, which will lead you into the Ghetto Vecchio." Noticing Melody's interest in the entrance, he explained, "This was one of the gates that was closed at night to keep il Ebrei in." Seeing Melody's horror at his words, Giovanni hastened to add, "Non adesso. No more. Back, long time ago back."

Remembering a book he had read on Venetian history before their trip, Rat added, "I believe that the practice ended in 1797 when Napoleon conquered Venice. At that point, the gates were torn down, and the Jews were no longer locked in from sunset to sunrise." He added, "The city then quickly fell under Austrian control, and many of the restrictions that Napoleon lifted were reinstated. However, the insistence that they live in the Ghetto was not. Even so, most Jews continued to live here and, I believe, still do."

"Sì, sì," Giovanni agreed. "Il Ebrei, they live here."

Melody and Rat disembarked from the gondola and made their way through the Sotoportego Ghetto into a narrow calle, immediately passing a bakery with a Hebrew star prominently placed in its window.

There were delicious smells emanating from the shop and Melody's grumbling stomach was a reminder of what a light meal she had eaten earlier. "Let us go in here and purchase a pastry," Melody suggested.

"Is this really the time to worry about your stomach?" Rat snapped.

In a quieter voice, Melody reminded him, "We do not know where we are going. Perhaps spending some coin will encourage locals to help us."

Rat realised the wisdom of his sister's words and nodded. They entered the bakery and were welcomed by a cheerful, motherly-looking woman wearing a simple, functional dress with an apron over it and with her hair tucked under a headscarf.

"Ciao," she said in a friendly tone.

"Ciao," Melody replied while inspecting the wide range of delicious-looking offerings. As she said that, a man dressed as she imagined a baker would be entered from the back of the shop with a basket of what looked and smelled like doughnuts.

Seeing Melody's interest, the woman pointed to the doughnuts and asked in English, "This?"

Melody nodded enthusiastically, "Sì, sì. Grazie."

The woman took a piece of brown paper, expertly wrapped it into a cone, and then placed several pastries into it.

As Rat paid, Melody eagerly took a bite of one of the still-warm doughnuts. It was as delicious as she'd hoped it would be: lemon-scented and covered in warm, sticky honey syrup. The woman appreciatively watched Melody's enjoyment.

"Excuse me, madam, but do you know an Antonio Graziano?"

Rat inquired.

They had clearly pushed beyond the limits of the woman's English, and she shook her head in confusion. Turning, she went through the door that the baker had come out of with the doughnuts, returning just a few moments later with a young man in tow.

Melody and Rat had been about to leave the shop when she returned, and the young man said, "Please, do not go. Mama said you asked her something, but she does not understand. Me, I speak the English gooder."

Turning back with relief, Rat repeated his question. The young man nodded his head sadly and replied, "We knew Signor Graziano, but he is no more."

"Yes, we heard of his death." Rat paused, "In fact, my sister here was the one who discovered his body while shopping for books."

Rat hoped that this explanation might suffice as an explanation for why they were asking after the man. The young man continued, "So sad. He was a true mensch, Signor Graziano."

Melody had heard Tuchinksy's grandmother, Bubbe, use the word mensch when talking about Wolfie. She nodded, "I did not know him well, but my slight interaction with him made clear that he was an honest and decent man."

"Sì, Signor Graziano, Zikhrono Livrakha, may his memory be a blessing, taught many of the Ashkenazi Jews in the Ghetto in cheder over the years."

There were so many words in that sentence that Melody and Rat didn't understand that they were both grateful when the young man explained, "Cheder is a Hebrew school for bambini."

"And Ashkenazi Jews?" Rat asked.

"Ashkenazi Jews came here from Poland, Germany, Russia and other countries to the north. The rest of us, those who fled the Inquisition, or other mamzer throughout southern Europe and North Africa who hate Jews, are Sephardim. We have our scuola. They have, as they say, their shuls." The young man then added,

"Signor Graziano's levaya, his funeral, is now in the Scuola Grande Tedesca in the Ghetto Nova."

Not that either Melody or Rat would have thought to ask the question, but the young man said, hoping to be helpful, "He would have been buried yesterday; Jews, we bury immediately. But it was shabbat."

Raising a question that hadn't occurred to her until that moment, Melody asked, "Where are people buried in Venice?" Clearly, they couldn't be buried in the watery city itself.

"Jews are buried on the island of Lido. When the levaya is over, the body will be taken out there by boat. Then, the family they return to sit shivah for seven days and nights."

None of this sounded conducive to questioning the family, but Melody did wonder whether they might still glean some information from this helpful young man. "I understand that Signor Graziano had one son still in Venice. I supposed that his other son, in Austria, was not able to return in time for the funeral."

"No, no. Avraham, or as he likes to be called now, Abe, was back in Venice anyway. So, that, at least, was a good thing. I know that it'll be a comfort to his brother, Moische, to have him home." In a lower voice, as if sharing a rather salacious bit of gossip, he said, "Moische is not able to handle things well. He is a grown man who still lived with his papa. A bit of a schlemiel." Melody didn't know what the word meant, but it didn't sound like a compliment.

"I heard that he is an artist," Melody said casually, hoping to keep the gossip coming.

The young man laughed and raised his eyebrows, "Artist. Sì, that is what he says. What kind of work is that for a grown man? If you want to paint, paint the outside of a house. Paint a boat, not a picture of a boat."

Melody couldn't help but argue, "Some of the great artists of all time were Italian men. What about Michelangelo?"

"Uffa! Moische Graziano is no Michelangelo."

Melody considered the distance between the bookshop and

the Ghetto and couldn't imagine the elderly, rather frail man who she had met walking it twice a day. "Signor Graziano lived in the Ghetto?" she asked.

"Tipo. When Signora Graziano was alive, they all lived in a house just off Campo di Ghetto Nuovo. But for the last few years, the signor has mostly lived in a little flat above the shop and has left Moische here, 'painting'."

Well, that was interesting, Melody thought. They would have to find a way to get in and search the flat. She caught Rat's eye, and it was evident he'd had the same thought.

The older baker came into the shop and yelled something at the younger man that Melody loosely mentally translated as, "Get back to work." They thanked the young man for his help and left the shop.

"What do we do next?" Melody asked.

"Well, it seems that we will not get to talk to either son for the next week. Though..." and he paused.

"You wonder how much of a coincidence it is that his son happened to be home from Austria?" Melody finished his sentence.

"Exactly!" For the first time, Rat wished that he could confide in his sister that his role in Venice was to do far more than merely be her chaperone. It was on the tip of his tongue to say something about what he had overheard at the party between Herr Peetz and Conte Foscari. However, he couldn't think how to explain why he was eavesdropping on them without explaining his role in the Secret Service Bureau. He knew that, even after being part of British Intelligence for more than forty years, there were very few people who had any inkling of Lord Langley's secret career. Tabitha, Wolf and the dowager knew, but that was only because of an unfortunate incident many years ago that Lord Langley was unwilling to expound on. What kind of operative would Rat be if he couldn't even keep his secret for two weeks?

They decided to wander further into the Ghetto; having come all the way there, it seemed foolish to go no further than one shop on the first street. The Ghetto was lively. Everywhere, people were shopping, children were playing, and women were hanging out their washing from their windows, merrily calling out to each other between houses. In many ways, the area did not seem much different than the rest of Venice; the architecture was the same, the narrow calles and endless bridges over canals. Yet, when they looked closely, they saw Hebrew lettering on buildings and the Jewish star on shops, and much of what the women were calling to each other didn't sound like Italian.

Melody and Rat wandered until they entered a large, open area. Reading the sign on a wall, Rat realised that they had made their way to Campo di Ghetto Nuovo. Looking around the campo, he thought there were a few buildings that looked as if they might be synagogues, each with rather distinctive arched windows and Hebrew writing on the buildings.

Just as he wondered which was the synagogue that Signor Graziano's funeral was taking place in, he saw a crowd of sombrely dressed people exiting from a mustard-yellow building over in one corner. Out of the crowd, six men emerged carrying a plain pine coffin. Melody hadn't been to many funerals, but whenever she had seen coffins, they'd been incredibly ornate and meant to demonstrate the wealth and status of the deceased. This coffin seemed more suited to a pauper.

Bringing up the rear of the coffin, Melody saw two men, probably in their late thirties or early forties, both of whom had noticeable tears in their garments. As the coffin bearers made their way out of the campo, people approached the two men and seemed to be paying their condolences.

"Let us get a little closer," Melody suggested. "I believe that those two men with the torn clothes are the family. Why would they go to their father's funeral in ripped jackets?"

It seemed that their conversation had been overheard by a nearby old woman, who explained, "Before the levaya, the family tears their clothes to symbolise grief."

Grateful to have found someone else who spoke fluent

English, Melody asked innocently, hoping that the old woman would overlook her previous words, "Whose funeral is it?"

"The gonif's funeral. Yimakh shemo, may his name be erased from memory." The old woman said these words with such venom. Melody couldn't reconcile this with the kindly old man she had met.

"What is a gonif?" she asked.

"What you British call a thief."

"Signor Graziano was a thief?" Melody asked in amazement. Was this little old woman just insane?

"Ha! If you only knew what I do," the old woman said with a cackle as she walked away from them.

This was indeed a different view of the deceased than others had expressed. Melody and Rat exchanged looks; were these merely the worlds of a crazy old woman, or had a whole new line of investigation just opened up?

CHAPTER 14

During the walk back to meet Giovanni at the gondola, Melody and Rat discussed what to do next.

"I believe that we need to search that flat as soon as possible," Melody said thoughtfully.

Melody told Rat that she'd been impressed with Ispettore Moretti. They had both heard Wolf and Tabitha complain about London's Metropolitan Police's incompetence and sometimes even venality. Rat certainly remembered Bruiser, long dead now, but once the epitome of a policeman who played both sides of the law.

"Ispettore Moretti struck me as an intelligent man who would not discount an idea just because it was expressed by a woman. His sergeant, I think his name was Vinditti, was another matter. It was all he could do to control his eye-rolling as I spoke. While Moretti listened to my thoughts on why this was not a robbery, I got the impression that Vinditti would be happy to write this off as such. I do wonder whether he will take the time even to search Graziano's flat."

"Regardless, I believe that we need to do so sooner rather than later. If nothing else, at some point, his sons will want to go through his possessions and perhaps even sell the bookshop."

They were each amazed by the other; Melody couldn't believe that Rat had not tried to dissuade her from investigating further and was willing to collaborate, and he couldn't believe how insightful his little sister was. Initially, Rat hadn't really stopped to wonder why Melody had wanted to go to the Ghetto to learn more about Antonio Graziano. Instead, he'd just marvelled at the lucky coincidence that his sister had been the one to stumble into the scene of a murder that had been discussed by two men he found particularly suspicious. Now, what amazed him was not this lucky coincidence but rather the thoughtful, intelligent observations that Melody had made.

As much as Rat had envied Wolf's friendship with Bear over the years, he'd also admired the professional partnership the man had formed with Tabitha. It had taken Rat some time and maturity to recognise the strengths that Tabitha brought to that relationship: her keen intellect, logical mind, and enormous empathy, which allowed her to put herself in the shoes of suspects and imagine what might have driven their crimes. As he and Melody walked through the twisting streets of the Ghetto, a brief thought flashed through Rat's mind: his sister was more like Tabitha, Lady Pembroke, than perhaps he gave her credit for.

Rat never doubted that his sister was intelligent; that had been obvious when they had first arrived at Chesterton House, unable to read and write. Four-year-old Melody had learned her letters and numbers almost as quickly as her older brother and had been able to best him at chess by the time she was six. Rat was not one of those who considered men above women in all ways that mattered. He had far too many intelligent, resourceful women in his life to ever be that hubristic. Yet, he had never shaken off the role of protective older brother who always knew best. Now, for the first time, it occurred to Rat that perhaps that would no longer be the case.

Melody and Rat realised that they needed to look through Signor Graziano's belongings immediately. Between his time working for Wolf when he was thief-taking and then his time studying under Lord Langley, Rat had learned many valuable skills, not the least of which was lock picking. This was a skill that a trained intelligence officer needed as much as an East End criminal did. Out of habit, Rat always carried a small lock pick in his pocket and today was no exception. A thought flashed through his mind: how to explain to Melody such a skill and his ready access to the necessary implement?

Perhaps it was believable enough that he remembered how to pick locks from his days working with Wolf. Melody certainly knew the stories of those days, even if she barely remembered her time living on the streets of Whitechapel. Could he just gloss over the pick in his pocket? Arriving at the bookstore after a gondola ride back from the Cannaregio district, it appeared that the answer was, yes, he could. If Melody wondered anything, she said nothing as he pulled out a small set of lock picks from his pocket and deftly picked the lock of the bookshop door.

Rat had been worried about passersby on the street or neighbouring shop workers. He needn't have been concerned. By the time they had arrived at the bookshop, it was almost time for the shops to close and their workers were too busy shutting up for the day to wonder about Melody and Rat.

Slipping into the shop, Melody shivered; it was eerily quiet. Though, on reflection, was it really any quieter than it had been when she had first visited, and Signor Graziano had been busy in the back? Not really. However, just the knowledge that a murder had taken place there recently made the murky, dusty shop feel disquieting.

"Do we want to search the shop first, or start with the flat?" Melody asked.

Rat considered the question: did the killer come looking for something? If so, did he find it, or was that why Graziano was murdered? Either way, looking around the messy, overstuffed bookshelves, he couldn't imagine where they would begin in the shop.

"Let us start with his flat," Rat decided. This then led to the question: how did they get to it?

Melody thought about the day that she and Luisa had visited the bookshop and had gone through to the back of the shop looking for the elderly bookseller. She thought about the dark blue curtain that separated the shop's front and back. Had there been a small staircase hidden in a dark corner? She thought maybe there had been. Indicating that Rat should follow her,

Melody made her way back in that direction. Just as she went around some particularly overloaded bookcases and walked into the dark alcove that led to the curtain, she saw a pile of boxes stacked in the corner and there, just behind the boxes, was the staircase that she had thought she remembered.

There wasn't much room to walk between the boxes, and Melody wondered how the frail and doddering Signor Graziano managed to squeeze through. The staircase was very narrow and twisting, and as Melody and Rat made their way up it, Melody again wondered how the elderly man managed this every day. The staircase led into a room that was as gloomy and dusty as the bookshop. A plate was on a small table and still had some bread and cheese that was turning mouldy, and a dried-up slice of apple on it.

"It seems as if Signor Graziano had been interrupted while he was having his lunch," Melody observed. No sooner had she said that than she considered the implication of her words. "I told the police inspector that I believed that Signor Graziano may have known his killer and certainly hadn't been surprised by him. This seems to confirm that theory."

Rat looked at his little sister with bemusement. "How can you possibly extrapolate that from a rotten apple?"

As Melody talked, she continued to take in the rest of the living room. "Luisa and I must have arrived here at perhaps eleven-thirty in the morning. So, the killer must have had Signor Graziano in the office by the time we arrived."

"How can you know that?" Rat asked, mystified at his sister's leaps of logic.

"Well, we called out to Signor Graziano about twenty minutes after we'd been in the shop, and when he didn't reply, we went back to the office and found him dead. My theory is that the killer heard us call out, and that's why he escaped out of the window instead of just walking back out through the door. It was evident that the two men had talked, and I found a cigarette butt that was quite burned down, so the conversation had been of some length of time. I am sure that if they had walked down the stairs while we were in the shop, they would have heard us. It is hard to imagine that the murderer would have just ignored the presence of two potential witnesses in the shop. Therefore, they must have already been in the office."

Rat replayed what Melody had just said and couldn't find any flaw in her logic. Considering the scene in front of them, she continued, "So, perhaps Signor Graziano was up here eating. The killer came into the shop, couldn't find him, called out and then our victim came down the stairs, and they went into the office to speak." The half-eaten meal implied that the old man hadn't been expecting his killer, but had he known him?

Deciding that they would not discover the answer to that question by looking at the plate of food, he turned and took in the rest of the room. It was a small, untidy, but not uncomfortable space. The walls were lined with bookshelves that were even more haphazard and dusty than the ones below. Apart from the table and the one chair by it, there was an old, sagging armchair that had seen better days. The stuffing was coming out of multiple holes, and the fabric was almost totally worn down. There was a small, equally old, threadbare footstool by the chair and a scratched and battered small side table.

On this table was a folder. Melody walked over and picked up the folder. Opening it, she found a few sheets of paper. One seemed to have a list of names on it with a few dated columns next to them. There were X's next to some of the names. The other sheets of paper had various things scrawled on them. Still, the combination of Antonio Graziano's handwriting and their limited Italian meant that Rat and Melody had trouble deciphering the words.

There were a few phrases that were underlined. Looking at one, Melody said, "This isn't in Italian, it's in German. Or, to be precise, it's a mixture of the two. Looking more closely, she continued, "I see the names Hermann Hesse and Thomas Mann. I think that at least some of these are German books."

"Well, Graziano was a bookseller. It would make sense. Did you see German books when you were perusing his shelves?"

"Honestly, it is such a jumble down there, and I was not really looking for them. Perhaps…" She considered the list in her hand, "Perhaps these are names of people who have ordered the books and the dates they were delivered."

That certainly made some sense, but there was something about the list that niggled at the edge of Rat's mind; he just couldn't think what it was. Then, he considered the conversation he had overheard between Conte Foscari and Herr Peetz, a conversation he hadn't told Melody about. Now, he considered just how much he might be able to share with his sister without divulging his mission in Venice. After all, he pondered, he had accepted her help, but how much use would that be if she was missing vital clues?

Finally, he made peace with his decision and admitted, "During Marchesa Casati's party, I overheard Herr Peetz talking with Conte Foscari about Signor Graziano's death."

Melody knew her brother well and it had been evident that he was weighing whether to share something with her. Whatever she had imagined he might be about to confide, that was not it. Rat continued, "Herr Peetz said, 'Graziano is a huge loss for us,' and then Foscari said something about being worried that this meant their plan had been discovered."

"What do you think they meant?"

Melody considered how she wanted to answer Rat. It was no secret that he had not liked Alessandro Foscari from the first moment they met. It had also been evident that he had been immediately suspicious of Herr Peetz. Melody had long known that Lord Langley had trained Rat to be a cryptologist, and she had begun to wonder recently whether his role had developed into something more. While Rat believed that Melody had no idea about the work that Lord Langley did for British Intelligence, he forgot how much time she had spent in the man's company as a child.

People often assumed that children weren't paying attention or didn't understand what was being discussed around them. However, Melody had always been an observant, bright child, and it had been evident to her for a long time that Lord Langley, or Uncle Maxi, as she referred to him, did some kind of intelligence work for the government. That he had been mentoring Rat in cryptology merely confirmed this. It wasn't a giant leap to imagine that Rat had progressed to other covert activities.

If Rat had been able to read her thoughts, it might have occurred to him to wonder why he had assumed that she had no idea about Lord Langley's role and, by extension, his own.

Finally, Melody decided that she was tired of pretending that she had no idea what was going on and said, "Do you think that Herr Peetz is involved in espionage for the Austrian government and that he is working with Conte Foscari?"

This was precisely what Rat thought and he wasn't immediately sure how to answer. Was this the espionage the British Government suspected was taking place? Of more immediate concern was the fact that Melody had intuited what was going on, or at least what Rat thought was going on. What else did she know? He reminded himself that just because Melody had guessed his suspicions, it didn't mean that she knew about Rat's role and his mission in Venice. Still, how to admit to the former without alluding to the latter?

Finally, unable to think of a better way to handle the situation, he simply said, "Yes. That is what I believe to be the case."

"I find it hard to believe that such a nice, sweet old man is up to anything so nefarious," Melody said in a determined voice.

"Well, an Austrian spying for Austria is hardly nefarious any more than an Englishman doing so for our government," Rat pointed out. "As for Signor Graziano, well, Italy's position in Europe is rather nuanced these days, to say the least. Britain and Italy have some colonial rivalries, and our government views Italy's naval build-up with caution. And, of course, Italy has been part of the Triple Alliance with Germany and Austria-Hungary for many years. Though, it is generally believed that its loyalty to those countries is not solid. After all, the movement for Italian unification, I believe they call it the Risorgimento, was at least in part a revolt against Austrian rule, including of Venice and the surrounding area."

Usually, Melody had little interest in history. Still, in the context of her murder investigation, she was glad that her brother had bothered to pay attention to his history lessons at least.

Rat decided they should take the folder and its papers with them. They looked around the rest of the flat but didn't find anything else of interest. Melody pointed out a medal on proud display and briefly wondered in what war Antonio Graziano had fought. Rat shrugged his shoulders, and with that, they left the flat.

CHAPTER 15

Arriving back at the palazzo, Rat went straight to his room to stow the folder and papers. Melody was stopped from following him by Rossi, who cleared his throat in the way that all butlers seemed to know how to do, regardless of country.

"Signorina, Conte Foscari is waiting for you in the salotto. Lady Bainbridge's riposo pomeridiano is going a little longer than usual. The conte has been here quite a while."

Before her illuminating chat with Rat, Melody would have been thrilled to receive a visit from the alluring Alessandro Foscari. Nervous, unsure of herself, but thrilled. Now, the knowledge that he might be an enemy of the Crown and actively involved in espionage against her country threw Melody into a panic; what should she say to him? Would he realise that she knew his secret identity? Was she a good enough actress to mask her feelings towards him now?

Collecting herself, she realised that at least she knew the answer to this last question: thanks to Granny's relentless insistence on training in deportment and etiquette, Melody knew that she was perfectly capable of controlling her reactions. As the dowager had said on many occasions, "When Bertie was alive, one needed to become adept at schooling one's features no matter how shocking and inappropriate the conversation or behaviour. It is a useful skill to master."

Melody walked towards the salotto, pausing before the door to take a deep breath and compose herself as the dowager had spent so many hours teaching her to. She then opened the door to find Alessandro standing in front of the window, looking out on the Grand Canal.

Hearing the door open, he turned, and a smile lit up his handsome face, "Ciao, Miss Chesterton."

He had asked her to call him Alessandro, but given what she now knew about him, this informality and friendliness did not sit well with her. However, if she was overly formal with him now, surely, he might become suspicious.

Realising that she must behave just as she would have if Alessandro had called on before her conversation with Rat, Melody answered in a sweet, measured tone, "Ciao, Alessandro. What a lovely surprise. Have you come to see Lady Bainbridge? I believe she is still taking her afternoon nap."

Alessandro crossed the room quickly, took her hand and kissed it, again lingering just a little too long. "No, bellissima, I came only to see you."

Melody blushed deeply. Despite her new feelings towards Conte Foscari, his compliment, in Italian at that, was utterly charming and hard to resist. He continued, "I am sorry that I did not get to say goodbye last night. I became caught up in a small business matter."

Small business matter! Melody thought. She knew exactly what that had been.

"It ended up taking me away from the party earlier than I had hoped and I missed the chance for our intimate tête-à-tête."

Given that a tête-à-tête was a private conversation between two people, Melody considered Alessandro's appendage of the word intimate to be grammatically unnecessary and yet romantically beguiling.

Determined to resist the man's charms, she answered in a cool tone, "You have nothing to apologise for. I had a delightful time and met some very interesting people." Melody paused. Would she be showing her hand if she mentioned Herr Peetz? Deciding that the risk was negligible and that she wanted to see Alessandro's reaction, Melody continued, "Rat and I met this delightful Austrian, Herr Dieter Peetz. Do you know him?"

Melody was usually quite adept at spotting when someone was about to lie to her. There was a micro-expression that normally flitted across their face as the decision was made to deceive. In Alessandro's case, there was no such tell-tale moment as he answered in the most guileless voice, "I do not believe I have had the pleasure. Of course, there were so many people in attendance last night."

If Melody had harboured any doubts or hopes that Rat was wrong about Alessandro's involvement in something villainous, this falsehood and its smooth delivery put paid to those doubts. It never occurred to her for a moment that Rat might have been mistaken; she had total faith in her brother. If he said that he had seen Alessandro with Herr Peetz and overheard them talking, there was no question that he had.

Melody was not sure in which direction to steer the conversation after this. Luckily, she was given a temporary reprieve by Rossi's entrance, bearing a tea tray. It was comforting to see that, despite her many years in Italy, Lady Bainbridge maintained some traditions from the country of her birth. Indeed, the pouring and drinking of tea and genteel nibbling on biscuits was a time-honoured way for the British upper classes to smooth over any social awkwardness, or worse.

Melody and Alessandro sat as Rossi poured tea. Finally, cups in hand and plates of delicious-looking little biscuits studded with almonds on their laps, Melody and her disarming guest were again alone.

Deciding to try another tack, Melody asked, "What is it that you do, Alessandro? You never said."

Of course, it was likely that an Italian aristocrat, even one mainly living in Britain, had no more need for employment than his British counterparts. Nevertheless, Melody was curious as to how he would answer.

"My father died a few years ago and I now run his many businesses." As if intuiting her thoughts, Alessandro continued, "I understand that it is considered quite gauche for the upper classes to taint their hands with commerce, at least in Britain.

However, my father was Italian and felt no such compunction."

Melody remembered the story Lady Bainbridge had told a few days before: Alessandro's father had married a wealthy heiress and restored his family's fortune. It seemed he had used his wife's money to launch himself successfully into business.

"What businesses are those?" Melody asked, attempting to keep her tone light.

"My father diversified into many industries. However, most of his investments were in publishing in one form or another. He started what is now the most popular newspaper in Italy. He then built on this foundation, often through acquisition, and we now own various smaller publications as well, including one here in Venice, *El Meso*."

Now, this was interesting, wasn't it? Melody thought. Didn't Herr Peetz say that he also published a newspaper in Vienna? Surely, this was too much of a coincidence. She considered mentioning Herr Peetz again in this context. Conflicted, she finally decided that given Alessandro's protestation that he didn't know the man, to refer to him again would be too suspicious.

Instead, Melody asked innocently, "So, do you consider yourself an Englishman or an Italian, Alessandro?"

He chuckled, "Ah, that is an interesting question. Is it not possible to be both? Can one not be two things simultaneously? Both husband and father, aristocrat and businessman, patriot and political critic?"

Melody found his last analogy particularly interesting. Is that what sat behind Alessandro's betrayal of Britain: A misplaced sense of political dissent?

"As per your examples, of course, one may be two things simultaneously. However, when it comes to nationalities at least, I would imagine that, at some point, one may have to choose sides. After all, if someone considered themselves French and British, presumably there was a point during the Napoleonic Wars when they would have to pick a side."

"Well, perhaps Napoleon is not the best example. I believe that many in France disapproved of him. However, your point is well taken. Luckily, at least for now, there is no reason for me to pick a side."

"And if there were?" Melody couldn't resist asking. She knew that the question was more provocative than perhaps she should venture to ask. Nevertheless, the moment was too fortuitous to resist asking.

"Let us hope that it does not come to that," Alessandro said, any hint of levity gone from his voice.

"You do not believe that we are headed to war?"

"I hope that we are not, but indeed it seems likely. However, I believe that, when it comes to that, Italy will not join Britain's enemies."

"How can you be so certain?" Melody asked with genuine curiosity.

"Italy, particularly Venice, has found it expedient to maintain economic ties with Austria-Hungary. However, it was barely fifty years ago that Italy fought for unification, Risorgimento, against the Austrians, and then allied itself with Prussia against Austria in the Austria-Prussian War. There is little love lost between the countries. Italy has been trying to play both sides, but I believe that when forced to choose, this country will never take the side of the Austrians."

Melody considered his words. Unless he was an outstanding actor, Alessandro's passionate words seemed genuine. Of course, it was possible that he truly believed what he said and yet didn't agree with what he thought was Italy's likely choice. Was his work against Britain intended to turn Italian sentiment towards Austria-Hungary and Germany? That would certainly explain why he was collaborating with Herr Peetz, an Austrian.

Just considering these machinations was giving Melody a headache. She had never had any interest in politics, let alone international ones. Uncle Maxi had tried to engage her interest in world affairs. However, she was far more inclined to listen to Granny, who made it clear that she considered all politicians, whether British or otherwise, as overgrown schoolboys who had never got over playing with tin soldiers.

Deciding to steer the conversation back to less dangerous waters, Melody asked how long Alessandro would be staying in Venice.

"I have no fixed schedule," he said. Then, in a more seductive tone, "It all depends on whether I find a reason to prolong my visit."

Melody blushed again; his tone could not be mistaken. Why was it that she always felt on such an unsure footing around Alessandro? His words felt dangerous and yet so enticing. She wasn't sure what he was offering, and yet she found their possibility so enticing. How did he manage that? It was not merely that he was handsome, though he was. Melody had certainly met many good-looking men in London. Yet none of them had Alessandro's mysterious allure. When he looked at her as he was doing now, Melody felt her skin tingle and her heart beat a little faster. Trying to reason against her reaction to the man, Melody reminded herself that perhaps his mysterious allure was nothing more than that he was a traitor.

Alessandro stayed for only twenty minutes longer, perhaps sensing that his private conversation with Melody was going to be interrupted eventually. Before he left, Alessandro managed to extract a promise that she would allow him to show her Venice at night from his gondola the following evening. It all sounded very romantic, and before she'd had a chance to consider her words, Melody found herself agreeing to the outing. As soon as she said this, Melody realised how furious Rat would be. He would likely have tried to forbid Melody from going even before they had realised Alessandro's likely treachery. Considering all this, Melody quickly added that, of course, Mary, her chaperone, would be accompanying them. Alessandro had accepted this with good humour and a plan had been formed.

Dear Diary, Rat was as furious as I thought he would be. He really does not like Alessandro, whether he turns out to be a traitor or not. What does he think will happen? That the conte will ravish me in the gondola in front of Mary? He may be only half British, but I am sure that half is gentleman enough not to try such a thing even if I were unchaperoned. And anyway, as I told Rat, Granny has always said that it is better to keep one's enemies close.

Anyway, we bickered about it, but I won in the end. Rat is eager to visit the consulate and wants to do it first thing tomorrow when it opens. He would not tell me the entire story but led me to believe that not only had Mr Ashby suggested the visit, but that Uncle Maxi knows Mr Burrows, the consul, from their days at Eton. Apparently, Rat has a letter from Uncle Maxi asking Mr Burrows to provide him with whatever assistance he may require. Of course, one does not need to be an investigative genius to deduce that Rat would not have been given such a letter unless he were in Venice in some kind of official capacity for the government. Under any circumstances, a large part of the consul's role is to assist British citizens abroad. So, there would be no reason to send him with a letter in the usual course of things.

Rat hopes that Mr Burrows might know something about the names on the list we found at Signor Graziano's flat. I still find it hard to believe that such a sweet old man was up to no good. However, Rat does have a point when he says that, as an Italian, Signor Graziano's supposed acts against Britain are not treason.

CHAPTER 16

The following day, just after lunch, Rat set out for the British Consulate. He remembered Xander telling him that it was in another palazzo on the Grand Canal. He hoped that Giovanni would know where.

Luckily, the ever-helpful Giovanni did know where he meant. Within fifteen minutes, the gondola was pulling up to an ornate, Gothic-style building with pointed arches and intricate decorative mouldings scattered liberally across its facade. It wasn't quite as palatial as Lady Bainbridge's palazzo, but it was charming, nonetheless.

Disembarking from the gondola, Rat walked up a few steps to a large oak door with an ornate copper knocker on it. A very British-looking young man answered the door, and when Rat brandished his letter from Lord Langley, the man indicated that Rat should follow him. They went through another door into a corridor that looked more suited for royalty than for British civil servants. Marble busts were lined up at regular intervals down the corridor, and portraits of serious and important-looking men covered the walls.

The young man walked Rat up to the third door, knocked, and then opened it. Rat was surprised to see Xander Ashby sitting at a large mahogany desk that was covered in papers.

Xander looked up, evidently equally surprised. "Mr Sandworth, what a surprise. Did we have a plan to meet that I have forgotten?"

Rat wasn't sure why he was surprised to see Xander. He'd known that the man worked for the consul, but he hadn't realised that his role was private secretary, as it seemed to be.

"No plan, I assure you, Ashby. I decided to take you up on your offer to visit. Actually, I have come to speak with Mr Burrows."

Xander raised an eyebrow slightly. "I hope everything is alright with you and Miss Chesterton," he said.

"Nothing is wrong. There is merely a matter I need to ask his opinion on."

Xander paused, then replied, "Unfortunately, the consul's day is very busy. Perhaps I can help you."

Rat considered the offer. He liked Xander Ashby and, despite Lady Bainbridge's warning, wasn't opposed to the idea of the young man courting his sister. What Lady Bainbridge had failed to consider when giving her counsel was that, despite being raised in the home of an earl and having a large, independent fortune, Melody was still the orphaned child of impoverished parents from Whitechapel. Given this, Xander Ashby, with his aristocratic lineage, was a fine catch for his sister. He knew that her interest in Xander was lukewarm at the moment, but he did not doubt that she could be persuaded with the right amount of wooing.

Despite his partiality towards Xander, Rat was not sure he was comfortable making his request of anyone other than Mr Burrows. One thing that Lord Langley had drilled into him over the years was the importance of keeping the circle of information as small as possible. The more people who knew something, the greater the chance of a breach of confidentiality, however inadvertent. He was only prepared to confide in Edwin Burrows because of Lord Langley's absolute confidence in the man.

Finally, a decision was made, Rat pulled out his letter from Lord Langley, though he didn't remove it from its envelope. "I really do need to speak to Mr Burrows immediately. I have a letter from Lord Langley, a very old friend of his, vouching for me and asking the consul to provide me with whatever aid I need."

It was clear from the look on Xander's face that he longed to know both why Rat needed such immediate help and why Lord Langley believed himself to be able to command that assistance. Instead, he held out his hand for the letter.

Fighting an almost overwhelming urge to remove the letter from the envelope and read it, he nevertheless knew that to doubt Rat's word was to insult his honour as a gentleman. Instead, he said, "I will go and show this to the consul. Please be patient while I speak with him."

In fact, it was barely any time at all before Xander reemerged from the room behind his desk. Returning the letter to Rat, he said a little tersely, "Mr Burrows is happy to give you a few minutes of his time." Saying this, Xander re-opened the door he had just shut behind him and invited Rat to enter.

The consul's office was so sumptuous that Rat wondered whether the Prime Minister's office could rival it. The furniture looked as if it wouldn't be out of place in King Louis XVI's Versailles, and the curtains were a deep, red-coloured velvet with a gold brocade. The wallpaper had red and gold stripes that added to the very regal air of the room.

Dominating the room was a large, imposing desk that was as different from Xander's in its utter lack of clutter and papers as could be imagined. Sitting at this desk was a rather unimposing middle-aged man who looked every part the civil servant he was. Rat was a big fan of Charles Dickens's work, and one of his favourites of the author's books was *Bleak House*. When he looked at Edwin Burrows, Rat immediately thought of the Dicken's character, Mr. Snagsby. While not a civil servant himself, Edwin Burrows perfectly fitted Dickens' description of Snagsby as "A mild, bald, timid man with a shining head and a scrubby clump of hair sticking out from the back of it." The similarity was so strong that Rat had to try hard not to smile at the thought.

Mr Burrows rose and held out his hand, "Mr Sandworth, I presume?"

Rat shook his hand and confirmed his identity.

"You may leave us, Ashby," Mr Burrows barked curtly.

Xander mumbled something and shut the door behind him. For just a moment, Rat wondered if the private secretary would eavesdrop on their conversation. However, he quickly reminded himself that Xander was a professional civil servant and surely knew better than to listen in on his employer's private conversations.

"So, you are Langley's ward, are you?"

"I am. I assume you read the letter?"

"Indeed. I will forever be in Langley's debt. Private matter from many years ago now. Suffice it to say, the man knows he may call on my help whenever he needs it. So, how may I help you?"

Rat had considered how much to reveal. He knew that Lord Langley's letter hadn't laid out either his own or Rat's role in the Secret Service Bureau. However, it had been challenging to think of how he could make his request while giving nothing important away.

Reflecting on what he'd previously decided, Rat said, "I need your help identifying some names."

Rat hoped that he might leave it there and that the consul would not ask any more. He was to be disappointed. "May I ask why you need this?"

Rat inwardly sighed. "I have reason to believe that they may be an important link in a murder investigation."

"Are you a member of the police force?" Mr Burrows asked, screwing his face up in confusion.

"Not as such," Rat admitted.

"And is this murder of a British subject? If so, I am not sure why I do not know about it."

"It is not," Rat answered, feeling increasingly uncomfortable both with how much he was stretching the truth and how much he was giving away.

"Then it is the murder of a Venetian. And you have some official interest in this murder that is not connected to the police force," Burrows stated rather than asking.

"I do," Rat admitted, then added, "I am afraid I cannot tell you more than that."

"I have total trust in Langley, and he seems to put similar trust in you. If you say it is important and yet you cannot tell me why, I will take your word for that. All I ask is that, if at some point this does involve a British citizen, you will inform me."

Rat agreed to this, if only because he doubted that anyone British was involved besides Melody and him. He had written out the names from Graziano's list on a fresh sheet of paper, and now he handed this to Mr Burrows, who took it and spent a minute or two reading.

"These all seem to be Italian names," he observed. "I am the British consul. Why would you ask me about Italians?"

"Well, firstly, because I hoped you might recognise some. But mostly because I have no one else to ask."

Burrows looked over the list more closely, then reached into his desk drawer and drew out a newspaper. Flicking through the pages, he finally stopped at one and said, "I thought that I recognised this first name. Silvio Verdi. I make a point of getting the local newspapers to glance through it. My Italian is serviceable. As well as writing for this more mainstream newspaper," he said, gesturing with the hand holding the publication, "I believe he publishes a more radical journal."

"When you say radical, what exactly do you mean?"

"Well, there are many loud voices encouraging Italian imperialism these days. At the moment, these voices are advocating for war with Turkey. A unified Italy is only fifty years old. As a youthful power in Europe, there were many Italians who sought colonial expansion within Northern Africa and believed that they should directly challenge the Ottoman Empire. However, as in Britain, there are also those who believe that Italy should direct its resources to domestic issues such as social reform and poverty. Silvio Verdi is one such voice. From what I understand, he was unable to publish his more radical opinions in the mainstream Venice newspaper, so he started his own publication. I don't remember its name."

"Do you have any copies of this journal by any chance?" Rat

asked hopefully.

"No. I am sorry I do not. However, I assume that the Marciana Library, or as the Italians call it, La Biblioteca Nazionale Marciana, will. It is located in St Mark's Square. I tell you what, I'll send young Ashby with you to show you where it is and help you navigate the almost certain Italian bureaucracy you will encounter there. And his Italian is not bad at this point. They will also have back issues of the other newspaper, if you need them."

"And you don't recognise any of the other names on the list?" Rat pressed.

"I do not. Can I show this list to anyone in Venice?" Mr Burrows asked.

"I would rather that you don't at this point. If you do have any more thoughts on any of them, please let me know."

"What about this? I am sending a diplomatic pouch back to London this afternoon. I could put this in and see if anyone back in the Foreign Office has any clue. But it'll take at least four days to get there and back, and that does not include time for review of your list. This will not be a quick solution."

Rat considered his options; while what the consul was suggesting wasn't going to be fast, it was also the only reliable and secure way he had to get the answers he needed at this point. He still had the original copy of the list, so he wasn't losing anything by taking Mr Burrows up on his offer.

The offer was accepted, and Mr Burrows walked Rat to the door. Xander was seated at his desk in the outer office and expressed his willingness to accompany Rat to the library.

Mr Burrows' final words to Rat were, "I will have my aide, Nicholls, send that information to London immediately."

Xander looked up, seemingly worried that someone else was being entrusted with important work. Mr Burrows smiled and said, "Not to worry, Ashby. You will be doing the more vital job of aiding Mr Sandworth with his research. Nicholls' Italian is negligible. Better he get the more dogsbody work of sending the pouch out."

Mollified somewhat, Xander led Rat out of the office. As they walked back down the corridor to the gondola, which was to take them to St Mark's Square, Xander asked casually, "Are you trying to find anything in particular?"

Rat didn't see any harm in telling the truth, and Xander's Italian could come in handy. Of course, he didn't share the entire story, merely that he was trying to learn more about the writings of a particular journalist and that Mr Burrows had suggested that the library would keep back copies of publications.

Xander didn't say much in reply, merely nodded. "What is the name of the journalist?"

"Silvio Verdi. It seems he is something of a radical."

Xander again made no reply for a few moments. Finally, he asked, "May I ask why you are so interested in this radical journalist?"

Rat didn't have a good response to this that wasn't the truth. Thinking on his feet, he said, "My guardian, Lord Langley, is, of course, a member of the House of Lords. He has been tasked with monitoring radicals and their writings in Britain, and as part of this, he is keeping an eye on similar thinkers elsewhere in Europe. Given that I was coming here anyway, he asked me, as a favour, to do a bit of research."

Once he'd said this out loud, Rat was quite proud of himself; it was a credible backstory for some of the poking around he would be doing over the next few days. Certainly, Xander didn't seem to question it.

CHAPTER 17

Rat returned to the palazzo not long before dinner and immediately went in search of Melody. He finally found her in her bedroom, in an armchair, reading one of the Italian-translated novels she had recently bought.

She looked up at his entrance, ready to forget their argument from earlier. "What did you discover?"

Sitting in the opposite, matching armchair, Rat rested his chin on his knuckles and considered Melody's question. "To be honest, I'm not sure. The consul, Mr Burrows, recognised one of the names on the list, a radical socialist journalist who saves some of his more extreme pieces for a slim journal he periodically puts out. I went to the library with Xander and read a few of this journalist's latest pieces, both in the regular newspaper and in his journal."

"You went with Xander?" Melody asked with curiosity. She still wasn't sure how she felt about the eager Mr Ashby, who, honestly, hadn't been so eager over the last few days. She hadn't heard from him since their trip to the Basilica and wasn't sure if she felt slighted or not.

"Yes, Mr Burrows asked him to accompany me and help with translations. I must say, when we left London, I thought my Italian wasn't bad. But since we've been here, I've felt quite out of my depth."

"I know what you mean. It is one thing to be able to sit through Don Giovanni and follow the plot, quite another to have regular conversations. It almost makes me think that Granny was right when she constantly harped on the importance of learning foreign languages."

"Well, foreign languages except French," Rat pointed out.

"Yes, except French. What is it that she has against France and its people?"

"I believe that she had never forgiven them for the French Revolution and executing so many of its aristocracy," Rat observed.

"Anyway, I am glad that Ashby accompanied me. He was a great help."

"Did you learn anything?"

"It seems that Signor Verdi is adamantly opposed to Italian nationalism. He sees Italy's Triple Alliance with Germany and Austria-Hungary as an entanglement that could drag it into conflicts that will only serve the ruling elite rather than the working class but will see the latter dying on the front lines of battle. There's more, but that's the general gist."

"So, why was he on Signor Graziano's list?"

"I'm not sure, but there were a couple of interesting pieces that were printed in the mainstream newspaper that he writes for. In particular, he published what he claimed were authentic internal memos from the Austro-Hungarian government discussing strategies to work secretly to suppress Italian nationalist movements and ethnic unrest. Another was supposed correspondence between high-ranking Austro-Hungarian officials expressing doubts about the loyalty of the Italian regions and discussing severe punitive measures."

"How can Austria-Hungary penalise Italians? They no longer rule this region," Melody argued.

"Indeed. And that was part of what Signor Verdi implied: that there is a secret plan to invade Italy if it doesn't fall in line in some future European war."

"Is it possible that these documents he claims to have are false?"

"It is always possible. But he includes photographs which certainly have the ring of authenticity about them. Either way, Verdi clearly hopes to stir up public opinion against Austria-

Hungary."

Melody considered Rat's words. "Is it possible that the plan that Herr Peetz and Conte Foscari were talking about was to disrupt this Verdi fellow's stories?"

"That had occurred to me. But then, why not kill him? Why kill Graziano? Anyway, it did sound as if the old man's murder had disrupted their plans, so I don't think that Foscari and Herr Peetz murdered him." Rat thought about what he had just said. "Of course, it's possible that one of them murdered him unbeknownst to the other and then merely pretended to be equally shocked when they met at the party."

"So now you think that Alessandro murdered Signor Graziano?" Melody said more indignantly than she intended.

"Why do you insist on this familiarity with the man?" Rat demanded, even though that wasn't really the most egregious part of what his sister had said. Focusing back on the rest of her sentence, Rat said irritably, "And why do you defend him? Can you not see how insupportable it is that you go out for a moonlight boat ride with Foscari as if you were courting? The man could be a brutal killer!"

"Conte Foscari did not kill Signor Graziano," Melody asserted with confidence.

"How on earth can you be so sure of that?"

"Because he does not smoke," Melody said as triumphantly as when she announced checkmate while regularly trouncing her brother at chess.

"Just because you have not seen the man smoke on the few occasions you have met does not mean that he doesn't smoke. Lots of men smoke but do not do so around ladies. You met him at a dinner party, at a masquerade ball, and apparently in this house this afternoon. None of those are circumstances under which a gentleman would smoke."

"Do not forget at the train station when we arrived."

"He might have just put out a cigarette or lit one after we left. None of your encounters with him qualifies you to state definitively that he doesn't smoke, at least on occasion." Finally,

Melody had to concede the point.

Deciding instead to address the other part of Rat's complaint, she pointed out, yet again, "If Conte Foscari is mixed up in whatever this is, is it not better that I stay close to him and find out what I can?"

She then told Rat what she had gleaned from Alessandro earlier, that much of his fortune was in publishing, particularly newspapers.

"That is interesting," Rat conceded. "Why did you not tell me this before?"

"Because you were being idiotic about him even calling on me and did not give me a chance!"

"And you say that he denied knowing Herr Peetz?"

"He did." Melody then told Rat the rest of her conversation with Alessandro, including his comments on the likelihood of Italy joining forces with its Triple Alliance allies if and when war came."

"So, what did you make of his words?" Rat asked, genuinely curious about his sister's observations of the odious Conte Foscari.

"They seemed heartfelt. Of course, it is entirely possible that he truly believes that Italy will either stay neutral or join with Britain and yet does not agree with that stance. Perhaps that is what sits behind his actions: a desire to change the course of history as he sees it, without intervention."

Rat considered her words. He couldn't believe he was playing devil's advocate in providing a defence for Foscari, yet he was too rational a thinker to allow his prejudice to cloud his judgement completely. "But why would Foscari want Italy to go to war against Britain? Even if he is half Italian, his mother is English, and Britain is where he was mostly raised and schooled."

It was a good question, and Melody didn't have an answer. Instead, she said, "I believe we need to learn more about Conte Foscari's business holdings and better understand what might motivate someone of his standing to hold such political views." Rat conceded that it was a good point, but how might they gain such information?

After pondering the question in silence for a few moments, Melody said, "I believe we have not fully utilised one of our best sources of information: Lady Bainbridge." Seeing Rat about to disagree and guessing his line of argument, she continued, "It is shocking that two young people who have grown up around the Dowager Countess of Pembroke and have seen the vital part she plays in Tabby Cat and Wolfie's investigations have nevertheless made such minimal use of another well-connected, intelligent older woman."

Rat wasn't sure that Tabitha and Wolf would agree with the characterisation of the dowager as having played a "vital part" in their investigations. He knew that often they considered the elderly woman more of a hindrance than a help. Nevertheless, he also knew they acknowledged that, even as her body became increasingly frail, her mental acuity had not dimmed in the slightest. More than that, the woman had an almost encyclopaedic knowledge of the whims, failings, and peccadillos of Britain's ruling class. Perhaps Melody was right; why had they so quickly written Lady Bainbridge off as merely a sweet, doddering old woman?

Finally, deciding that they had nothing to lose by talking to their hostess, Rat said, "Then there is no time like the present. We need to dress for dinner. Perhaps this can be the topic of discussion over our evening repast."

Melody agreed. Before they parted, they discussed just how much to share with Lady Bainbridge. Of course, Rat still hadn't shared everything with Melody, so this was an even more loaded conversation for him. Finally, he asked, "What do you think we should tell Lady Bainbridge?"

Melody took a deep breath, then, looking her brother straight in the eye, she said, "I believe that we should share that you are working for Uncle Maxi on behalf of the British Government and are investigating a possible link between the death of Antonio Graziano and Alessandro Foscari."

Rat gasped. While it had been increasingly apparent that his sister had some sense of the job he was doing, hearing her state it so plainly was still shocking.

"Are you denying that this is why you are in Venice with me?" Melody asked, almost amused by the look on her brother's face.

Rat then spoke aloud his real fear, "Was I so clumsy in my actions that it has become obvious? Did I fail to be sufficiently discreet?"

Suddenly, all of Melody's amusement at the situation melted away, and she moved closer to her brother and put a sympathetic hand on his arm. "Rat, I can assure you that no one else has any suspicions. You have been the soul of discretion. However, I know you better than anyone. Moreover, I have long suspected some of this."

"You have?" Rat said in amazement. "Why?"

"Rat, I have spent a lot of time around you and Uncle Maxi talking together since I was a little girl. Did you imagine that I was not listening in on your conversations? It has long been clear to me that he has some sort of intelligence role for the government and that he was grooming you to join him in some capacity."

Rat thought back to the games of chess that he and Lord Langley would play while discussing the political situation in Europe and Langley's role in monitoring possible espionage. He then thought about the little girl sitting nearby playing quietly with her dolls or her dog. It was true; they had both never considered that she was paying any attention to their conversations or that, even if she was, she would understand and remember what they were discussing. In many ways, this realisation made him feel a lot better; the oversight was as much Lord Langley's as his, maybe more so given that Rat had also been a child.

Melody continued, "So, now we have that out of the way, I am assuming that you did not merely stumble across Herr Peetz and Conte Foscari at Luisa's party but instead were suspicious when you saw them together and followed them." Rat nodded. "Good! Now, we are getting somewhere. While I do believe that we can trust Lady Bainbridge, I also understand the need to give out as little information as possible. Therefore, here is what I believe we should say." She then outlined her plan. Again, Rat did little more than nod in agreement.

Finally, the siblings parted ways to dress for dinner. Meeting up a short while later in the salotto, they each gave a brief nod to acknowledge the plan they had discussed earlier. Lady Bainbridge preferred to eat dinner earlier than was customary in London circles, at least when she dined at home. Because of this, she rarely indulged in pre-dinner aperitifs but instead moved quickly to the dining room to begin her meal.

Melody and Rat were the first to arrive in the room, but Lady Bainbridge soon followed and, as expected, quickly indicated to Rossi that they were ready to eat. This suited Rat and Melody's purposes; they would prefer the relative privacy of the dining room, where the servants usually retired between courses, to the salotto, where Rossi was often hovering, ready to anticipate his mistress' every need.

Rossi tended to stay in the room for the soup course because it was brief. However, he usually left once he had served the primi, which tonight was Risotto alla Zucca, pumpkin risotto with pieces of scattered fried sage leaves on top. Once Rossi was out of the room, Melody and Rat exchanged a glance and began.

"Lady Bainbridge, Melody and I need your assistance."

The elderly woman looked up from her risotto and asked in a quizzical tone, "What on earth would two young people need help with from an old woman like me? However, I am happy to be of assistance if you believe I can be."

"As you know, when I was out with Luisa, we came upon a dead body," Melody began.

"Yes. Awful stuff. That poor bookseller. I never visited his shop myself, but I know that Luisa was fond of the man. And for an innocent young woman such as yourself to stumble upon such a scene, well, I cannot imagine what dear Tabitha would have to say about my lack of care."

Given how many crime scenes Tabby Cat had witnessed over

the past fourteen years or so, Melody doubted she would be as horrified as Lady Bainbridge imagined. However, she let this observation pass and instead said, "It seems that my brother is in Venice, not merely to chaperone me."

"Is he not, dear?" Lady Bainbridge asked in a somewhat distracted voice. Her wine glass was empty, and she was busy looking around for Rossi to refill it. Wanting the elderly woman focused on their conversation, Rat reached for the bottle and refilled her glass.

Melody continued, "As you know, Matthew is Lord Langley's ward. Lord Langley has acted as something of a mentor to my brother over the years, training him to be of service to his government."

Lady Bainbridge looked over at Rat, "Really, dear? How exciting. Of course, I do not know exactly what 'of service' means, but it does sound thrilling and rather like something out of a novel. You know, *The Prisoner of Zenda* is one of my favourite books." She paused for so long that Melody and Rat wondered if she had totally lost the thread of their conversation. However, eventually, she seemed to rejoin them and asked, "And so how can I be of help?"

Melody and Rat both breathed sighs of relief; they had hoped that Lady Bainbridge wouldn't probe too deeply into what being "of service to his government" entailed, and they had been correct. Grateful to be spared the need to divulge more information about his role and that of Lord Langley, Rat picked up the narrative. "I would like to know more about Conte Foscari."

"Dear Alessandro? Surely you cannot imagine that a man as handsome as that would be involved with anything as sordid as murder?"

Tempted to ask what good looks had to do with moral character, Rat nevertheless let the thought pass and instead said, "Well, to be honest, I am not sure." Then, gesturing to include Melody said, "We are not sure. That is why we need to know more. It may be that the information you can provide will help clear his name."

"Well, when you put it like that, I am happy to tell you all I know. Though, I am unsure how much help I can be. Ask away."

"The other day, you told us about Conte Foscari's parents' marriage and his early life. It seems that his father used the fortune Foscari's mother brought into the marriage to create an impressive business empire that Foscari, Alessandro Foscari that is, now manages. How much do you know about that business?"

"Well, probably no more than the average person who floats around Venetian society does. Alessandro's father founded what is now the most popular newspaper in Italy. He also acquired some smaller, regional newspapers, including one in Venice. Alessandro has expanded the business and now owns newspapers across France and Spain as well."

Lady Bainbridge took another sip of wine and a forkful of risotto and continued, "And then there are his other businesses, though I am not entirely sure what they all are. I know that he does something in mercantile trading because when I once decried the quality of Italian tea, Alessandro said he would ensure that a case of British tea was on his next boat to Venice, and he was as good as his word. In fact, he shipped me so much that we are only now coming to the end of it. When he came to dinner the other evening, he promised to send me a new shipment. Darling man."

Melody thought about what Lady Bainbridge had said, then asked, "So, is all his trade between Britain and Italy?"

"Heavens, no! In fact, I believe that is the least of his business. Most of his trade is within continental Europe, particularly between Austria and Italy. I do not know the details, though I do remember sitting between Alessandro and another Italian businessman at one dinner party and having to endure a rather boring conversation about shipping Italian agricultural products to Austria and shipping industrial goods back to Italy. Apparently, from what I could tell, Austria-Hungary is more advanced in the manufacture of machinery, textiles, and chemicals but enjoys the superior fruits, vegetables, wine, and olive oil enabled by Italy's delightful climate."

Melody and Rat exchanged knowing looks. Melody reflected again on what she had learned from many years of watching Tabby Cat and Wolfie investigate crimes: Who benefited? Who wanted revenge? Who had a reason to hate the victim? While it still was unclear what part Antonio Graziano's death played in it all, it was not hard to see how Alessandro benefited from Italy maintaining close ties to Austria-Hungary rather than aligning itself with Britain: money.

CHAPTER 18

As they left the dining room to return to the salotto for coffee and tea, Melody whispered to Rat, "I believe it is for the best if Mary does not accompany me tonight with Conte Foscari. I want to lull him into speaking openly to me, and it is best if he does not feel inhibited because my maid is there."

Speaking louder than he intended, Rat exclaimed, "Are you mad? You expect me to agree to you going out on a moonlit boat ride alone with a man who, even if he is not a murderer, is still almost certainly a lothario."

"Well, you do not know either thing for sure, and anyway, his gondolier will be there," Melody countered.

Lowering his voice again so as not to catch Lady Bainbridge's attention, Rat said, "A gondolier I am sure he compensates well to pay no attention to what goes on in that gondola."

Realising that they needed to find a compromise, Melody suggested, "What if I insist that we take Lady Bainbridge's gondola and that Giovanni rows us? You cannot imagine that he will look the other way if I am in any way insulted."

Rat would have liked to have argued against this suggestion, but it did seem reasonable. In all honesty, as much as he liked and respected Mary, she was far too much under Melody's thumb to be an appropriately moderating force for all his sister's wilder behaviour. Instead, he said grudgingly, "Fine. However, if he is unwilling to change gondolas, then I insist that you refuse to accompany him."

"I will agree to that," Melody conceded.

Alessandro had said that he wanted them to take in the sunset and so would call for her at eight-thirty. Given how early dinner had been, Melody had time to change her dress. She wanted to look alluring, but there were also the practicalities of getting in and out of a gondola. Finally, over Mary's protestations, she decided on a simple muslin dress that wouldn't get spoiled by some splashes of water but also had a rather daringly low-cut neckline. Melody wasn't sure how she had persuaded Tabby Cat to purchase it. Perhaps it was because she had not actually seen it on Melody, who had somewhat more décolletage than one might expect in a girl of her otherwise slim frame. Hanging up, the dress seemed quite demure; it was only when Melody wore it that it was so provocative.

To prevent Rat from seeing her in the dress and insisting that she change immediately, Melody took a pretty embroidered shawl and draped it demurely across her before she descended to meet Alessandro.

Rat and Alessandro were waiting for her in the palazzo's vestibule. "I have informed Conte Foscari that you wish to take Lady Bainbridge's gondola and gondolier tonight," Rat said in a rude tone that made quite evident why he would say such a thing.

Alessandro raised his eyebrows slightly but replied in a gracious voice, "Whatever will make Miss Chesterton most comfortable. Is your companion not joining us, though? "

"Unfortunately, Mary has developed something of a sore throat and headache, and I insisted that she go to bed and rest," Melody lied smoothly.

She walked towards Alessandro, who held out his arm. Melody took the proffered arm, and they turned to leave. "I will be waiting up for you," Rat said to their departing backs. No one answered him.

Alessandro informed his gondolier that he was to wait for his return and then stepped into Lady Bainbridge's waiting gondola before holding out a hand to help Melody in. As she took his hand, Melody artfully allowed her shawl to slip down off her shoulders, exposing her neckline. She could see that Alessandro had noticed and was gratified by the desire she saw flare in his eyes.

Melody sat on the bench seat in front of Giovanni with her back to him, and Alessandro sat beside her without asking permission. Both had been raised in households filled with servants and were accustomed to forgetting that they were being observed by those who waited on them. With their backs to Giovanni, it was even easier to forget that they were not alone.

The sun was just beginning to go down, and Alessandro turned and said something in rapid Italian to Giovanni. "I told him to go down to the mouth of the Grand Canal, where it opens into Bacino di San Marco, St Mark's Basin, and that we will stop by the Basilica di Santa Maria della Salute to get the best view of the sunset," Alessandro explained.

As Giovanni pushed off from the porta d'acqua, Melody settled against the cushioned back of the seat. However, she was too acutely aware of Alessandro's presence to relax. While there was at least an inch between them on the bench, she felt as if her skin was prickling with electricity at his closeness. While there was a cool enough breeze that evening that Melody was glad she had brought her shawl, she nevertheless felt almost uncomfortably warm as she caught the aroma of his cologne. There was a citrusy scent of maybe lemon or bergamot with base notes of amber and sandalwood; it was intoxicating. Even more than that, there was an underlying male muskiness that she couldn't put a name to but could sense with every fibre of her being.

Melody was so aware of Alessandro and his effect on her that she almost wished she had brought Mary with her, if only to protect Melody against her own baser instincts. Perhaps reacting to her confusing feelings, Melody pulled her shawl more tightly up and around her.

They floated along in silence for a few minutes, then if only to break the tension that she felt, even if he didn't, Melody said, "Lady Bainbridge said that you have a trading business in addition to your publishing business."

"Were you asking about me, Miss Chesterton?" Melody might have been worried that she had shown her hand, except that the words were said in a light, jesting tone.

"I might have been a little curious," Melody acknowledged. She knew that her best move was to play the innocent ingenue, asking questions about topics she would pretend not to really comprehend. "I understand nothing about commerce. My guardian, Lord Pembroke, has many businesses that he has control over in addition to the Pembroke estate. I know that he has a man of business, a steward to help him and many people managing those businesses, but even so, I have no idea how he does it."

Alessandro sat back and seemed pensive for a moment. "My grandfather was something of a wastrel and drunk and gambled the family fortune away. He left my father with not much more than a title and a villa in Tuscany that had not been maintained in twenty years. If my father hadn't married my mother, I cannot imagine what might have happened. Anyway, while Mama brought a small fortune with her to the marriage, my father could never get past the thought of how close he had been to being completely destitute and decided that a small fortune wasn't sufficient to ensure that neither he nor his family ever faced ruin again."

Given that Melody had started her life in the kind of abject poverty that Alessandro probably couldn't even imagine, she listened to his story with compassion for his father's fears.

"Papa felt that to protect his family, he needed to diversify his businesses as much as possible. Over time, he became a partner in a trading business, a publisher, and a shipbuilder. I believe that he even was a part owner of a nightclub for a while. As long as he saw a path to sustainable profits, he was interested in investing. He died quite recently, and, as his only son, I inherited everything. In his never-ending quest to ensure his fortune and his family, my father had demanded that I learn every aspect of his business and be ready to take over whenever it was necessary. Neither one of us thought that would be as soon as it turned out to be."

Melody put a hand on his arm, "I am so sorry for your loss, Alessandro." Melody had almost no memory of her parents. All she had were shadows of memories that she wasn't even sure were real, rather than merely based on stories that Rat had told her over the years. Nevertheless, she couldn't imagine losing Tabby Cat or Wolfie, Rat or Granny, or any of her loving, warm extended family. Lord Langley was a beloved uncle, and she would never forget the gentleness with which Bear would get down on the floor and play with her when she was little. Just the thought of losing any of these people made her anxious.

Alessandro put his hand on top of hers. "Thank you, Melody," he said very gently. "It was difficult, particularly at first, but my father trained me well. And now, I find myself running this commercial empire that he built, questioning myself at every turn as to whether my decisions are what his would have been." Just when she thought that Alessandro would say no more on the topic, he said quietly, almost as if to himself, "My greatest fear is that I fail to protect the business he fought so hard to build."

This was a rare moment of vulnerability and a side of Alessandro that Melody had yet to see. She liked it. A lot.

After a while longer, it was clear that they were close to the end of the Grand Canal and would soon emerge into a larger body of water. Alessandro pointed to her right, "This is the Basilica di Santa Maria della Salute," he said as Giovanni moved the boat close to the shore.

The sun was about to disappear into the horizon, and the sky was a watercolour masterpiece of dramatic pinks, oranges and yellows. Melody looked up at the massive, octagonal church dome that dominated the skyline. "It is beautiful," she said, admiring its dramatic, Baroque grandeur contrasted against the magnificence of the sky.

"Not as beautiful as you are," Alessandro said, leaning towards her.

Melody realised that as they had made their way down the Grand Canal, her shawl had slipped off her shoulders, exposing her décolletage again.

Alessandro turned and whispered in her ear in a seductive tone that made Melody shiver, "You look delicious in that dress, Miss Chesterton. Might I hope that you wore it hoping to entice me?"

Melody had no idea how to answer this, mainly because it was true. Just as she was deciding how coy to be, she felt Alessandro take one of the ringlets that hung loose over her shoulders and entwine his fingers in it, managing to stroke her shoulder as he did so.

This time, her shiver was noticeable, and Alessandro said in a low, sultry voice, "I think that you are not as innocent as you make out, Melody."

Her name sounded so delightful and yet shocking when said in the tone Alessandro was using. Melody knew that, by all rights, she should pull away and admonish him, but she found she was unable to do either. Instead, she found herself leaning towards Alessandro. He clearly noticed her movement, and Melody felt his hand rest more firmly on her shoulder, and then a finger began to trace its way down her arm. She let the shawl drop entirely, put her head back, and shuddered in a paroxysm of desire. Melody had never felt this way before. She wasn't sure what was happening, but she knew that she didn't want Alessandro to stop.

Her neck was exposed, and Melody suddenly felt his lips gently brushing the delicate skin under her ear. Oh my! Now, she really felt out of her depth. Alessandro worked his way up her neck along her jawline with his butterfly kisses until he reached her face. Then, turning her head gently towards him, Alessandro kissed her lips.

Melody had been kissed twice before. Once was when she was fifteen, and she kissed her friend's sixteen-year-old brother as a dare, and the other time was recently, at a ball, when an over-eager suitor had managed to trap her in a dark corner of the ballroom. She still remembered how wet and unpleasant that kiss was before she managed to shove her suitor away and slap his face. Alessandro's kiss was nothing like that. It was slow and tender as his tongue gently prodded her lips open. As the kiss deepened, Melody found herself lost in its passion. At that point, anyone could have been watching, and she wouldn't have noticed or cared. All she knew was that Alessandro's arms were around her and, before she knew it, she was pulled onto his lap.

Melody knew for certain that this was the point when she should have stopped him, but she was unable to. Instead, she found herself wrapping her arms around his neck and tangling her hands in Alessandro's thick, dark hair. She felt that she might lose herself altogether to this man's kisses, happily abandoning propriety just to feel her skin next to his.

Melody's breath became ragged as Alessandro whispered in her ear, "I see you desire me as much as I do you, mio bellissimo tesoro. Mia cara. I had hoped that the prim, good little English debutante persona was just a facade. But I never imagined that beneath it was such a fiery temptress."

She knew that should have been the moment that she stopped him, if not earlier. His words should have been taken as an insult to her feminine virtue rather than a spur to her grasping of him even more passionately. However, Melody truly could not help herself. She was so beyond stopping Alessandro that she might have been prepared never to make him stop, no matter where he next placed his hand. In fact, she was so beyond reason that she pulled his head down to her chest, throwing her head back again in ecstasy as he began kissing along her neckline.

Melody didn't know a lot about conjugal relations between a man and a woman. Other debutantes would giggle as they whispered silly girlish statements about what they had heard from newly married friends and sisters, but Melody had never had much time for such things. She wasn't sure exactly what she was prepared to abandon herself to, but she knew how much she desired it, whatever it was.

Suddenly, the kisses stopped. Alessandro gently put his hands around her waist and placed her back on the seat next to him. He could see the hurt and confusion in her eyes as she wondered if she had done something wrong. Was that not how one was supposed to kiss? Did he find her behaviour too wanton?

Alessandro caressed her face and said in a tone both gentle and resigned, "I cannot do this, Melody. You are a maiden, not a woman of the world. It would not be right. As much as I want to."

"Do I not get a say?" Melody asked rather sullenly, unsure of what she was asking to have a say in.

Leaning over, Alessandro placed a gentle, avuncular kiss on her forehead. "No, you do not get a say because you do not understand what you are agreeing to." Melody had no answer to this.

They said very little on the return trip to the palazzo. As she exited the gondola, Melody caught Giovanni's eye and flushed with embarrassment. Somehow, she had forgotten that he was witness to her abandon. The gondolier kindly averted his gaze, prepared to pretend he witnessed nothing.

As he left her at the door to the palazzo, Alessandro kissed her forehead again and whispered very gently, his words caressing her ears, "Arrivederci, Mia Cara. Until we meet again."

Melody would have liked to have escaped to her bedroom without having to talk to anyone, but true to his word, Rat was waiting for her in the salotto. Luckily, she had the forethought to pull her shawl around her shoulders as she heard him coming to meet her.

"That was quicker than I expected," Rat observed. "You barely caught any moonlight."

"We watched the sunset," Melody said defensively. "It was beautiful."

"More to the point, was it useful?"

Melody indicated that he should follow her up to her bedroom. She found Mary there but sent her away so they could talk. In truth, she wasn't sure that the trip had been very productive, at least for the investigation. It was a given that she wouldn't be sharing what else happened in the gondola with Rat.

She felt that she had failed in her task, giving in to passion when she was supposed to be conducting an interrogation. However, she felt that she had gleaned some information at least, though she wasn't sure how pertinent it was.

"Conte Foscari's father worked very hard to build up the business, determined to make it as diversified and resilient as possible. It seems very important to the conte that he honours his father's memory and life's work."

"Important enough to meddle in international affairs to aid his business ventures?" Rat asked.

Melody considered the question. "Perhaps," she answered hesitantly. "There is no doubt that Alessandro, I mean Conte Foscari, feels that it is his very personal mission to protect what his father built. The question is: how far would he go to do that?"

Even as Melody said this, she felt incredibly guilty for betraying Alessandro's trust. He had told her that in a rare moment of vulnerability and she had exploited that for the sake of the investigation. Was it always true that the ends justified the means? Or at least, was it true in this instance?

She had no more to tell Rat and was happy to retire for the night, confused, ashamed and yet aware that she felt more truly alive than she had in a long time.

CHAPTER 19

*D*ear Diary, I am consumed by such inner turmoil that I do not know which way to turn. I cannot believe what happened last night with Alessandro. More than anything, I cannot believe what I wanted to happen. I know that Tabby Cat, Wolfie and Granny would be very ashamed of me, to say nothing of what Rat would think if he had an inkling. I know that a respectable young woman does not allow herself to be seduced – at least, I think I was allowing myself to be seduced. A young woman must be an untouched, perfect flower if she wishes to be respectable and win herself a husband. But is this what I want?

Granny has made it very clear that I do not have to marry unless I wish to. She certainly could have made my fortune a dowry, yet she chose not to. I know that there is more to life for a young woman in 1911 than to be a wife and mother. Yet, to deliberately choose to go down a different path, particularly when it comes to my virtue, is to cross a bridge with no return.

And then, if that all were not enough, there is the very real possibility that Alessandro is a traitor. While one can make a case that Signor Graziano and Herr Peetz may be acting in their country's interests, even if they are not acting in Britain's, Alessandro is half-British. He was raised and schooled there. To work against Britain, even if, and it's a big if, he believes he is acting in Italy's interests, is to be a traitor. Of that, there is no doubt. Yet, there was a moment last night when it was the most absurd thing to imagine him doing something so awful.

I feel that I need to confide in someone, but who? Who will understand me and not judge my actions? Perhaps the only person I *know in Venice who may not be bound by the rigid British moral code is Luisa. Dare I talk to her about this?*

By the following morning, after a restless night, Melody had decided to call on Luisa to ask for her advice. In London, it would never do to call on a casual acquaintance before noon, even before early afternoon, really. Based on something that Luisa had said, Melody suspected that the woman was not an early riser, even by aristocratic standards, and so this was even more the case. Given this, Melody decided she would have to put her visit off until later in the day.

Melody found Rat eating breakfast alone. The dark circles under his eyes suggested that his night had been no more restful than hers. She gratefully accepted a cup of coffee from Rossi and selected a couple of pastries.

"You look as tired as I feel," Melody said, trying to put her relationship with her adored older brother back on a more even keel after their disagreement the night before. Part of what had kept Melody tossing and turning all night was that Rat had been right; he hadn't wanted her to go out alone with Alessandro for fear that the man might take liberties. Despite Melody's protestations that her virtue would not be compromised, that was precisely what had happened. And what was worse, she had been a willing participant.

Melody couldn't bring herself to admit that, despite Rat's insistence that she at least be rowed by Giovanni, the gondolier had not been the protector that Rat had hoped. To be fair, Melody was quite sure that if she had protested in any way, Giovanni would have stepped in. However, given her evident enthusiasm, it was not a servant's place to interfere. A servant's only job in a situation such as that was to avert his eyes and pretend he heard nothing. Nevertheless, Melody wasn't sure she'd be able to look Giovanni in the eye anytime soon. Whatever must he think of her?

Rat looked up from what was his second cup of coffee that morning and replied, "We need to find that journalist, Silvio Verdi."

Melody had been thinking the same thing at two o'clock in the morning and nodded. "Do you know which newspaper Signor Verdi works for?"

"Yes, it's called *El Meso*, or *The Middle*. Xander explained that there are two other major newspapers in Venice, *La Gazzetta di Venezia*, which is quite conservative and *Il Secolo Nuovo*, which was founded by the Italian Socialist Party and supports the kind of causes you'd expect it to. Based on what Verdi wrote in the journal that he published, it seems that his private views align far more with *Il Secolo Nuovo*, but a man must earn coin however he can. Even a socialist, it seems."

"*El Meso*? That's who he works for? I am sure that is the newspaper that Alessandro said he owns. He was telling me that his father founded the most popular newspaper in Italy but then also owned smaller, regional newspapers. I am assuming that it is called *The Middle* because it has more middle-of-the-road political views?" Melody asked.

"That would be my assumption," Rat agreed. "Though, I'm not sure precisely what we can deduce from that, at least for our investigation. I asked Xander a little about the various newspapers. He told me that *La Gazzetta di Venezia* is very supportive of Italian colonialism and nationalism. As such, it is quite supportive of those who would annex those northern, Austrian-held territories still inhabited by ethnic Italians. However, it also advocates for stability and national security, so tends to balance this nationalistic rhetoric with more pragmatic support for the Triple Alliance, at least to some extent."

"I assume that the socialist newspaper feels otherwise," Melody guessed.

"Indeed. As you might expect, that newspaper strongly condemns the Triple Alliance, denouncing it as a militaristic and imperialist entanglement which does not serve the interests of the working classes." Rat took another sip of coffee and continued, "Foscari is a businessman. It does not surprise me that he takes the most pragmatic position."

"Yes, though, I am surprised that he allowed Verdi to publish that exposé of Austria-Hungary's intent towards the Italians if he supports the Triple Alliance."

"He is not the editor," Rat pointed out. "He is the publisher of many newspapers who spends much of his time away from Venice. Do you really think that he has oversight of the day-to-day pieces published in any of his newspapers, let alone a small regional one? Perhaps that is why he has returned to Venice, to deal with this situation. Regardless, we need to talk to this Verdi. I believe that Lady Bainbridge has *El Meso* delivered. I imagine that the newspaper's address is listed somewhere on the front page."

Thirty minutes later, armed with an address, Rat and Melody settled into the gondola after directing Giovanni to take them to the Strada Nova in the Carnareggio district. Melody felt very uncomfortable when she faced Giovanni for the first time since the previous evening. She needn't have worried; Italians were not as prudish about passion as the English, and Giovanni did not judge the young lovers nearly as harshly as one of his London counterparts might. Regardless of his personal feelings, Giovanni was paid well by Lady Bainbridge and had a job that was both stable and easy. He knew better than to give any indication that he, a servant, had any thoughts at all as to the behaviour of Lady Bainbridge, her friends, or her guests.

Forty-five minutes later, they found themselves back in the gondola. Their trip to the newspaper's offices had been brief and unfruitful; through a brief conversation using faltering Italian on their side and a smattering of English on the other side, Melody and Rat had learned that Silvio Verdi had not turned up for work that day. No, that was not usual, the man was most diligent. No, he hadn't sent word as to why.

The only thing that anyone could tell them was the man's address, provided by a petite, dark-haired young secretary who shyly offered it in perfect English just as they were leaving. This caused Rat to fume once they were back in the gondola, "If she could speak English all along, why did we have to act out that ludicrous scene in the newsroom that felt like something out of a low-brow comedy of errors?"

Melody smiled indulgently; for an intelligent, educated man, Rat could be very stupid and blind sometimes. "She didn't say anything because she is the lone female in that newsroom and knows that it is her place to be seen and not heard. I am sure that her opinion has never been valued, that is if she has ever been allowed to voice one. I can only imagine how her male superiors would have taken it if she had shown them up in such a way, and in front of visitors."

Grudgingly, Rat acknowledged the truth of her words. "But it's 1911. Surely men are used to women in their workplaces by now."

Melody laughed again, "Yes, as the people who file their papers, make their tea, and answer the telephone. Not to stand with them as equals and voice opinions worth paying attention to. Perhaps in a hundred years, this will be different, but I do wonder if things will change so much."

As Melody said these words, she thought about their relevance to her situation. She did not need to work; Granny's gift of a fortune had ensured that. However, if she did not want to accept the role of wife, mother, and hostess that society expected her to conform to, what did she want to do with her life? She thought of Cousin Lily, who, despite now being a viscountess, nevertheless had made a name for herself in the botanical sciences. Melody knew that women were slowly entering many of the professions that had been closed off to them in the past, but did any of them really interest her?

Shaking off these difficult thoughts, Melody said, "Let us hope that Signor Verdi is at home. It's possible he was suddenly called out of town, which is why he was not at the newspaper."

"Perhaps. But we have no other avenues of investigation at this point, so let's try."

The Strada Nova, where Silvio Verdi lived, was in the Cannaregio district, where the Jewish Ghetto was located. Rat had given the address he had been told to Giovanni who nodded, then pushed off. Venice was such a complicated maze of streets and canals that neither Melody nor Rat knew how Venetians managed to have it all mapped out in their heads. Somehow, it didn't matter where they asked Giovanni to take them, he not only knew the best way by boat but was then able to give them directions for how to wind their way through the labyrinth of calles. This time was no different.

They disembarked a short time later. After a few wrong turns and two linguistically challenging conversations as they asked for directions, they found themselves on an unremarkable calle in front of an equally unremarkable house. Rat knocked on the door, and after a few minutes, it was answered by a woman who had the boarding-house landlady look that seemed to transcend cultures and perhaps even continents. She wore an apron over a plain, ill-fitting housedress and a scarf over her hair. What was most noticeable about the woman was the strong alcoholic odour that seemed to ooze from her every pore. Rat had smelled enough gin wafting off prostitutes and others in Whitechapel to know that wasn't the landlady's beverage of choice. He idly wondered what the cheap, easily accessible Italian equivalent of gin was. Maybe grappa?

As soon as she opened the door, the woman started talking in a torrent of Italian that was well beyond either Melody or Rat's command of the language.

Finally, Melody turned to Rat and said, "I think we called her away from the stove and it'll be our fault if the food burns. Or something like that."

Rat nodded and said to the landlady, "Signor Verdi?"

The landlady then went off on another lengthy, passionate rant that seemed to include something about not being given money on time. Either that, or she was complaining that they had mice. Melody wasn't entirely sure which. Nevertheless, after a final few sentences, which the landlady spat out, she turned, pointed up a narrow, dingy, uncarpeted staircase and said, "Lassù, sulla destra."

They followed her directions up to an equally dingy, poorly lit hallway. There were only two doors, so they chose the one that most seemed to correspond to "on the right." Rat knocked at the door, but there was no answer. Then he knocked again and called Silvio Verdi's name and said he wanted to ask him a few questions.

He turned to Melody, "What should we do? I assume the landlady wouldn't have pointed us up here if she didn't believe that Signor Verdi was at home. Perhaps he slipped out without her knowing."

Melody shook her head, "I have a bad feeling about this. I cannot say exactly why, but I think we need to go in."

Rat was prepared to pick the lock, but it seemed he didn't need to utilise that skill on this occasion; a test of the doorknob made clear that the door was unlocked. The shutters seemed to be closed, and the room was very dark. Rat called out again for Silvio Verdi with no reply. There was a gas light on the wall and Rat pulled the chain, illuminating the room and casting its light upon a body on the floor. A moment's observation made evident that the man, Rat assumed it was Silvio Verdi, had been shot through the heart.

Melody gasped, "Oh no! Is he dead?"

Rat couldn't imagine how the man would still be alive, but he went over and checked for a pulse, just in case. "He is very dead. By the temperature of his body, I would say he has been dead quite a while."

Melody took a deep breath, tried to compose herself, and joined her brother. Touching the body, she said, "Yes, rigor mortis has fully set it but has not started to dissipate yet. I believe he has been dead for less than twenty-four hours."

Rat looked over at his sister in surprise, "How on earth do you know about such things?"

"I read books!" Melody said indignantly. "I also attended a few lectures at the Royal Academy with Cousin Lily, and one of them was on new forensic methods. I did not understand all of it, but what I did understand was very interesting."

Looking around the room, Melody observed, "Given that the curtains, such as they are, are closed, I am assuming whoever did this committed the crime last night."

Rat agreed with her observation. Melody continued, "The thing I do not understand is how someone came in here and shot this man, then left without someone, at least the landlady, seeing or hearing something."

"Did you smell the alcohol wafting off the landlady? And it's not even noon. I can only imagine how dead to the world she is by evening. Someone with even a passing acquaintance with the woman might guess that. And as for anyone else not hearing anything, Wolf was telling me recently about a new device, still in its early stages, but nevertheless available, called a firearm suppressor. Basically, it works to silence a gun. Perhaps our killer used one." Then, noticing a pillow lying near the body, he added, "Or perhaps he just shot him through this and muffled the sound." Looking more closely at the pillow, they noticed it had an obvious bullet hole through it.

Melody considered Rat's words; they certainly made sense. "So, is our theory that the killer somehow got entry to this house while the landlady was drunkenly asleep in her parlour, then shot Signor Verdi silently, and that this all happened sometime yesterday evening?"

"I believe it is," Rat concurred.

"Then, the outstanding question is: are we dealing with two killers or one?"

"Venice is not a large place, and by and large, not a crime-ridden one, at least for serious crimes. It is hard to believe that two killers are going around shooting men simultaneously. This must be the work of the same man who murdered Signor Graziano."

Rat continued, "In London, the police can run tests on bullets to see if they have come from the same gun. I wonder if such technology is available in Italy, specifically in Venice?"

This question led to a more immediate question: did they summon the police or leave the body for someone else to stumble across?

As if reading each other minds, they both came to the same

conclusion, almost simultaneously. "Even though it may seem highly suspicious that I was the person to come across both murder victims, we must be the ones to summon the police," Melody decided.

"I agree. After all, who knows how long it might be before that drunken sot of a landlady thinks to come up here. And when she does, she will inevitably tell the police about the English man and woman who came to call. It will seem far more suspicious at that point that we never reported the murder."

They were in total agreement on their course of action, but were both flummoxed by the most salient point of their upcoming conversation with the Venice police: why did they want to talk with Silvio Verdi? After all, it was one thing to be browsing in a bookshop and stumble across the body of its owner, but they had gone searching for Signor Verdi and needed a plausible explanation as to why.

"Given that we found that list, it is probably safe to say that the police either didn't come across it or didn't find it relevant," Rat said thoughtfully. "Therefore, they have no idea that Silvio Verdi is in any way connected to Antonio Graziano."

"I am assuming that we do not wish to draw their attention to this connection, at least for now," Melody surmised.

"I think that will gain us nothing. In the best-case scenario, they brush off the connection as insignificant. In the worst case, they accuse us of meddling in police matters. Either way, drawing their attention to this fact is unlikely to facilitate my mission. While it is, of course, important to apprehend a killer, there are far larger issues of British national security to consider. Those can be my only concern at the moment."

Rat said these words with a professional air that made Melody's heart swell with pride; her brother was a serious, thoughtful, and evidently very competent agent of the British Government. He'd come a long way from his time as a Whitechapel street urchin.

Opening the curtains, Melody looked around the room. There wasn't much to see. Now that sunlight was streaming into the room, they could see the body more clearly. For some reason, Melody had formed a mental image of the journalist as a young man, but she had been wrong. He had wispy grey hair and looked almost as old as Antonio Graziano.

There were some books on a shelf and a medal next to them. Moving closer, Melody peered at it and said, "I believe this is a similar medal to the one we saw at Signor Graziano's flat. Perhaps that is just a coincidence. Or perhaps it is not. Should we mention this to the inspector?"

Rat shook his head. "If we do that, then we will have to admit that we searched Antonio Graziano's home." Melody realised he was right. Even so, she wondered about the significance of the matching medals.

CHAPTER 20

Rat and Melody sat in Ispettore Paolo Moretti's office. The sleep-deprived inspector looked at them warily. "Explain to me again how you happened to stumble across yet another dead body," he said in Italian, which was quickly translated by the young policeman who happened to speak fluent English, who he'd managed to find on their arrival.

On the way to the police station, Melody and Rat had discussed what they would say to explain why they had sought out Silvio Verdi. Finally, they had agreed that the safest and most credible explanation was a version of the one Rat had used previously: that Lord Langley was tasked with monitoring radicals and their writings in Britain and had asked Rat to keep an eye on similar thinkers elsewhere in Europe while he happened to be escorting his sister. They hoped that Ispettore Moretti was unfamiliar with the workings of the House of Lords and that the entire story would be believable enough. Now, through the translator, Rat told that story.

Finally, when Rat was finished, Ispettore Moretti and the translating policeman, Cavelli, exchanged a few sentences before the translator turned back and asked, "This House of Lords, is it like our Senato del Regno?"

Melody knew nothing about Italian politics or its governmental structure. Still, Rat had read enough before their trip to know that Moretti was asking about the Senate of the Kingdom, loosely translated.

"Sì. Yes. It is like that," he answered.

Moretti's English stretched to understanding that answer

and he asked, in his very limited English, "Who is this Lord Langley?"

It seemed that the young policeman's English did not include the terms ward and guardian, so Rat spent some minutes explaining the concept. Finally, the policeman translated what he had said into Italian and Moretti nodded his head in understanding, then spoke some rapid Italian.

The translator asked, "So, you believe that Signor Verdi was one of the radicals you are watching?"

Melody and Rat had realised that this was the weakest part of their story. It was in Britain's interests that Italy not join forces with Germany and Austria-Hungary in any war, so why would Verdi's writings be considered radical?

Rat thought back to some of the pieces he had glanced at in Verdi's journal and decided that it was his other pieces on worker's rights and the evils of capitalism that made the most sense for Britain to be worried about. Rat considered Britain's current ruling Liberal party and its progressive policies. As it happened, it did make some common cause with the Labour party and its more moderate socialism. However, he doubted that Moretti had his finger on the pulse of British politics and assumed that he could gloss over these nuances.

Instead, he answered, "The British Government is worried about the spread of socialism at home and abroad. Signor Verdi's radical publication is one that our Government monitors." This seemed to satisfy the police inspector.

Melody considered whether to share her thoughts on the time of death and her rationale for how the killer managed to enter the house and shoot Verdi without the landlady hearing anything. However, with a glance at Rat, who was evidently weighing a similar decision, she decided that she wanted to remove Moretti's attention from her and Rat, not refocus it.

Instead, she rose, followed by Rat, and said, "As I said before, if you have any more questions for us, we are staying with Lady Bainbridge."

Moretti nodded and let them go. As the door closed behind

them, the inspector said to the young policeman, "Cavelli, there is more going on with those two than they are admitting. I don't think they are the killers, but I don't believe in coincidences. When was the last murder we had in Venice? Two, maybe three years ago? And that was a crime of passion. Two men killed, shot within days of each other, and Miss Chesterton discovers both the bodies?"

The young man nodded along as Moretti stood and emphasised, "Non sono mica nato ieri!" No, he wasn't born yesterday, and he would be keeping a close eye on the oh so innocent-looking Miss Chesterton and her brother with a different last name.

As they walked towards the fondamenta where Giovanni had dropped them, Melody and Rat discussed this very subject. "That Inspector Moretti is no fool," Rat observed.

"I agree. He was not confident enough in his doubt to call us liars to our faces, but I doubt he believed much of our explanation. We need to be careful, Rat."

Rat knew that his sister was right. As if their task wasn't challenging enough, they now also had to be careful of arousing any more police suspicion.

By the time they had arrived back at the palazzo, Lady Bainbridge had already had luncheon and had retired for her afternoon nap. However, Rossi had thoughtfully set aside a cold collation in anticipation of their return. Gratefully, Rat and Melody tucked into various salamis and other cured meats, a variety of delicious cheeses, tomato and basil salad, and some more of the crostini with whipped salt-cod, Baccalà Mantecato, that Melody had so enjoyed at Luisa's party.

As they ate, they discussed their investigation. "Is it possible that the killer had seen Signor Graziano's list with Silvio Verdi's name on it?" Melody wondered.

"Or perhaps it was enough to see some of the articles he has published recently and that those drew our killer's attention.

Melody thought back to their conversation from the previous day. "I remember that yesterday, you questioned why our killer did not murder Silvio Verdi instead of Antonio Graziano if the aim was to stop him publishing supposed proof of Austria-Hungary's secret plans for Italy. Well, now he has killed Verdi, so where does that leave us? Is it possible that Signor Graziano was somehow the one feeding Silvio Verdi material for his articles?"

Rat considered the question. "I think that we need to find out more about the other names on that list." Then he added, "This theory is reasonable except when we consider Herr Peetz's conversation with Foscari and the fact that Graziano's death disrupted their plans."

This was a flaw in their logic, but Melody's counsel was that they not focus on this contradiction for now. "Perhaps you misheard or misunderstood without more context." Begrudgingly, Rat allowed that it was possible, even if he didn't believe that he had misconstrued the conversation between Foscari and the Austrian.

Just as they were finishing eating dessert, Rossi entered the room and cleared his throat meaningfully. "There is a young gentleman to see you, signorina. A Signor Ashby. I left him in the salotto."

Given that this was Melody's second gentleman caller in as many days, she didn't blame Rossi for a slight lifting of his eyebrows as he announced Xander's visit.

"Do you think that Xander has discovered something else about Silvio Verdi after your trip to the library the other day?" she asked.

Rat laughed, "I believe that he would have asked for me if that were the case. I think it is far likelier that this is a more personal visit."

Melody blushed. While her vanity had been mildly wounded by Xander's seeming loss of interest in pursuing her, that had been her only feeling about his absence over the last few days. There was no doubt that the young Englishman did not set her heart racing the way that Alessandro did. Maybe that was a good thing, she thought, remembering their gondola ride the evening before with shame. Melody was unused to being so out of control of her emotions and particularly her actions; wasn't it better to be with someone who clearly was more enamoured of her than she was with him? Someone whose touch didn't sear itself into her flesh.

Making a decision, Melody threw down her serviette and sprung to her feet. "Please serve tea, Rossi, and tell Mr Ashby that I will only be a few minutes." She hadn't done much more than wash her hands on their return to the palazzo. Now, Melody wanted to run up to her bedroom and ensure that she looked somewhat more presentable than she suspected she did at that moment.

Luckily, Melody found Mary in the bedroom tidying up. Mary quickly brushed Melody's hair and repinned some of it, leaving the rest hanging down her back. Melody changed out of the workaday muslin dress she had worn that morning into a far more stylish, light blue one that she knew she looked very pretty in. Finally, feeling more appropriately attired to meet a suitor, she made her way back downstairs.

As Melody walked into the salotto, Xander leapt to his feet. Rat had compared the young man to an over-eager Golden Retriever dog when they had first met. Now, with his reddish-blonde hair falling into his eyes and a goofy smile on his face, Melody thought something similar and almost expected his tongue to loll out of his mouth with doggy joy.

"Miss Chesterton," Xander gushed, rushing forward to take both of her hands. "I do hope you will excuse my tardiness in calling on you again. Please believe me when I say that only the most urgent business kept me away."

Despite her previous fit of pique, Melody found that she could not be angry or even pretend to be angry with the contrite young man. To do so would be like kicking a puppy. Instead, she smiled and said, "Mr Ashby, do not give it another thought. Of course, you have been busy."

As she said this, Melody moved towards an armchair and indicated that Xander should retake his seat. Rossi had followed her into the salotto and now poured tea for them both. There was a plate of very Italian-looking biscuits that tempted Melody, even though she had just finished luncheon. Deciding that she needed to restrain herself, she nevertheless encouraged Xander to take one.

Finally, settled back in her chair with her cup of tea, Melody said teasingly, "So, is all your urgent business finished, Mr Ashby?"

"Please do call me Xander," he said. "And yes, for now, the most urgent business has been dealt with." He paused, then said in a hopeful voice, "As such, I was hoping that I might persuade you to visit the Accademia Gallery with me this afternoon. It is a great favourite of mine, and I try to visit it whenever I can."

As it happened, Melody had been hoping to visit the Gallerie dell'Accademia. Titian's *Bacchus and Ariadne*, which hung in the National Gallery, was one of her favourite paintings, and she knew that the Accademia had many paintings by the artist. In particular, she wished to see his *The Assumption of the Virgin*, a large altarpiece illustrating the Virgin Mary being lifted into heaven by angels while surrounded by the apostles. Melody was in no way a devout person, but there was something about religious paintings that stirred something in her. Perhaps it was no more than a response to the painter's fervour.

"I would love to join you, Xander. The Accademia is on my list of places I must visit while I am here. Let me get my hat and gloves. I do not believe it is far, is that correct?"

"Indeed, it is probably not even a ten-minute walk from here. It is just by the Accademia bridge, on this side of the Grand Canal."

Five minutes later, Melody and Xander exited the palazzo through the entrance that led to the Calle dei Cerchieri. Xander had offered his arm and Melody had taken it, noticing that Xander's arm under his jacket felt more muscular than she would have imagined. Trying to be surreptitious as she glanced at his profile, she noted that Xander really was quite handsome. Of course, it was a very different kind of handsome to Alessandro's sultry dark, brooding eyes, chiselled features and broad shoulders, but still a handsome face.

Melody tried to imagine bringing Xander home to Chesterton House. What would everyone make of him? She thought that Tabby Cat would like him well enough. Wolfie would appreciate that he was a man who earned his own living, however much it was due to circumstance, but what would Granny think? Melody had a nagging suspicion that the dowager countess would disapprove, though she couldn't quite put her finger on why. Perhaps it was nothing more than that she would consider him too pedestrian for Melody, who she frequently pronounced to be extraordinary. Of course, those were merely the words of a doting grandmother; Melody didn't at all feel as if she deserved such a title.

CHAPTER 21

M elody always enjoyed walking around museums and art galleries. There was something so peaceful and soothing about the stillness and quiet one found in them. Even if the artefacts in a museum were not particularly interesting, wandering through rooms, occasionally glancing at exhibits, and reading a description now and again made for a lovely afternoon.

She particularly enjoyed going to the National Gallery, sitting on a bench, and letting the paintings' beauty casually wash over her without trying too hard to understand the meaning of the pieces. Whenever she did so, she was reminded of Mr Eager, who ministered to the English community in *A Room with a View*, leading his flock through the Basilica of Santa Croce in Florence. She thought about him pompously lecturing his pious audience on the Giotto frescoes only to have his pretentious interpretation poohpoohed by the down-to-earth Mr Emerson.

As he was in the Basilica, Xander was a wealth of information in the Gallerie dell'Accademia. Some of his great store of knowledge about the paintings they saw was interesting, but much of it was quite tedious. Melody longed to just linger in front of some of the paintings, not thinking too much about what the artist may have meant or what art historians had written books on. Instead, Xander might have been Mr Eager, except there were no Emersons to rescue her. Melody tried to tune out most of what Xander was droning on about. Luckily, he seemed rarely to need a response from her.

When Melody could take no more of Xander Ashby ruining

her experience of a museum she had looked forward to visiting, she suggested that they find a place where they could sit and have a drink. Xander was all too eager to continue their outing and led her out of the museum and down a fondamenta to a small bar called Enoteca Schiavi. There were only two small, round tables outside. Inside, it appeared to be a wine store; bottles lined the crowded shelves. On the bar was a case with what looked like little sandwiches and other snacks.

Despite her late lunch, Melody found she was peckish. Pointing inside the store at the snacks, she asked, "Would it be possible to get a couple of those? Whichever you think best."

"Yes! Cicchetti," Xander exclaimed. "Venetians eat these in the late afternoon with a glass of wine. Take a seat out here. I need to order inside and will get you a variety to try. Is there anything in particular you do not like?"

"I am not a fan of oily fish," Melody said. "However, I do love that salty cod spread that they put on rounds of toast."

Xander disappeared inside and soon came out with two glasses of white wine, followed by a waiter with a large plate with far too many cicchetti for the pair of them to finish. The wine was light, crisp and chilled. Melody took a few cicchetti off the large plate and put them on the smaller plate the waiter had put in front of her. Everything was delicious and it was a lot of fun to have the small bites interspersed with sips of wine. As they sat there, Venetians began to arrive. Most either leaned on the bar as they ate and drank, but some sat on the steps of the nearby bridge, laughing and enjoying the late afternoon's cool breeze.

When her initial hunger was satiated, Melody patted her mouth with her serviette and said, "It was very kind of you to accompany my brother yesterday."

"It was my pleasure to be of assistance. Mr Sandworth said that he was monitoring radical thinkers in Europe on behalf of his mentor, Lord Langley." Xander said this casually, and Melody assumed that Rat had told the story they had agreed upon.

Xander continued, "Are there other journalists he needs to

research? I would be happy to return with him and help translate if there are."

"Thank you, Xander," Melody said gratefully. "As much as I am enjoying travelling, it means a lot to have someone from home who is willing to help." Xander gave her his puppy-dog look of devotion in return for her kind words. Melody considered the young man's evident desire to be of service to her and asked, "Might I ask you something more personal, Xander?"

"Of course, Miss Chesterton."

"The night we met at Lady Bainbridge's party, it was clear that you and the Conte Foscari do not care for each other. May I ask why?"

Now, Xander looked more like a bulldog, his face scrunched up with displeasure at the mention of Alessandro's name. "He is a cad. A half-breed, insolent cad. He believes that his father's money and an Italian title permit him to swan around both England and Italy, satisfying his appetites with whatever and whomever he pleases."

Realising how angry he had sounded, Xander relaxed his face back to its normal appearance, but he said in a lowered voice of caution, "Please be careful around Foscari, Miss Chesterton. He is not all he appears, and he certainly is no gentleman."

It was all very vague and yet sinister sounding. Melody thought about the previous evening when Alessandro almost certainly could have taken what he pleased and yet did not. That seemed to be the action of a gentleman rather than the cur that Xander was portraying.

Of course, Melody could hardly defend Alessandro using that example. Instead, she said gingerly, "My experience of Conte Foscari has been quite counter to your description."

Xander's unhappiness with her words could not have been more apparent. Nevertheless, he answered in a measured tone, "Please, Miss Chesterton, do not take my warning lightly. I would never forgive myself if Foscari were to take advantage of your sweet, innocent nature in any way."

Sweet and innocent? Is that how Xander saw her? Just an

airheaded, naive debutante? It was a good thing he didn't know about her passionate response to Alessandro in the gondola. Whatever would he make of that?

The conversation was making Melody increasingly uncomfortable. Drinking the last of her wine, she said, "It has been a lovely afternoon, Xander, but I believe I should be returning to the palazzo."

Sensing a change in the tone of their conversation, Xander said in a concerned voice, "I hope I have not offended you in some way, Miss Chesterton. I merely wished to warn you."

"You did not offend me. However, I find myself quite fatigued all of a sudden. Would you mind walking me back?"

Xander paid for their wine and cicchetti, and they began walking back to the palazzo. Arriving at the rear door to the building, Xander turned towards Melody and took her hand. Raising it to his lips, he said very gently, "Miss Chesterton, you must know that I admire you excessively."

Melody looked at his sweet, hopeful face. What would it be like to kiss Xander? Deciding that she would like to find out, she leant forward and touched her lips gently to his. Initially surprised by her bold gesture, Xander pulled away slightly.

"I am sorry, Xander. I have shocked you with my forwardness," Melody said in embarrassment. What on earth had come over her?

Xander quickly recovered from his shock, put his arm around Melody's waist and pulled her in towards him. Xander's lips were soft, and his kiss was gentle but insistent.

Just as Melody felt the kiss start to deepen, Xander pulled away again and let her go. "Miss Chesterton, Melody, I must apologise. I do not know what came over me. That was not the behaviour of a gentleman," Xander said in a flustered voice. "Will you ever forgive me?"

"Xander, I kissed you. There is nothing to forgive, except perhaps my brazenness."

"You are perfection, Miss Chesterton." And with that, Melody opened the door to the outer courtyard, leaving Xander staring at her with adoring eyes.

Dear Diary, I kissed Xander Ashby. I felt that it was a matter of scientific investigation as much as anything else. I do not believe that the two other kisses in my life were a sufficient basis for comparison with Alessandro's. But Xander is a handsome, charming, if rather verbose at times, young man. His adoration of me is evident, and so I felt he would make an excellent point of reference.

I am sure you are eager to learn what I learned from this study. Xander's kiss was very nice. Very nice, indeed. I am sure if he had kissed me prior to my trip to Venice, I would have swooned and been sure I was in love. Well, perhaps not in love. However, I am sure that I would have been quite taken with Mr Ashby. Unfortunately, compared to kissing Alessandro, this was quite pleasant but stirred nothing deep within me. Cook's rice pudding is very tasty and comforting, and I am happy to have it once a week. Still, it does not rouse me to the heights of delirious pleasure that Lady Bainbridge's chef's Zabaione did when it was served the other day.

Melody had intended to visit Luisa that afternoon, but those plans had been thrown into disarray with Xander's visit. Having given up the notion of talking with her new friend that day, Melody was delighted to find an invitation to dine with the marchesa for that evening.

"Chère amie, je suis inconsolable. I know that this is very short notice, but amongst dear friends, such things do not matter. Please join me for dinner at eight tonight."

Melody was curious about the cause of the marchesa's ennui and eager to discuss Alessandro with her. She made her way up to Rat's bedroom to tell him about the invitation.

He opened the door with a sour look on his face. "What on earth is the matter with you?" Melody asked.

Rat moved aside to let her in and then, closing the door, replied, "Oh, it's nothing new. I am just frustrated by this investigation. Besides now having two dead bodies on our hands, I am not sure what progress we've made. Perhaps I am not cut out for international intrigue after all."

"Poppycock!" Melody said in a tone that was so like the dowager's that Rat had to smile. "I have seen Tabby Cat and Wolfie manage situations like this a hundred times. They feel they are getting somewhere and then come to a dead end and must try a different path. Uncle Maxi once told me that he felt that the trait that Tabby Cat and Wolfie shared that, more than perhaps anything, made them such good investigators was tenacity; they do not give up. No matter what, they keep going until they are sure they have found out the truth. And that is what we will do."

Rat smiled at Melody's words; she was right, of course. "Then what do you suggest we do next?" he asked.

"I think that we must talk to Antonio Graziano's sons. I know that they are in their mourning period, but we have no choice. Perhaps, if we go early enough in the day, we can catch them before their prayers start or whatever it is they do. Honestly, if we tell them that we are investigating their father's murder, I find it hard to believe they will refuse to talk to us. And if they do, we are no worse off than we are now."

Rat nodded; his little sister was right. That was what they would do the following day. "Thank you, Melody."

"What for?"

Walking towards his sister, he took her hand and then pulled her into a warm embrace. "Thank you for being here. I was so nervous about this first mission and so sure that I had to keep it all a secret from you. It never occurred to me that Little Miss Melly, the precocious know-it-all who I used to view as needing my protection, would reveal herself to be my best chance to succeed."

With tears sparkling in her eyes, Melody hugged her brother tightly. "It was always Rat and Melly, remember? Nothing's changed about that. We may speak like toffs, and we may never need to worry where our next meal is coming from again, but a part of us will always be Whitechapel street rats who only have each other."

Finally, pulling out of his embrace, she informed her brother that she would be dining with Luisa that evening. "Don't you find her a little odd?" Rat asked with genuine curiosity. From her bizarre outfits to her extreme menagerie, the marchesa seemed a curious choice of companion for his sister.

"Luisa is an original. She lives her life as a performance. But not the kind of fake show of manners that so many in aristocratic circles do, at least in London. Instead, she lives it as a vibrant, colourful extravaganza of a performance. Yet, underneath it all, I believe that she is a very sensitive, quite shy soul. I find this juxtaposition to be fascinating," Melody admitted. "However, it is more than that; she inspires me."

"Inspires you? Whatever do you mean?"

"It is inspiring to find a high-born woman living as she does: apart from her husband and child and uncaring about the judgement of society."

"Surely you don't mean to emulate the marchesa?" Rat asked, horrified at the thought.

Melody placed a reassuring hand on his arm. "Of course not, you silly thing. However, I believe there are lessons I might learn that might help me determine how to carve out a path for myself that is more than a woman of my class, in this age, might be expected to walk."

CHAPTER 22

Arriving at the marchesa's palazzo before sunset and for something other than one of her extravagant parties gave Melody the opportunity to appreciate what an oddity the building really was. It was very evident that it had been intended to have more than one storey, but the crumbling, overgrown facade obfuscated whether the others had never been added or if the building was a ruin of its former glory.

Standing on the terrace of the palazzo waiting for Melody to disembark was one of Luisa's African manservants. Melody had remembered seeing quite a few other African servants at the party. This one was wearing a very ornate tunic and wore a white turban. If Melody hadn't remembered that he had been the one to hand her a glass of champagne days before, she might have assumed that he was a royal guest.

The manservant bowed and said in perfect English with only a hint of a foreign accent, "The marchesa welcomes you and is awaiting you in the garden."

As she did the night of the party, Melody walked through the hallway connecting the terrace to the garden, glancing to her left and right at what she could see of the palazzo's other rooms. The night of the party, the garden had been so full of people and servants that, while it had seemed almost otherworldly, Melody hadn't fully appreciated its beauty. Now, she realised what an oasis Luisa had created for herself in the middle of the city. The garden was a charming mixture of pieces of art, exotic flowers basking in patches of sunlight and leafy trees providing welcoming shade.

Under one such tree, Luisa sat at a wrought iron table. On the table, there was an ice bucket with a bottle of champagne in it and a platter with snacks that looked like the cicchetti from earlier that day.

Even sitting down, it was clear that Luisa was wearing another outfit that bordered on a costume: a bright red silk high-collared blouse with a large bow tied at the neck topped what looked like wide-legged black, linen trousers. While it wasn't unheard of for women to wear trousers, particularly if they were cycling or doing some other outdoor activity, wearing them as evening attire was scandalous. Large, gold hoop earrings hung from Luisa's ears as if she were a gipsy at a carnival, and this impression was only heightened by the dark kohl around her eyes and her scarlet, painted lips.

However, Melody barely noticed any of this as she took in the sight of Luisa's cheetah lying by the side of her chair. The big cat was quite beautiful, its creamy fur dotted with evenly sized and spaced black spots. The animal was majestic but also quite terrifying to behold. While it seemed to be sleeping, perhaps even sedated, nevertheless, there was something quite terrifying in the raw power that seemed coiled up in the animal, even when it was at rest.

The cheetah's collar was made of very fancy-looking leather covered in metal studs. It was attached to a chain that was connected to a hook embedded in a large rock.

Seeing Melody's nervousness, Luisa said languorously, "Cara, you do not need to fear Shaitan. He is, as you say in English, a pussycat." Then Luisa laughed at her pun. Apparently recognising his name, Shaitan raised his head. Large, round golden eyes looked at Melody with a curiosity that was hard not to imagine might have been that of a hunter assessing its prey.

There were three other chairs besides Luisa's, and Melody made sure to take the one furthest away from Shaitan, who quickly lowered his head back onto his paws and seemed to go back to sleep.

Luisa indicated to her manservant that Melody's champagne flute should be filled. "It is so lovely to see you, Melody. We did not get much time to talk at the party. You enjoyed yourself, sì?"

Enjoying the first sip of the champagne as its bubbles hit her tongue, Melody nodded. "My brother and I had a lovely time. The palazzo and this garden looked so magical and the whole party was unlike any I have ever attended. The food, the wine, the company, the costumes, it was all quite marvellous."

Luisa indicated that Melody should choose some cicchetti. Once she had a few mouthwatering-looking pieces on her plate, Melody remarked as casually as she could, "I met one particularly interesting gentleman from Vienna, a Herr Dieter Peetz."

"Ah yes, dear Dieter. I have not known him for very long. It seems it has been many years since he was last in Venice. Herr Peetz has travelled here with his daughter who is some kind of special envoy to the Austrian exhibit at the Biennial. I was introduced to him by the charming Conte Foscari."

"Have you known the conte for very long?" Melody asked, trying but failing to keep a note of jealousy out of her voice.

Despite Melody's efforts, her tone had not been lost on Luisa and she raised her eyebrows, "He is a very handsome man and charming. Certainly, I see he has charmed you, ma chérie." As if reading Melody's thoughts, Luisa continued, "Alessandro and I have been friends since I first came to Venice. But only ever that; amici. Good friends. He has the mind of a banker, not an artist, which is what I look for in a paramour."

Melody was mildly scandalised by Luisa's plain speaking about such a topic, and while she appreciated the kindness behind the woman's words, she was also concerned about what they suggested. "Conte Foscari and I also no more than friends," she hurried to say.

As soon as the words were out of her mouth, Melody realised that she was working against her intentions for this evening; she had wanted to ask Luisa's advice about her feelings for Alessandro. She couldn't do that if she denied having any.

Deciding to match Luisa's honesty and transparency, Melody amended her statement, "Well, perhaps a little more than friends." She said this while looking down at her hands. Now, she glanced up nervously, unsure what the marchesa's reaction might be. What she saw writ large on the other woman's face made her heart sink: pity.

"Amore," Luisa said in a sympathetic voice. Then she sighed and repeated it, "Amore. I see it on your face."

"No, not love!" Melody exclaimed in more of a a horrified voice than she intended. At this, Luisa's eyebrows shot even higher, and she smiled knowingly. Melody realised what her disavowal had implied, and she said in a panicked tone, "No, Not that. Well, I am not sure exactly what you think, but all we did was kiss."

There, she had said it. She hadn't intended such candour, but perhaps it was for the best. At least now, Luisa knew everything. Or almost everything.

The other woman said nothing for a few moments. It seemed as if she were considering her words carefully. Finally, she spoke, the same sympathy tingeing every word, "You are a lovely young woman, Melody. You are lively, intelligent, so fresh and vibrante. That is our Italian word. Do you know what it means?" Melody nodded, and Luisa continued, "It is no surprise that you catch the eye of a man like Alessandro Foscari. But Alessandro is a man who takes you to his bed, not to the altar. Capisce?"

Melody did understand, only too well. It was another way of saying what Alessandro himself had said to her; he took lovers, nothing more. A part of Melody had wanted to protest then and she wanted to do so again now; she was not looking for a husband. However, while that was true, that didn't mean that she was ready, perhaps would never be ready, to allow herself to fall so entirely from grace and become a man's mistress.

Despite Tabby Cat's attempts to shield Melody from society's most tawdry gossip, she had heard and read enough to know how many aristocratic men kept a mistress. She was sure that Wolfie and Uncle Maxi did not, but they were unusual. Some men flaunted their mistresses, taking them to restaurants and the theatre. Most kept them hidden from the view of their wives and friends in discreet houses in slightly less fashionable areas, such as Chelsea. When she thought of such women, Melody imagined gaudily made-up faces and barely covered bosoms. That was not a life she desired for herself and certainly not one that Tabby Cat and Granny expected her to lead.

Deciding that perhaps she had the answers she had been looking for, Melody decided to pivot the conversation back to less risqué ground. "So, tell me more about Herr Peetz."

Before answering, Luisa said, "I thought we might eat out here tonight, if that is acceptable to you, Melody. It is such a lovely evening." Melody indicated that was acceptable and more servants appeared from the shadows with dishes, cutlery and linens.

As the table was being set, Luisa answered, "I do not know much about Dieter Peetz, only that he is a publisher of newspapers and journals in Austria, which is how I assume he and Alessandro know each other."

Just as Melody was beginning to think that this line of inquiry would not bear fruit, Luisa added, "Of course, I am sure that their shared political sensibilities also attracted them to each other."

Melody leaned forward, trying not to sound too eager as she asked, "What shared political sensibilities are those?"

"I do not know the details, but my understanding is that Herr Peetz uses his major newspaper to advocate for peace and is strongly against the warmongering of Austria-Hungary and Germany. I believe that one reason he is in Italy at the moment is that some recent pieces his newspaper has published, which were particularly critical, have made him a target, and he felt it was safer to leave the country for the time being."

Well, that was interesting. But if Herr Peetz were publishing similar articles to those written by Silvio Verdi, then it would seem the men were on the same side.

"And you believe that Alessandro, Conte Foscari, shares these views?" Melody asked.

"Sì. Alessandro's father, like many older Venetians, despised the Austrians. From what Alessandro has said in the past, his father used his newspapers to advocate against the Triple Alliance, and his son has continued where he left off."

This was a very different view of things than the one Rat had suggested. Melody's relief at the thought that Alessandro was not the villain they were looking for quickly turned to resignation; his innocence or guilt could not matter so much to her. Still, even if he could be no more than a friend, she was happy to think that she probably hadn't been such a poor judge of character. Though if that were the case, where did that leave their investigation?

Melody wondered if Luisa might know more about the medals proudly displayed in the homes of both dead men. She casually mentioned the medal in Antonio Graziano's home. She hoped that Luisa, who seemed to have her head in the clouds so much of the time, would either not notice or dwell on when and where Melody had seen the medal. Luckily, the fanciful marchesa skipped over that detail just as Melody had hoped she would and instead asked what the medal looked like.

When Melody described as much as she remembered, Luisa said thoughtfully, "Sì. I think I know what you are describing. It is the Medaglia della Liberazione di Venezia given to those brave men who helped liberate Venezia from the Austrians in 1866, which led to its unification with Italia. I remember dear Antonio once telling me about his involvement in the Risorgimento, which agitated and then fought for unification."

Luisa paused and smiled sadly. "Do you know that even all these years later, Antonio would host meetings of his Risorgimento comrades. He was a true patriot."

This was certainly interesting. However, Melody was unsure where this piece of information fitted into the investigation. Shifting her focus and thinking about Rat's plan for them to talk with Antonio Graziano's sons the following morning, Melody wondered if Luisa might have more details about which house was theirs. All she and Rat knew was that it was off Campo di

Ghetto Novo.

She asked the question of Luisa, who considered it for a few moments before answering, "I do know that he often stayed in the flat above the shop, but yes, there is a house in the Ghetto where Moische lives and has a studio. I did visit it once, to look at his art as a favour to dear Antonio. He knew that I have many friends who are artists and some who are patrons of the arts. He begged me to look at his son's paintings and see if I felt I could help him."

"And did you?" Melody couldn't help but ask.

Luisa wrinkled her nose as if smelling a foul odour. "Per Dio! The paintings were terrible. The man has no talent. What could I say? I wanted to be kind, but I could not ask any of my friends to help him, let alone be his patron. In the end, I selected the least terrible of them and bought it. I came home and told my man to burn it."

"Do you remember which house it was?" Melody asked hopefully.

"Sì. It has a green door. It is the first house after the small bridge leading onto the campo to the right."

The rest of their meal was uneventful. Luisa was a delightful companion and shared many amusing stories with Melody as they dined. After finishing the bottle of champagne and then one of red wine, they ended their meal with a delicious, sweet wine Luisa called Vinsanto, into which they dipped long, hard, almond-studded biscotti.

By the time she returned to Lady Bainbridge's palazzo, everyone else was in their beds. Feeling a little tipsy, Melody's last thought before she fell asleep was that she wished to live a life as sparkling and full of beauty and excitement as Luisa's.

CHAPTER 23

The next morning, Melody and Rat set off for another trip to the Jewish Ghetto. Now that they knew they were going to the Campo di Ghetto Novo, Giovanni was able to drop them off right by the bridge Luisa had described. The house with the distinctive green door was not hard to spot.

During the gondola ride to the Cannaregio district, Rat and Melody had discussed how to introduce themselves and explain why they were intruding on a house in mourning. Finally, they decided that the most respectful thing to do was to tell a limited version of the truth; having discovered the body of Signor Graziano, Melody felt an obligation to learn more about why he was murdered and to try to help identify his killer.

Now, pausing nervously before the Graziano family house, Melody wondered if that story would make any sense to strangers. Why would a young Englishwoman and her brother care? And more to the point, why would they not think that the police would do a sufficiently good job tracking the killer down?

As if sensing her concerns and perhaps sharing them, Rat laid a hand on her arm and said, "Let us try to be as truthful as we can be without revealing my real role in this." Melody nodded; they could try.

The door was opened by a stern-looking older woman in a severe black dress. Melody's first thought was that she might be a housekeeper, but then, noticing the tear on the shoulder of the woman's dress, she suspected that she was a close relative, perhaps Signor Graziano's sister. Using faltering Italian, Melody offered her condolences and explained, or tried to explain, that she knew it was not a good time to call but that they needed to speak to the Graziano brothers about their father.

The old woman did not say anything as Melody stammered through her introduction. It was not immediately clear if the woman had understood what Melody had tried to convey, but then she stepped back and indicated that they should follow her.

The house was dark and narrow. Stepping into the hallway, Melody saw what she assumed was a mirror covered in a black cloth. They followed the woman into a living room in the front of the house where another mirror was covered and a candle burned on a low table, even though it was barely ten o'clock in the morning. The woman told them to sit and wait.

Melody and Rat perched on the edge of an old, battered couch. Melody looked around the room. The most noticeable thing about it was three low stools over in one corner. They had been waiting a few minutes when two unshaven men wearing jackets with the fabric ripped on one shoulder entered the room. Melody recognised the men from the funeral they had observed on Sunday.

Standing, Rat said in shaky Italian, "My name is Matthew Sandworth, and this is my sister, Melody, who had a passing acquaintance with your father. We are so sorry for your loss."

Well, at least that is what he had intended to say. What he actually said was not quite that, and the taller of the men quickly recognised that his English was better than their visitors' Italian and replied, "Thank you for your kind words, but we are sitting shivah, and this is not a good time for social calls."

Relieved to be speaking English, Rat replied, "We realise that and would not have disturbed you and your brother at this time, except that we have questions we must ask you, and time is of the essence." He then repeated what they had planned to say.

The two men each took one of the low stools and sat on it while Rat and Melody sat back on the couch.

Seeing their looks of curiosity, the brother who had spoken before explained, "As mourners, we must be low and uncomfortable to reflect our sadness and loss." He then introduced himself; he was Avraham, the brother visiting from Vienna, and his brother, who did not speak English, was Moische.

"It must be of some comfort to you that you were already visiting from Vienna and had time with your father before his death," Rat said. He meant nothing by the comment except to make small talk but was interested to see how Avraham Graziano visibly tensed at his words. What was that about?

Melody had noticed it as well and picked up the conversation, "Had you been back in Venice for long before your father's death?"

"Perhaps a week," Avraham said in a tight voice. "May I ask, why you are concerned about my father's death? The police suggested that they believe it might be a botched robbery."

Melody had to repress the urge to sigh loudly at these words. Even though she had explained very clearly to the inspector why this could not have been a robbery, that was still the conclusion the police had drawn. She did wonder if they still believed this after Silvio Verdi's death.

"Did you know that another man was shot yesterday?" she asked. "A journalist called Silvio Verdi." Avraham's response was interesting; it was evident from the look of shock on his face that he had not heard about the second murder, but it was equally evident that he knew the name.

Deciding that there was nothing to be lost by being as candid as possible, Melody continued, "I discovered your father not long after he was killed, and my brother and I also came upon Signor Verdi's body."

"And the police do not think this is an unlikely coincidence?" Avraham said sharply, suspicion now suffusing his face. "Why are you here? And what do you have to do with these murders?"

On the spur of the moment, Melody decided to tell a lie. "In London, my brother and I are private investigators." Avraham's incredulity at the notion of a young woman, or perhaps any woman, performing such a role was evident. However, he said nothing and let her continue. "I was shopping in your father's bookstore with the Marchesa Luisa Casati, a friend of your father's, when we stumbled upon his body. I made certain deductions at the scene of the crime, which I shared with the police on their arrival. Subsequently, my brother and I searched the flat above the bookshop, and we found a list of names. Silvio Verdi was at the top of that list."

Melody had glossed over the part where Rat had picked the lock on the door of the shop, and they had entered the flat without permission. It was clear that this detail had not been lost on Avraham, yet he chose to ignore this revelation and instead said, "You found a list? What did you do with it?"

"I showed it to Mr Burrows, the British Consul in Venice, and he recognised Signor Verdi's name as that of a local journalist," Rat explained.

"Did you leave the list with him?" Avraham demanded with increasing urgency.

"No. I still have the list." Rat told a half-truth. He did have the original but didn't mention that he had given Burrows a copy. "In fact, I have it with me," he said, reaching into the inner pocket of his jacket and retrieving the folded-up paper.

Seeing it, Avraham leapt off his stool and grabbed it out of Rat's hand.

Melody jumped up, "What on earth do you think you are doing?" she challenged.

"I am taking back something that you stole from my father's home," the man said coldly. The only way you could have searched my father's quarters was if you broke into the shop. Perhaps I should call the police and report that."

Rat could see that the situation was getting out of hand. Touching Melody's hand, he gently pulled her back down to sit behind him. Then, turning back to Avraham Graziano and attempting to defuse the tension, he said, "You are correct; we did enter your father's home without permission, and we took something that perhaps we should not have. However, we did this only because we believe there may be more to your father's murder than the police are saying."

"He is dead. That is all that Moische and I need to know," Avraham said, indicating to his brother, who had sat through this conversation in a state of uncomprehending confusion. "We will be saying prayers for our father shortly. I think you should leave." And with that, he turned and exited the room. His brother stood, shrugged his shoulders, and then followed him. Melody and Rat were left to let themselves out.

Standing outside the green front door, less than fifteen minutes since entering it, Melody said, "So, what do we do now?"

"Honestly, I'm not sure. I'm hungry and don't feel like returning to the palazzo just yet. Why don't we return to the gondola and ask Giovanni to take us somewhere for an early lunch? Perhaps sharing some wine and a hearty meal will help us think more clearly."

In another twenty minutes, they were sitting under the shade of an awning outside of an osteria that Giovanni had said was owned by his aunt and uncle and that made the best risotto in Venice. He left the gondola tied up and escorted them to the restaurant, disappearing into the kitchen to greet his family and have his own meal.

There was no menu, just a choice of fish or meat for their main course. Working men were starting to gather at the tables next to them and inside the restaurant, and carafes of red and white wine appeared on tables, including theirs. Less than five minutes later, the waiter put a large plate of battered, fried seafood in front of them and said, "Fritto Misto di Mare."

Melody took what seemed to be a shrimp and popped it in her mouth; it was delicious. They ate from the plate as they talked.

"Avraham knows more about this than he admitted," Rat observed.

"I thought the same thing," Melody agreed. "Did you see how tense he became when we mentioned that he was visiting from Vienna? And then his reaction to the list was quite violent. I was shocked." Rat agreed. They had expected to find grieving sons who perhaps resented their intrusion into their mourning period. Instead, they found a man who seemed desperate to keep his secrets close, even if those secrets were somehow related to his father's murder.

Melody had slept late that morning and had not wanted to tell Rat about her conversation with Luisa in front of Giovanni. Now, she told him everything that the marchesa had said about Herr Peetz and Alessandro.

"So, she believes that Dieter Peetz has sought refuge in Venice because of incendiary articles that his newspaper has printed?"

"Well, not just that he printed them but that he somehow had access to secret government papers."

"Just as Silvio Verdi seemed to. That cannot be a coincidence," Rat concluded.

"Neither can the fact that Herr Peetz has fled Vienna, which is where Avraham Graziano lives and is visiting from." Rat agreed; there were too many things pointing back to Austria-Hungary and the publishing of documents that might have the power to expose Austria-Hungary and challenge its alliance with Italy.

Melody then considered her conversation with Luisa about the medals and Antonio Graziano's involvement in the Risorgimento.

"If Silvio Verdi's medal was the same, then that is something else that links the two men," Rat observed. "Did Luisa know anything more about these meetings of the Risorgimento?"

"No. That was all. I think we need to talk with Herr Peetz," Melody concluded. "While I do not know how precisely, I do not doubt that he is involved in something that, even if indirectly, led to the deaths of Antonio Graziano and Silvio Verdi."

"How do we go about finding him?" Rat asked. "Foscari has already denied knowing the man, so we cannot approach him for help, even if I were inclined to," he added.

"Do you not remember what Herr Peetz said when we met him? He said that he has a home away from home at the Hotel Bauer-Grünwald. That is a very Germanic-sounding name, which is why I assume he feels so comfortable there. Giovanni seems to know every landmark in Venice. Let us see if he knows that hotel. We can go there when we are finished eating."

It took them three more courses of risotto, braised chicken, and a simple but lovely chocolate tart to finish eating. After paying, Rat asked the waiter to send Giovanni out to them. He explained to the gondolier where they wanted to go. Giovanni gave a very Italian shrug that Melody had learned meant some combination of "yes", "that's no problem", and "of course I can do that."

CHAPTER 24

The Hotel Bauer-Grünwald was on the Grand Canal, not far from where they had disembarked to visit the Basilica days before. It was another glorious, neo-gothic, grand Venice building. A red awning with the hotel name picked out in gold lettering distinguished it from the neighbouring palazzos. A very smart doorman kept watch over who could enter the hotel. Luckily Melody's elegant olive-green jacket and matching skirt and Rat's smart suit made a sufficiently good impression for the doorman to smile in welcome and open the door.

Inside, the hotel was all opulence; the red and gold theme was repeated in the carpet and window shades. In truth, Melody thought the whole thing was a little overdone and might have benefited from a more restrained design hand, but there could be no doubt that this was a place of luxury and exclusivity.

"I wonder if they will be prepared to let Herr Peetz know that we are here," Melody whispered.

Rat considered the question. He had heard Wolf speak many times about the usefulness of a title and how, when necessary, he would take on the persona of his imperious grandfather, the late earl, to gain cooperation from people he believed would be cowed by aristocratic grandeur. It was not something Wolf enjoyed doing, but its efficacy was beyond doubt.

Indicating that Melody should follow his lead, Rat approached the front desk, threw back his shoulders, and did his best impersonation of Wolf impersonating his grandfather.

The man behind the desk was small and sallow-skinned. His

jet-black hair appeared artificially dark and was slicked back with far too much pomade. Tomasso Rinaldi was, in fact, the assistant manager of the hotel. He had only recently risen to that position and adored lording his new status over the rest of the staff. Signor Rinaldi took great pride in his ability to identify and fawn over those of high birth. He was particularly obsequious towards the British upper classes, believing that they exhibited better breeding than the Italian nobility. Rat could not have found a more willing player in his charade.

It had been many years since Rat had successfully erased any evidence of his East End origins from his speech. Nevertheless, he now made a conscious effort to round his vowels and clearly enunciate every word. "My good man, I am the Earl of Langley and need your assistance." Rat had chosen to borrow Lord Langley's identity, sure that his mentor would agree that the deception was warranted given the circumstances.

While the young man in front of him didn't look quite grand enough to be an earl, Tomasso Rinaldi knew enough about the eccentricity exhibited by so many of Britain's aristocracy and quickly arranged his features to display maximum deference. "Certainly, your lordship. You have come to the right person. Tomasso Rinaldi is known for his ability to provide whatever assistance our guests might desire."

It took Rat a moment to realise that the assistant manager was referring to himself in the third person. "I am not a guest of this establishment, but rather wish to inquire of one."

Under normal circumstances, Tomasso Rinaldi considered himself the soul of discretion when it came to the comings and goings of the hotel's guests. One didn't rise to the level of assistant manager without recognising the value of subtlety, diplomacy, and tact when speaking to and of the good and great who passed through the doors of the Hotel Bauer-Grünwald. However, he balanced these well-honed skills with an unctuous willingness to do whatever was necessary to ingratiate himself within the highest echelons of both Venice's permanent and temporary high society. In plain speech, he was willing to toady to whomsoever he felt better placed in any given circumstance.

"I would be most happy to provide whatever information I can," Tomasso said, making the split-second decision that an earl likely outranked most of their current hotel guests.

"I believe that you have a Herr Dieter Peetz staying here."

Tomasso breathed a sigh of relief; there was no need for him to feel any inner conflict at this request. Without a doubt, not only did an earl's needs trump Dieter Peetz's right to privacy, but Rinaldi had a particular disdain for Austrians. "We do indeed," he replied.

"Do you know if he is currently within the hotel?" Rat asked.

"Certainly. I believe that I saw him go through to our dining room earlier." As he said this, the assistant manager pointed ahead to a fine-looking oak door with "Dining Room" etched out in large, gold lettering on it.

They went through the door and found the large, elegant dining room mostly empty except for the man they were looking for, seated at a table in the corner of the room. His snow-white halo of hair made him easy to spot immediately. It seemed he was finishing up his meal with a cup of coffee and a slice of tart.

Herr Peetz was reading a book as he ate and didn't notice Melody and Rat approach his table. Finally, when they were almost upon him, Rat cleared his throat, and the old man looked up.

Taking his reading glasses off, he peered at them, seemingly confused at first, then with recognition. "What a surprise seeing you here, Mr Sandworth, isn't it? And your charming sister, Miss Chesterton. I thought that you were staying with Lady Bainbridge. Have you moved to this hotel?"

"May we join you, Herr Peetz?" Melody asked.

"Ja. Please do. Though you will have to pull up an extra chair."

Rat took a chair from the neighbouring table, and he and Melody sat down.

"We are here looking for you," Rat said.

"Me? I am honoured, but why?" the Austrian asked after putting down his fork and pushing his plate away from him.

Rat and Melody exchanged glances; they hadn't talked about how to handle this conversation. Rat gave the slightest of nods to indicate that his sister should take the lead. He had recently come to realise that Melody did a good job, whether consciously or not, of using men's preconceptions about a pretty young girl to her advantage during interviews. Men underestimated her; they didn't expect blunt, insightful questions from Melody, which took them aback, making their first reactions far less guarded and more telling.

While they had not discussed how to approach Herr Peetz, Melody had considered the question during the gondola ride and had made some deductions. Now, she said in a very sweet, innocent voice that utterly belied the words she was uttering, "Herr Peetz, we know that you are involved, somehow, in smuggling classified documents out of Austria for publication in Italy, as well as in your own newspapers. We believe that you are doing this to sway public opinion away from the Triple Alliance. What we do not yet know is how you are involved in Antonio Graziano's murder."

To say that Dieter Peetz looked shocked at Melody's words would not do justice to the look of horror and fear on the man's face. Speaking in a voice so low that Melody and Rat had to strain to hear his words, Herr Peetz said, "Nein! Nein! You do not understand. We cannot talk here. Come to my room, 107. I will leave now, and you will follow me in fifteen minutes. No sooner. Do you understand? I will explain everything then."

With that, the man rose from his chair and scurried out of the dining room. It had all happened so quickly that neither Melody nor Rat had thought to prevent the man from leaving. Now, they sat at the table, looking at each other with uncertainty.

"Perhaps we should not have let him go," Rat suggested.

"He seemed very nervous. It is possible that he believes he is being watched. After all, two men involved in this scheme have been murdered."

Melody's words distracted Rat from his concerns about Herr Peetz. "What scheme do you think this is?" he asked. "You seem to have pieced something together, or at least you may have."

"I do not want to say too much here. As you said, there may be a reason that Herr Peetz was unwilling to speak in public even though there seems to be almost no one else around. However, I do share your concern about trusting him. I do not think we should wait the full fifteen minutes that he suggested."

Neither of them was sure what to do; Melody's accusation had shaken the old man, that was clear. But why? To barge into his room now would demonstrate a lack of trust, and they wanted Herr Peetz to trust them with the truth. However, did they trust him? Certainly, they had no real reason to. Merely looking like a slightly doddering, sweet old gentleman did not seem sufficient cause for credibility.

Finally, when a very long, uncomfortable five minutes had passed, Rat stood and announced, "I see no reason why the man needs a quarter of an hour to prepare to tell us the truth. If he believes he is being watched, then we have already been seen together. If he is not, then what matter is a few minutes here or there?"

Rat was right, or he was probably right, Melody thought. She followed him back out to the hotel lobby, where Tomasso Rinaldi was still manning the desk. Rat assumed that room 107 was on the ground floor, but the hotel was large enough that it was not obvious where they should go to find it.

Tomasso saw the young English couple coming towards him and straightened up, prepared to serve the aristocrat further. Let it not be said of Tomasso Rinaldi that anything was too much trouble for hotel guests – well, the right kind of guests, at least.

"Your lordship, is there something more Tomasso Rinaldi can help you with?" the man said with an oily smile, again confusing Rat with his use of the third person to refer to himself.

"We are to meet Herr Peetz in his room, 107, and need directions," Rat explained.

If Tomasso had been mildly interested initially as to what the young English earl wanted with the absent-minded Austrian, that now became intense curiosity. He had watched the couple enter the dining room and then, not many minutes later, Herr Peetz had left it in a hurry, leaving the other two behind. Now, they were here asking the way to the man's room. And that was to say nothing of the man who had been so enigmatic when leaving an envelope for Herr Peetz earlier. What on earth was going on?

Tomasso's mother had raised him with various oft-repeated principles, one of which was: don't question the actions of your betters. This philosophy had served the assistant manager well in his life and career and had likely contributed to his recent professional advancement. Whatever he might think about the eccentric, sometimes even outlandish, requests and behaviour of the hotel guests, Tomasso was always as helpful, some might say sycophantic, as he felt necessary.

Tightly controlling his features and his tone so that there could be no perception that he was in any way questioning the other man's actions, Tomasso said smoothly, "If you go down this hallway to the right, just past the stairs, you will find the gentleman's room."

Rat nodded his thanks, and he and Melody followed the instructions. Rat rapped on the door, but there was no answer. He knocked again and called out, but nothing.

"How can he not be in there?" Melody said. "Surely, if he had left the hotel, that man at the front desk would have said so."

"Perhaps he slipped out while Mr Rinaldi's back was turned or when he was helping another guest."

Making their way back to the lobby, they mentioned this possibility to Tomasso, who informed them that he had not left the desk, even for a moment, since they had entered the dining room. Only one person had wandered into the hotel, apparently lost. He had approached the desk and asked a question. Even so, Tomasso was certain that he would have noticed if Herr Peetz had left the hotel during this brief conversation.

Was it possible that the old man had taken ill suddenly on returning to his room? Melody wondered aloud.

"I assume that you have a master key for all the rooms," Rat said to the assistant manager.

"Indeed. If you believe that Signor Peetz might be in some kind of trouble, Tomasso would be happy to enter the room and check on him." The assistant manager did not doubt that the protocols in place for entering guests' rooms without permission fully covered being asked to do so by an earl.

Coming out from behind the desk, Tomasso indicated that Melody and Rat should follow him as he made his way to room 107. Knocking and calling out for Herr Peetz and receiving no reply, Tomasso used his master key to open the door. Standing behind the assistant manager, Rat and Melody peered into the room. It wasn't large and seemed to have no private bathroom. Given this, it was immediately apparent that the room was empty. Nevertheless, the assistant manager moved into the room and started checking every nook and cranny as if he believed that the Austrian was hiding under the bed or in the wardrobe.

Looking around the room and noticing some drawers that were pulled out and an open window, Melody whispered to Rat, "He's gone."

Her brother nodded his agreement. Moving over to the window, he realised that a chair had been pulled up next to it, which explained how an elderly man had managed to get up onto the windowsill. Looking out of the window, Rat realised that it wasn't a long drop down to the calle behind the hotel.

Tomasso saw Rat inspecting the window. While no written hotel rule stated explicitly that hotel guests should exit their rooms through the door, there was one that said that they needed to deposit their room key with the front desk whenever they left the hotel. If Dieter Peetz had jumped out of the window with his key in his pocket, then there had been a transgression, however minor. Certainly, the Hotel Bauer-Grünwald did not want to gain a reputation as the kind of establishment where its guests felt the need to escape out of windows on a regular basis.

Sniffing his disapproval, the assistant manager promised, "If the gentleman should return, Tomasso Rinaldi will make clear that this kind of behaviour will not be tolerated at the Hotel Bauer-Grünwald. If an earl wishes to speak with one of our guests, he should be allowed to. Is there somewhere I can contact you if he returns?"

Rat doubted that Herr Peetz would be returning any time soon, but just in case, he let the assistant manager know that he could be found at Lady Bainbridge's palazzo. Tomasso nodded his approval; a palazzo owned by someone called Lady Bainbridge was an appropriate establishment for an earl's stay in Venice.

CHAPTER 25

L eaving the hotel, Rat indicated that Melody should follow him around to the back of the building. There were already crowds of people headed to San Marco, and they had to push their way through the throngs of avid tourists headed to the Basilica and the Doge's Palace. Eventually, they came to the calle Rat believed the hotel backed onto. It was too much to hope for that they might catch sight of Herr Peetz; Rat did not doubt that even though he was less than spry, the old man was long gone. Venice was an easy place to get lost in if one wanted to.

Melody followed Rat, deep in thought. Why had Dieter Peetz run from them? The most obvious answer was that he had been involved, directly or otherwise, with the two murders. Prior to twenty minutes earlier, she would have pooh-poohed the idea that someone of Herr Peetz's age could have been the man who killed Antonio Graziano and then escaped out of the window. However, that fallacy had just been exposed when the man escaped out of the one in his hotel room; Herr Peetz was more agile than he looked.

What Melody couldn't understand is why the Austrian might have killed Silvio Verdi, a man who seemed to share his political views and wrote similar articles to the ones that Herr Peetz's newspaper published. Was it possible that there were two killers after all?

As she and Rat walked up the calle, she said, "Rat, is it possible that we have been looking at these murders from the wrong angle? Or at least a skewed one?"

Rat looked over at his sister, "What do you mean?"

"Well, we have been working on the assumption that two murders, a few days apart, must have been committed by the same man. After all, what are the odds that they're not? However, they might be connected to the same activities and yet perpetrated by different killers. Perhaps the list Antonio Graziano had in his flat was a list of journalists to target and Silvio Verdi was on the top of that list. Maybe Herr Peetz, who we believe has similar views to Signor Verdi, somehow knew that the journalist was being targeted, paid Signor Graziano a visit, and killed him. Then, as some kind of retribution, a different killer murdered Silvio Verdi."

Even to her ear, this was convoluted. If Melody had learned anything from Wolf over the years it was to keep theories simple. The more complicated and outrageous a conjecture, the less likely it was to be the correct one. It was evident, even from her view of Rat's profile, that he was suitably sceptical of her hypothesis.

"I know, I know. That really does not make much sense. If both men were part of the Risorgimento, why would Signor Graziano target Silvio Verdi? I do wish that we could have learned something more concrete from Avraham Graziano. Clearly, he knew something about the list we found, or at least had a sense what it was. Now, we do not even have that."

Rat stopped for a moment and turned towards her. "I made a copy."

"You did? Whatever made you that prescient?"

"Well, I made one copy to take to the consulate in case Mr Burrows wanted to keep it. That's the copy that he sent to London. While I was making that copy, I thought that there might be other people I would need to leave it with, so I made an additional copy. I still have that in my room." Rat had always been methodical and careful, something that the headstrong, wilful Melody often teased him about. Now, she was grateful for her brother's foresight.

They arrived at the point in the calle where the back of the hotel seemed to start. Rat remembered the layout of the corridor that Herr Peetz's room was on and counted down windows. Arriving in front of an open one that looked like the same window they had looked out of earlier, they stopped and looked around. Suddenly, Melody caught sight of a piece of paper on the ground.

Stooping to pick it up, she unfolded it and read, "I have your daughter. The Austrian pavilion. Tonight, at 11 pm. Meanwhile, I am watching you. Do not do anything stupid or talk to anyone."

"There's a daughter?" Rat asked.

"Yes. Don't you remember that Herr Peetz pointed her out at the party? Also, Luisa mentioned her in passing when I went to dinner. It sounds as if she has been kidnapped. Is that why he jumped out of the window? Because he had been warned not to talk to anyone, and our arrival scared him."

"Perhaps the note had been put under his door, and he only saw it when he returned to wait for us. Or at least that seems to make some sense," Rat suggested. He took the note from Melody and reread it. Then, he folded it up and put it in his jacket inside pocket where the list had been earlier.

"Does the fact that someone has taken his daughter suggest that Herr Peetz is the hero of our story or the villain?" Melody mused.

Rat shook his head, "This isn't a novel, Melody. We are dealing with international intrigue. It's quite possible, even likely, that they are both villains. There is a reason that the phrase 'no honour amongst thieves' is a common one."

"What are you suggesting? That Herr Peetz is in league with whoever kidnapped his daughter and that they have now turned on each other?"

"It's possible," Rat replied with a shrug of his shoulders. In truth, he had no idea what was going on and this new twist just seemed to complicate things even further. He looked up and down the calle; Dieter Peetz could be anywhere.

"I don't think there's anything else to be done here, at least for now," he admitted despondently, shrugging his shoulders again. He had no idea what to do next, but he suspected that a more experienced operative would already have a strategy with multiple possible tactics depending on eventualities. Rat acknowledged to himself that they were in this situation because of his greenness.

Melody knew her brother very well. Even though they hadn't lived in the same house for the last fourteen years, they had still spent a lot of time together. Throughout her childhood, Melody had visited Lord Langley multiple times a week and Rat had always been welcome to visit her in the nursery at Chesterton House, something he did most days, often taking his evening meal with her. Despite her frequent frustrations with his overprotectiveness, she had never forgotten being a scared, hungry four-year-old waif on the dangerous streets of Whitechapel when her big brother provided food, shelter, and security.

Looking at her Rat now, Melody could guess the insecurities that plagued him, and she suddenly felt protective towards her brother. "Rat, this is not your fault. None of it is. I cannot imagine how anyone else might have managed this situation better."

While he knew what Melody was trying to do and appreciated the effort, he couldn't help replying ruefully, "I wouldn't even be as far as I am without your assistance. Do other agents need to rely on their younger sisters and, even then, muck everything up?"

It was clear that there was no point in trying to talk Rat out of his doldrums. Instead, Melody suggested, "Let us return to the palazzo. Perhaps a cup of tea will help us clear our heads." She thought about the corkboard that Tabitha and Wolf had long utilised to help them organise their thoughts on investigations. Did Lady Bainbridge have anything similar that they might use?

During the gondola ride back to the Dorsoduro, neither Melody nor Rat spoke, each lost in their thoughts. Finally, just before they pulled up at the fondamenta, Melody said in a determined voice, "We must go to the meeting tonight at the

Austrian Pavilion."

Rat had been thinking a similar thing, but his idea differed from Melody's in one crucial aspect. "We will not be going anywhere tonight," he told her firmly. "I will be going, alone."

One of the many skills that Lord Langley had insisted Rat learn was how to use a gun. For his eighteenth birthday, his mentor had gifted him his own Webley & Scott .32 Pocket Revolver which Rat had made a point of packing for this trip. While he had never had cause to use his gun outside of practice sessions, he felt reasonably confident in his ability to use the firearm if necessary. What he didn't feel at all confident about was bringing his sister into such a situation.

Melody had anticipated this response and replied calmly, "Unless you plan to lock me in my bedroom, I will be joining you tonight, even if I have to follow in a separate gondola."

Unbeknownst to Rat, Melody also knew how to use a gun. Mingled in with lessons on how to curtsey should one meet the King and the appropriate small talk for state dinners, the dowager had insisted that lessons in self-defence be part of the young woman's education. For her most recent birthday, the dowager had given the young woman a Derringer Pistol. The dowager had informed Melody that James Purdey III, of James Purdey & Sons, Mayfair, purveyors of firearms to generations of royalty, had assured her that, small and compact, the gun was easily concealed in an evening bag and was the choice of the Queen Mother herself, Alexandra of Denmark. Like Rat, Melody had brought her gun to Venice, concealed in the same small, locked box that contained her diary. Even Mary did not know she had it with her.

Brother and sister stared at each other across the gondola in a standoff; Rat did not doubt that Melody would follow through on her threat to follow him. How much more dangerous might that be? Finally, realising that the only way he maintained any control over the situation was to accept her company, he said, "If you come with, you have to do what I say. At all times. Is that understood?" Melody nodded in agreement.

Giovanni pulled the gondola up to the palazzo for them to disembark. Rat stood, but Melody remained seated. "I am going to talk to Conte Foscari," she informed her brother. "Alone."

There was so much wrong with that statement that Rat wasn't sure where to begin. "What on earth are you planning to discuss with that man?" he demanded. "You do realise that he is up to his ears in whatever this is, don't you? He might even be our killer."

Melody had been considering this for most of the gondola ride. "I do not believe that Alessandro is a killer." Rat winced at Melody's use of the man's first name. Ignoring him, she continued, "He is involved, but we do not know on what side or why. Those questions need to be asked. Given the conversation you overheard at Luisa's party, we know that Alessandro was involved with Herr Peetz somehow. They both own newspapers that have published pieces against the Austria-Hungary government's stance. That would imply that they are friends, not foes."

Rat was unconvinced. "Even if what you say is true, and that is a big if, that does not mean that they didn't kill Signor Graziano. As I said earlier, perhaps he had Silvio Verdi's name on a list because he was planning on exposing the man's sources. Maybe Graziano was in favour of the Triple Alliance. After all, his son does live in Vienna. Surely you are not claiming that murder is acceptable as long as it is of our enemies?"

Melody looked at him quizzically, "Given your role, you might want to consider what you are claiming about such a subject." She did not want to say more in front of Giovanni, but her point was obvious: government-sanctioned killing of enemies didn't only happen during wartime. If Rat wanted to work for the Secret Service Bureau in the field, he would not only have to make his peace with that reality, but he might be called upon to be the one doing the killing. Was he ready for that?

CHAPTER 26

However irritated he was to see her go, Rat did not stop Melody from taking the gondola to visit Alessandro. She had hoped that Giovanni knew the Foscari palazzo and was not disappointed. Earlier in the week, Lady Bainbridge had said it wasn't far, and it wasn't. The palazzo was also in the Dorsoduro, though closer to where it met the San Polo district.

The journey was so short that Melody barely had time to consider how she would explain her visit. She had been so fired up with righteous indignation at Rat's attempt to prevent her going that it had not occurred to her that Alessandro might give her visit a more romantic interpretation than she intended. As soon as this occurred to her, Melody became flustered. The man had rejected her forcefully only two evenings prior. Would he view her purported desire to question him as merely a ploy to be in his presence? The mere thought was enough to make Melody consider asking Giovanni to turn the gondola around. Her own thoughts almost sufficed to do what Rat's stern words were unable to achieve: make Melody second guess her plan.

Giovanni was beginning to pull the gondola towards the canal's edge, and she had only moments before they would arrive at Alessandro's palazzo. Just as she was about to ask the gondolier to turn around, Melody considered what the dowager would do in this situation. Granny had a force of personality that struck fear into the hearts of even the most hardened criminals. She never let herself be affected by what others might think of her, as much as her family often wished otherwise.

When the dowager had come into Melody's life, the woman was already elderly. Nevertheless, neither her age, gender, nor the expectations of how a woman in her social class should behave had ever stopped the Dowager Countess of Pembroke from striding forth, ready to take control of any situation. If she were in Melody's shoes, there is no doubt that Granny would not have turned back. And so, Melody took a deep breath and didn't stop Giovanni from pulling the gondola up to the porta d'acqua.

Seeing Alessandro's gondola tied up, Melody was unsure if she hoped that indicated he was home or not. Either way, the die was cast, and she thrust out her chin, allowed Giovanni to help her out of the gondola, and climbed the two steps to the door. Pausing a moment before fully committing to her plan, Melody finally used the door knocker to rap decisively on the door.

The door was opened by Alessandro's maggiordomo, who cocked an eyebrow at the young woman standing alone at the door. Melody's immediate thought was that British butlers knew better than to let their thoughts be evident on their faces. It seemed that inscrutability wasn't in the job description in Venice.

"I am here to see Conte Foscari," Melody said in Italian. "Please tell him that Miss Chesterton needs to speak with him urgently."

The maggiordomo's face showed that he could only imagine one reason that an unaccompanied young woman might come looking for his master. Melody was glad that the man had quickly turned his back to her, so he couldn't see how flushed she became at this realisation. However, he didn't question her further and made it clear that she should follow him.

Even though she was glad not to be challenged, the butler's immediate acquiescence made Melody wonder how often young women turned up at Alessandro's door. The thought that the butler lumped her in with those women mortified Melody even more.

Melody was led down a hallway and through a door into an impressively grand sala. However close to destitution the Foscari family might once have been, it was evident that

Alessandro's father had done more than enough to restore their fortunes. Everything about the receiving room was understated elegance. Melody had been in enough drawing rooms in her young life to recognise expensive furnishings that felt no need to call attention to their cost. The overall effect in this room was a stylish simplicity that nevertheless left one in no doubt as to the wealth of the palazzo's owner.

The butler indicated that Melody should take a seat on a cream, silk-upholstered sofa. She perched on the edge, too nervous to even relax back into the sofa's luxurious cushions. His job done, the man left the room, shutting the door behind him having not said a word. Was he merely reticent or did he not believe her Italian up to a conversation?

If she were waiting in a London drawing room, Melody would expect to be served tea and cake not long after arrival. Her only experience of afternoon customs in Venice was in Lady Bainbridge's home, which hewed closely to those of upper-class London society. Just as she was wondering whether Italian afternoon social calls followed any of the same rules of etiquette as Britain, the door opened, and Alessandro entered.

Somehow, Melody had forgotten just how handsome he was. His striking green eyes were sparkling now with something that, if Melody had to put a name to it, she would have reluctantly called laughter. Yes, the man seemed amused by her presence in his home.

Coming towards her, he bowed low over Melody's proffered hand, his eyes flickered up to meet hers. "What a delightful surprise, Melody," Alessandro said in a tone whose underlying amusement matched the look she had seen in his eyes.

If Melody could have erased the past fifteen minutes and instead listened to Rat and not come, she would have. Suddenly, she saw herself through Alessandro's eyes: a naive young girl who had got in over her head in the gondola the other evening and read more into their kiss than he had intended. All Melody wanted to do at that moment was to make clear that her presence in his home had nothing to do with any feelings for him. And, of course, that was because she had no such feelings.

Unsure how to immediately disabuse him of any assumptions he may have jumped to, Melody said in a very businesslike voice, "Conte Foscari, I wish to discuss the two recent murders with you."

Alessandro raised an eyebrow, though, whether at her formal use of his title or at the topic she wished to talk about. "And what do you have to do with these murders, Miss Chesterton?" He stressed the formality of his pivot to her last name.

Melody considered how many of her cards to lay on the table. "You may not have heard, but Luisa, the marchesa, and I stumbled across the body of Antonio Graziano, the deceased bookseller."

"I may have heard some rumour that alluded to that. And the second murder?"

Melody had forgotten to check the morning newspapers, so she wasn't sure what, if anything, had been reported about Silvio Verdi's death. Deciding she had little to lose by repeating the story that she and Rat had been using, she explained why they had been looking for the journalist and how they had come across his body.

Alessandro let her finish and then said, "Two bodies in less than a week. A more superstitious man than I might say that you bring bad luck." As he said this, he smiled, indicating he was teasing. Then he continued, "But I still do not understand what you wish to discuss with me."

Deciding that if she was in for a penny, she was in for a pound, Melody plucked up all her courage and replied, "I know that you lied to me when you said that you do not know Herr Peetz. My brother saw the two of you talking at the marchesa's party and overheard you speaking of Signor Graziano's death."

Alessandro's face was impassive as she made this accusation. The silence when she stopped speaking went on so long that she wondered if he would answer at all. Finally, he leaned forward with his elbows on his knees and steepled his fingers. "And what did your brother believe he overheard?"

"That Signor Graziano's death was a loss for you and caused worry that your plan had been discovered."

His face still giving nothing away, Alessandro asked, "And what do you and Mr Sandworth believe was meant by that?"

Deciding that she had gone too far to pull back now, Melody looked him in the eye and said, "My brother thinks that you may be working against the interests of the British Government."

"Do you agree with your brother?" Melody wasn't sure if she was imagining it, but she thought that perhaps his words were tinged with a little sadness as he asked this question.

"I do not know. Luisa told me that Herr Peetz has published articles that have angered the Austria-Hungarian imperial government and that he has taken refuge in Italy for the time being. We know that the deceased journalist, Silvio Verdi, wrote for one of your newspapers which published some of his exposés. We believe these may have been written using secret papers smuggled out of Vienna. My brother thinks he may have done this against your wishes."

Melody paused; if she went any further, she was potentially risking her investigation and showing too many of her cards to Alessandro. However, if she didn't tell him what she knew, how could she gauge his reaction? Finally, throwing caution to the wind, she said, "Matthew and I searched Signor Graziano's flat above his shop."

At this admission, Alessandro's eyebrows shot up, but he said nothing. Melody continued, "We found a list of books with some names next to them. The first name on the list was Silvio Verdi, and now he is dead as well."

"And you believe that both men were killed by the same person?"

Melody then explained the deductions she had laid out for the inspector days earlier. Alessandro was visibly impressed with her reasoning, and Melody couldn't help but feel proud and happy that he might come to realise that there was more to her than a silly debutante.

He then asked the question to which Melody had no answer,

"Do you think that I am the killer?"

Melody paused just too long, and she saw a look flit across Alessandro's face; was it hurt? Was that possible? Why would he care what she thought?

"I did not kill those men," Alessandro asserted. "Nor do I know who did. I can tell you that it wasn't Dieter Peetz."

"The man you claimed not to know," Melody said with more bitterness than she meant to show.

Alessandro had the good grace to look chagrined. He got up from the armchair he had been sitting in and moved to sit next to her on the sofa, taking one of her hands as he sat. The move was so quick that Melody barely registered it until her hand was in his. He held her hand in both of his, looking down at their conjoining, saying nothing.

Finally, he looked into her eyes with an intensity from which she wanted to turn away. But she didn't. Instead, she held his gaze, as painful as it was to do so. "Miss Chesterton, Melody, I wish I could tell you everything, but I cannot. There is too much at stake."

"And you do not trust me?" she said, finishing his sentence.

"I cannot trust anyone."

"Yet you are asking me to trust you. To believe you."

Again, he looked ashamed at her words. With one hand still holding hers, Alessandro touched her face gently with the other, gossamer-light strokes of his fingertips on her cheek. "You are so beautiful and so young. You deserve a world as wonderful as you are, but, alas, that is not the world we seem to be living in. There are forces at work determined to drag us all into war."

His words broke the spell that he had woven with his touch. Pulling away from his caress, Melody asked sharply, "And which side do you wish Italy to be on when Britain goes to war with Austria-Hungary and Germany?"

"How can you ask that? Britain is my home. I was raised there."

Instead of answering his question directly, Melody said with genuine compassion, "It must have been hard to grow up torn between two countries, two cultures."

Alessandro laughed darkly. "You have no idea. I was never British enough at Eton or Oxford. But when I came home to Venice, I did not speak the Venetian dialect fluently and did not know every calle and fondamenta like the back of my hand. I was never enough of each and always too much of both. That someone like that cocky fool, Ashby, feels he can look down on me says everything you need to know. It doesn't matter if his father lost his title and his fortune. It doesn't matter that they had to sell off the family estate, that the girls have no dowries, and the boys all must work for a living; he still thinks he's better than me, and most people in society agree with him."

He had dropped her hand and turned away as he said this. Taking his large hand in her dainty one, Melody said gently, "I know what it is like to be viewed as never good enough."

"You? You are the ward of an earl! I doubt that people look down on you."

"I am the ward of an earl, but I spent my first four years of life penniless in the East End of London. When I was four, my parents died, and Matthew and I became homeless orphans. If we had not fallen into the Earl of Pembroke's sphere and if he had not taken us in, my life would be very different today."

This was not the first time that Melody had considered the vagaries of fate, but it was the first time she had ever spoken of them to anyone other than Rat. She knew what would have happened to them; Rat would have ended up joining Mickey D's criminal organisation, and she, well, if she were lucky, she would have found herself married to a drunk who beat her regularly and saddled her with a brood of dirty-faced children already. If she were unlucky, she would have already spent a few of her prime years as a prostitute catering to the working men of Whitechapel. This so easily could have been her life, perhaps was destined to be her life, except for a quirk of fate that usually took her breath away even to contemplate.

CHAPTER 27

*D*ear Diary, whatever am I going to tell Rat? He dislikes Alessandro, though why I cannot say, but he formed an immediate distrust of the man. Once he hears what I have to report, his reaction will merely feed off that distrust. To say that I just believe Alessandro will hardly suffice. However, I do. The question Rat has every right to pose is: why does my instinct to trust Alessandro trump his distrust? I have no good answer to that. I am trying not to let my attraction to the man colour my judgement. However, if Rat knew about what had happened in the gondola, he would not only be furious, but he would never trust my defence of Conte Foscari again.

I am unsure how to view my visit to Alessandro's palazzo this afternoon. One thing that I believe I can say with certainty is that, after hearing me speak, he was disabused of the notion that I was merely a lovesick young girl fabricating a reason to call on him. Nevertheless, I am not sure that I advanced the investigation at all. Perhaps that is not entirely true; he vouches for Herr Peetz, and if I believe Alessandro to be innocent of the murders, then surely it follows that I should take his endorsement of the Austrian seriously.

Of course, perhaps Alessandro does not know everything about Dieter Peetz. However, the man we confronted earlier today seemed scared, not dangerous. Diary, I do trust Alessandro's judgement about Herr Peetz. And if I do, where does that leave us?

Rat will be furious, but sitting there with Alessandro, I decided to tell him about the note we found alluding to the kidnapping of Fräulein Peetz. His reaction was interesting; he became quite still and even quieter as if he were deep in thought. Finally, he asked if

Rat meant to go to the Austrian Pavilion tonight and when I said that we both were, he said, "I beg of you, Miss Chesterton, leave this alone." That was really the end of our conversation. I do not know what to make of it. Alessandro neither provided a rationale for his plea nor a promise that he intends to come to Herr Peetz's aid. But is that what he plans?

By the time Melody had finished writing in her journal, she had a headache. She remembered Rat once alluding to the early days of Tabby Cat's involvement with Wolfie and how they'd had reason to distrust Lord Langley. She knew that there had been some incident involving her that had cemented that distrust for some time, though no one would tell her exactly what happened. Yet, somehow, over a matter of a few months, the relationship between them and Lord Langley had gone from deep distrust, even dislike, to its polar opposite. Indeed, within a year, their feelings had so metamorphosed that Lord Langley was named as Melody's joint guardian with Bear in the event of Tabby Cat and Wolfie's death.

Melody reflected on what the transition period from deep distrust to utter faith must have felt like. Of course, Tabby Cat's emotions were not clouded by attraction to Lord Langley, or at least that was Melody's assumption. Did that make the move towards trust easier or more difficult?

Realising she was wool-gathering when she should be telling Rat about her visit, Melody put her diary away and steeled herself. On her return to Lady Bainbridge's palazzo, Melody had rushed to her room to collect her thoughts. However, she knew that she couldn't avoid her brother for much longer, and more to the point, they needed to discuss their plans for that evening.

Melody found Rat in his bedroom, sitting in an armchair in front of the unlit fireplace, deep in thought. Looking up at her entrance, he said nothing, merely raising his eyebrows in question.

Sitting in the other armchair, Melody summoned all her courage and confessed everything. Despite his evident growing irritation, even anger, Rat said nothing until she had finished.

Then, shaking his head in exasperation, he sighed and said, "How could you be so naive, Melody? There is no good reason to trust Foscari and many reasons not to. It is bad enough that you insist on accompanying me tonight, but now you have added a whole new layer of danger to the expedition by alerting the conte."

Trying to avoid a repeat of their ongoing argument about Alessandro's trustworthiness, Melody instead suggested, "Perhaps it is time to alert Ispettore Moretti to what we believe is going on."

Rat's feelings about this suggestion were evident on his face before he spoke. "To do so would be to admit that I am unable to handle this investigation alone on behalf of the British Government," he said in a tight voice.

"Rat, Lord Langley had no idea what he was sending you into when he asked you to accompany me to Italy. Do you truly believe that, if he had, he would want you to manage such a situation alone? We are dealing with a cold-blooded murderer, after all."

Despite himself, Rat smiled. "But I am not managing alone, am I? You insist on accompanying me." His tone may have been lighter, but the set of his mouth made evident his continued determination to handle this situation without asking for help from the Venetian authorities.

By this time, it was just past five o'clock in the afternoon. They had barely five hours to arrive at a plan for disrupting Herr Peetz's rendezvous at the Austrian Pavilion. Melody looked at her brother, who, despite his posturing as the more worldly, mature one of the two of them, was not much older than she was. It was clear from the note that they had intercepted that a young woman's life was now at risk. Melody did not want to doubt Rat and certainly didn't want him to feel she had no faith in his abilities. Nevertheless, how could she justify not doing everything she could to rescue Herr Peetz's daughter?

The more she pondered her predicament, the happier she was that she had told Alessandro about the abduction. He seemed like the kind of man who could handle any situation. At least she had to hope that he could. In the end, Melody couldn't find it in her heart to secretly contact Ispettore Moretti against her brother's wishes. However, she hoped that Alessandro would consider doing so.

There was an awkward silence. Melody's evident doubts about her brother's ability to handle their situation hung between them, heavy with her fears and his insecurities. It became so uncomfortable that when there was a knock at the door, Melody sprang up, eager for any excuse to leave the room.

"Miss Melody, that nice young Mr Ashby is downstairs to see you," Mary announced. She knew both the siblings so well and could tell that words had been exchanged. However, a slight raising of her eyebrows in Melody's direction was the only comment on the situation Mary would allow herself.

Melody was so eager for an escape that she rushed out of the room and downstairs to see Xander without even wondering why he was visiting. That time in the late afternoon, almost early evening, was at the very edge of what polite society considered acceptable for a social call. She assumed that Xander hadn't been invited for dinner; surely Lady Bainbridge would have mentioned that. Also, it was far too early for a dinner guest to arrive. Only as she was about to enter the salotto where Rossi had said that the young man was waiting did she pull up sharply and wonder if their kiss the day before had somehow provoked this visit.

Trying to compose her face into the kind of neutral, bland expression that Granny had said one must always wear during social calls, Melody forced herself to enter the room. Xander stood by the fireplace with his back to her. Hearing someone enter, he spun around and, on seeing that it was Melody, his face broke into a smile of such sweet devotion that, at least at that moment, she forgot all about her kiss with Alessandro. Wouldn't it be lovely to be looked at in that way every day? For a brief moment, Melody imagined looking at that handsome, adoring face every morning over tea and toast and every night before she fell asleep.

Xander crossed the room in a few long strides, took both her hands in his and brought them to his lips. "Miss Chesterton, please forgive me, but I could not stay away. After yesterday, well, you know, I..." he stammered, getting redder in the face with every mangled word.

Finally, taking pity on the young man, Melody extricated her hands and said kindly, "You never need to ask forgiveness for paying me a visit, Mr Ashby. Xander. I hope that you and I are good enough friends that we need stand on no such formalities."

As she said this, Melody sat on the sofa. She was rather taken aback when, instead of sitting in one of the nearby armchairs, Xander sat down next to her and took one of her hands.

"Miss Chesterton. I would like us to be more than good friends. I would like to court you, if that is agreeable."

The pronouncement was so old-fashioned and quaint that Melody had to fight the urge to smile at his words. Not that Melody had much experience of such things. However, at least said by Xander, asking for permission to court her seemed like something that might have been said when Tabby Cat was a girl, perhaps even further back in Granny's time. Melody wasn't sure if she should be charmed or put off by the anachronism. Suddenly, she was flooded with the memory of Alessandro's kisses, his arms around her, the fire that coursed through her body at his touch. Shaking her head to try to dispel such thoughts, Melody decided that Xander's old-fashioned charm was, if not preferable, then safer.

Making up her mind, Melody said quickly, before she could second-guess herself, "I would like that very much, Xander."

The young man moved a little closer to her on the sofa, gently put his arm around her waist, and gave her a chaste kiss on the lips. It was a nice embrace that didn't confuse Melody at all. The kiss didn't cause her heart to pound, her palms to sweat, nor make her want to throw all caution to the wind. Just as with their kiss the previous day, it was safe, comfortable, and easy. The kind of kiss Melody could easily imagine enjoying for a lifetime.

Just as Melody was ready to lean further in towards Xander and encourage him to greater heights of passion, the young man pulled back. "Miss Chesterton, Melody, might I have the pleasure of taking you out for an early dinner this evening? I do have some important consulate business I have to take care of later, but I can certainly spare a few hours for your charming company."

Melody thought about all the precious time she was wasting just entertaining Xander now and how much planning was needed if she and Rat were to turn up prepared at the rendezvous spot later that evening.

"Xander, under normal circumstances, I would love nothing more. However, I also have some tasks I need to accomplish this evening. In fact, I should be applying myself to them even as we speak. I would love to take you up on the invitation tomorrow night, if that is convenient for you, that is."

Retaking her hands, Xander looked into her eyes, utter infatuation suffusing his features, and told her that it would always be convenient for him to spend time in her company. And after uttering those words, Xander left.

Melody sat for some minutes contemplating the courtship she had just agreed to. She did not love Xander, of that, there was no doubt. However, there was something about Xander Ashby that reminded her of the safety and security she had always felt around Wolf and Lord Langley. While the dowager rarely advocated for marriage these days, one piece of advice she had given Melody when she had turned seventeen was, "It is always best to be loved more than you love in return." Reflecting on this advice, Melody decided that, even if she never matched Xander's adoration, it would not be unpleasant to spend a lifetime as its recipient.

Finally, realising that she was wasting even more time on such thoughts, Melody instead put her intellect to better use by considering how best to manage the situation she and Rat were walking into later. For that was the large question mark hanging over their plan to interrupt Herr Peetz's appointment at the Austrian Pavilion: what were they walking into? Was the person who had abducted Fräulein Peetz their murderer, or was it possible that this was wholly unrelated to the killings? It seemed unlikely, but it was possible. Perhaps Herr Peetz had gambling debts, and the kidnapping was an attempt to force repayment.

Rat had suggested that Herr Peetz and their killer might have been in league and were now turning on each other. As much as she allowed that to be a possibility, it didn't feel right to Melody. She thought about their meeting earlier with the Austrian. He had not seemed unhappy to see them when she and Rat had first approached in the hotel dining room. It was only once Melody had accused him of being involved in the smuggling of stolen documents in Vienna and suggested that he might have something to do with Signor Graziano's death that the man became agitated. She considered his words, "You do not understand." His reaction had not seemed disingenuous but rather an authentic, heartfelt response. He might have denied all knowledge of what Melody had accused him of, but he hadn't. He didn't deny the basic facts she had laid out, only her interpretation of them.

Then Melody reflected on their visit to the Graziano house that morning. When she had first let slip that she and Rat had broken into the bookshop to search Signor Graziano's flat, his son hadn't been overly concerned. What had agitated Avraham Graziano was the mention of the list. And then she remembered his reaction to the news of Silvio Verdi's death and her intuition at the time that Avraham knew the name, and not just because he read the Venetian newspapers. Finally, she considered the connection she and Rat had made at lunch between Herr Peetz and Avraham Graziano both visiting from Vienna.

Melody had an epiphany and jumped to her feet. She hoped that Rat was still in his bedroom. She knew what they needed to find out for the final puzzle pieces to slot into place.

CHAPTER 28

"Repeat what you just said," Rat demanded, shaking his head in confusion.

"I think that Avraham is the link, somehow. I was thinking back to what Luisa told me about Signor Graziano's sons: one is an artist, and the other, Avraham, lives in Vienna and works in a library."

"So? I still don't understand what you see," Rat exclaimed in frustration.

Melody had burst into Rat's bedroom to find him where she had left him when she went to meet Xander, sitting in front of the fireplace, deep in thought. Now, she moved to reseat herself opposite him and took a moment to calm herself and to try to explain in as calm and methodical a manner possible the insight that had just hit less than ten minutes earlier.

"Let us consider what we know," she began. "We know that articles are being published in newspapers in Italy and Austria purporting to expose nefarious schemes within Austrian-Hungary directed at Italy and its citizens. Not only have those pieces been published, but they have quoted supposedly stolen documents and have even included photographs of said documents. Obviously, someone within the Austrian government or civil service, or close to them, is stealing these documents. I supposed we would call someone doing something similar in Britain a traitor."

Even as she said this last sentence, Melody reflected again that treason was in the eye of the beholder; one man's traitor is another man's hero.

Rat considered her words and thought about the papers Lord Langley had given him to read. "There are certainly various factions in Austria-Hungary and within Germany who are against the war that is looming. From what I've read, the Austrian Social Democratic Workers' Party is just one of the groups that is passionately anti-war because of what it sees as the inevitable exploitation of the lower classes. However, there are also many intellectuals and other figures who bemoan the belligerence of their country and its allies. Then there are the usual pacifist groups. Certainly, there are more than enough reasons that someone within the government in Austria might want to provoke Italy and its subjects to turn away from the Triple Alliance."

Melody acknowledged Rat's words and continued, "So, someone steals the documents and photographs them or makes copies. Then, they have to find a way to get these distributed to publications in Italy and Austria. I am assuming one does not just send such things by mail."

"There definitely needs to be a covert way to move the material. Perhaps they use couriers, but that would seem to hold too many risks."

"Exactly. So, there needs to be a way to get evidence of what Austria-Hungary plans out of the country and disseminated to news organisations that will not seem out of the ordinary in any way." Seeing that her brother was not following where her thoughts had led her, Melody continued, "Think about the list we found."

"Yes. It was a list of names."

"And what else was listed?" she asked patiently.

"I don't remember. Was it books?" Rat asked, his frustration evident.

"Exactly. The list had books by German authors, perhaps also Austrians. I saw the name Arthur Schnitzler. Is he Austrian? Anyway, the point is, it was a list of books."

"Graziano was a bookseller. Surely it is not surprising to find a list of authors and their works in his home," Rat remarked.

"Rat! Why are you not getting this?" Melody snapped, her patience at an end. "Yes, he is, well was, a bookseller. His son works in a library in Vienna. Somehow, stolen documents are getting transported from Vienna to Italy."

Finally, Melody saw Rat's eyes light up. "You believe that Avraham Graziano is secreting documents in books that the library is shipping to Venice?"

"I do. I cannot imagine that he was shipping them directly to his father. That would seem too suspicious. There must be an intermediary at a library here in Venice. Perhaps Signor Graziano then borrowed the books, removed the documents, and distributed them to journalists, which is why Silvio Verdi's name was on the list. It was a record of which books from the library had material for particular journalists. I would bet anything that the other names on that list are also journalists writing for newspapers, or perhaps they are other people in Italy who might influence public opinion somehow."

Melody paused again and considered her theory. "Perhaps Avraham sends his father letters recommending books for him to read, or something like that. They must have had some way to secretly communicate which documents are in which books and to do so in a way that would not raise any suspicions, particularly if the communications were intercepted."

"Melody, I think you're right. You're amazing," Rat gushed. Melody blushed with pride at her brother's praise. "What is Herr Peetz's role in this, do you think?"

This had been something that Melody hadn't worked out yet. She shook her head. "I am not sure, honestly. We know that his newspaper publishes anti-war pieces. Perhaps he also receives some of the stolen documents and that is the extent of his involvement."

"Yet, what I overheard Herr Peetz discuss with Foscari suggests otherwise. They talked of their plan being disrupted. Surely that indicates that, if nothing else, Dieter Peetz was aware of Antonio Graziano's role as a link in the chain connecting whoever is stealing these documents in Vienna to their eventual publication in Italy."

Too late, Rat realises the implication of his words, which Melody seized on immediately and victoriously. "Ha! So, by your logic, Alessandro is also on the side of good, trying to prevent Italy from joining the war as Austria's ally."

Loath to concede the point, yet boxed in by his own words, Rat held his hands up in surrender. "You win. Yes, all the evidence points to Foscari being, if not on Britain's side, at least not on Austria's. However, that doesn't mean that I now trust him. It certainly does not mean you were right to tell him about the abduction of Herr Peetz's daughter."

Rat looked at the clock on the mantlepiece. "We only have a few hours. What are we going to tell Lady Bainbridge to explain why we are not joining her for dinner?"

"Well, that I can answer easily; she told me earlier that she is out for the evening, and we will be dining alone. We will still need to eat something. I will ask Rossi for something light that we can eat up here so we can talk in private." At this, Melody rose and left the room to find the maggiordomo. She returned a few minutes late and said that Rossi would be bringing some tramezzini and other refreshments up shortly.

Settling back into the armchair, Melody asked, "So, what is our plan?"

Rat considered the question. "The piece of this we still don't understand is why the two men were murdered and by whom. I think we need to consider this question, if only to have some sense of what we might be walking into this evening."

This had been another piece of the puzzle that Melody had also considered, to no avail. She had delighted in Rat's praise and hated to be unable to follow-up her earlier deductions with one equally laudable. Desperate to surprise her brother with another brilliant hypothesis, she pondered the question again.

Finally, Melody asked, "Luisa said that Herr Peetz had left Vienna because of the government's displeasure at the pieces his newspaper was publishing. Is it too much to assume that they have also noticed the pieces being published in Italy? If they have seen copies of secret, internal government documents reproduced in Italian newspapers, the Austrians must have realised that there was a leak that somehow led to those journalists."

She paused, then added, "Here is the part I do not have any answer for: one might posit that both men were murdered over the list. Except, what does the list really show? Surely, the Austrians can extrapolate which journalists are being fed documents just by tracking what is being written about and by whom. At least, from what we saw, it is a list of names and a list of books. As you said, Signor Graziano was a bookseller; even if someone came upon that list, what would it tell them?"

"Well, you pieced together the method by which the information is carried between Vienna and Italy. Why couldn't someone else?"

"Well, to begin with, we are not sure that I am correct. We merely have a hypothesis at the moment which has yet to be tested and proved correct," Melody told him.

Rat smiled, "You may have been spending too much time with Cousin Lily. Her scientific terminology has rubbed off on you. But your point is well taken. However, let us assume, for the time being, that you are correct. After all, isn't that what scientists do: assume the possible truth of a hypothesis until they can test it sufficiently to either confirm or discard it."

Melody nodded, and Rat continued, "So, we have a working hypothesis. Given that, what might an operative working on behalf of the Austrian government have been able to extrapolate from such a list? More to the point, how would he even have known it existed?"

His sister considered his words. As they sat in silence, there was a knock on the door, and Rossi entered with a tray of food. As well as the promised tramezzini, there were little savoury pastries, wedges of cheese and slices of salami. There was a bowl of black olives in oil and herbs and another bowl with sauteed artichoke hearts in it. Finally, there was a basket filled with warm rolls. To top off the feast, and because it was Italy, after all, there was a bottle of red wine and two glasses.

Rossi laid out all the food on the table near Rat's chair, then left Rat and Melody to their meal. Their lunch felt like it was many hours ago, and Melody realised she was famished. She loaded up her plate in a very unladylike manner, then settled back in her armchair. Neither sibling spoke for some time as they satiated their immediate hunger.

Finally, washing a third tramezzini down with a gulp of wine, Rat said, "Let us not worry about how this Austrian operative, who we are assuming is our murderer, found out what Signor Graziano and the others were doing. As you pointed out, the results of their operation were evident enough to anyone paying attention to the sudden flurry of anti-Austrian news articles. So, our killer, let's call him Mr X for now, is sent to Venice to investigate."

Immediately, Melody could see the flaw in Rat's argument, "But why Venice? Does it not seem unlikely that these articles are only being written for Venetian newspapers? While it is true that the people of Venice have a particularly recent unpleasant history with Austria, how much can the citizens of one city influence? These articles must have been placed in newspapers all over Italy, don't you think?"

"So, what do you believe made Mr X target Venice?"

Melody considered the question. "Well, I think there are two possible options: either Herr Peetz had already been identified as a person of interest, and when he left Vienna, Mr X followed him to Venice."

"That's it!" Rat exclaimed, not even letting Melody get to option two.

"Well, I agree, it is very likely. However," his sister counselled, "we need to consider option two: that Mr X was already in place in Venice. After all," she said slyly, "you were sent here by the British Government. Venice's proximity and complicated history with Austria clearly makes it a city of interest to your overlords. So, why not also to Mr X's?"

Rat had to concede his sister's point. Then he added,

"If we assume that the Austrians were suspicious of how supposedly secret information was making its way into Italian newspapers, perhaps Mr X was watching Silvio Verdi and the other journalists and came to suspect that Antonio Graziano was involved. Maybe he was killed because he would not reveal his son's role and help lead the Austrians to whoever is leaking the documents." This made sense and Melody nodded her agreement.

Taking another sip of wine, as he considered whether he had room for one more tramezzini, Rat said thoughtfully, "Regardless, we have even more reason to be very cautious tonight. Mr X did not kill by accident or as a last resort. This man had the forethought to pick up a pillow to silence his gun; he knew what he was doing. He might even be a trained assassin."

As her brother said this, Melody wondered for the first time whether Rat had been similarly trained for such assignments.

CHAPTER 29

Finally, they had a plan of sorts. Rat wasn't confident it was foolproof. He wasn't even convinced it was particularly good. However, it was all they had managed to come up with. Rather than waiting until the rendezvous time of ten o'clock to enter the pavilion, they would situate themselves there earlier and lie in wait.

Melody had pointed out that the note hadn't said where in the pavilion. "How large are these places?"

Rat's counter was that if Mr X hadn't specified where, then it would either be obvious when they arrived, or he intended to meet Herr Peetz in the vestibule. Melody wasn't sure she agreed with this assumption. She had formed a mental image of a very sadistic Mr X. In her view of the killer, he might enjoy throwing Herr Peetz off kilter by making him wander through the pavilion, looking for his daughter.

One of the things that Melody and Rat quickly realised was that not only did they not know exactly how to get to the Giardini Della Biennale, but they also had no idea where in the gardens the Austrian Pavilion was located nor what security there was likely to be. As they considered who might not only know the answers to these questions, but be someone they believed they could trust, they concluded that Giovanni was the most likely person. They already knew that the gondolier could find his way to any spot in Venice. They had to hope this skill extended to the parts of the city not immediately accessible by canal. And as for trusting him, well, while they could not be one hundred percent certain of anyone outside of each other, there was no reason to believe the man was anything other than a longtime, loyal servant to Lady Bainbridge.

While they both needed to change their outfits for their evening adventure, Melody would need longer to devise an appropriate costume for covert activities than Rat. Given this, she returned to her room to see what Mary had packed that might be appropriate while Rat went to talk to the gondolier.

Rat assumed that, just as with the Lord Langley's and Wolf's drivers, when they weren't in the carriage house polishing the new Rolls Royce motor cars, they were to be found in and around the servants' quarters, most likely the kitchen. Rat hadn't explored this part of the palazzo, but he had spent enough time in the great houses of Britain to be able to guess his way. Indeed, as he walked down the hallway past the dining room, Rat saw a plain oak door whose handle was well-worn. Pushing on the door, the immediate change to a more functionally decorated hallway confirmed he was going in the right direction.

While it had been many years since Rat had been a servant at Chesterton House, he had never forgotten his humble origins and had always treated the servants there and at Langley House with particular respect and care. In return, the servants at both homes were universally chuffed to see the young boy elevated to circumstances they could not even imagine aspiring to. As he moved into adulthood, he continued to walk that line with a deftness and sensitivity that was not lost on the inhabitants of both houses, from the highest to the lowest ranks.

Now, it occurred to Rat that he was in a house where no one knew of his background, amongst servants who only saw him as a guest of their mistress. He could not assume the familiarity he did at home and needed to be aware of the servants' likely alarm at finding him in their midst.

Because they hadn't had to serve a formal dinner, the staff had been allowed to take their meal at a more leisurely pace than usual, and Rat found them all assembled in the kitchen, sitting around a long, plain oak table. He was happy to see that Giovanni was amongst them.

At his entrance, all the servants rose, most with bemused looks on their faces. "Please, don't let me interrupt your dinner," Rat stammered in broken Italian. "Sit. Please." The servants followed his command but shared looks of curiosity. Rat continued, "Giovanni, might I speak to you briefly?"

The gondolier rose and indicated that Rat should follow him through a door off the kitchen. Rat had never been more grateful that Giovanni understood and spoke English, however broken it was. He let the other man lead the way. Giovanni took him into a small room that, from the looks of it, was the housekeeper's office. Rat took a seat behind the small, tidy desk, and indicated that Giovanni should take the other chair.

On his way down to the kitchen, Rat had considered what reason he might give Giovanni to explain why they needed his help. It was a given that he couldn't tell the truth, but it was also impossible to imagine how he might explain the need for a nighttime break-in without some kind of plausible explanation. Finally, he'd decided on a limited version of the truth.

"Giovanni, as you may know, my sister discovered the body of the bookseller, Signor Graziano, some days ago." The gondolier nodded his head. Rat continued, "She felt the need to learn more about the murdered man and to try to understand why he had been killed." If Giovanni wondered why a well-bred young English woman wasn't content to leave such an investigation to the police, he was too good a servant to comment. Yet again, he kept any thoughts he might have on the behaviour of Lady Bainbridge and her guests to himself.

This had been the easy part of the explanation. Now Rat paused, then explained, "In the course of trying to learn more about the murder, we discovered that a young woman has been kidnapped and that her abductor is holding her hostage in the Austrian Pavilion at the Giardini Della Biennale." This wasn't exactly true and didn't make a whole lot of sense taken out of context, but it was close enough to the truth. No need to go into who Herr Peetz was and how he had escaped from them out of the window. Instead, Rat then made his request: they needed help getting to and entering the gardens after dark. Was this something Giovanni was able and willing to help them with?

Rat was particularly sensitive to the willing part; he did not doubt that if he commanded the gondolier to help them, he would. However, he had no desire to have the man break the law merely because he felt he had no choice but to help.

"Sì, signor. Giovanni, he will help you," the man assured Rat. "When I was bambino, Giovanni and brother Paulo would go to i giardini. We would, how you say? We sneak in. My family's home it minuscolo and i giardini they are grande. Capisci?"

Rat thought about the cramped tenement he and Melody had lived in when their parents were still alive. Yes, he understood what it was like to be a child who yearned for space to run in.

Giovanni continued, "Giovanni take you in the gondola, then we walk and I show you how get in." It did occur to Rat to question if the secret entrance the gondolier had used as a child was still there, but he didn't want to show a lack of trust in the man. Instead, he told Giovanni what time they wished to arrive at the Austrian Pavilion and the man indicated that they should leave at least an hour to have sufficient time to get there and enter the gardens. Rat had already decided that they would not take Giovanni into the Giardini Della Biennale with them. Rat had no idea how dangerous the situation might become, and while it seemed he had no choice but to allow Melody to accompany him, he could control how much he involved the gondolier.

Looking at his watch, Rat realised that if they were to leave at eight o'clock, they didn't have very long to prepare for their expedition. He indicated that Giovanni should return to his meal and that they would meet him out by the gondola at the allotted time. Then, Rat returned to his room to change his clothes and prepare himself.

Unlike Melody, Rat had expected that he might become involved in nocturnal, covert activities and had packed accordingly. He didn't want to attract attention on the streets of Venice, so he needed to be dressed in a manner that would not be considered bizarre. He had a lightweight, black suit whose material was soft enough that it wouldn't impede his mobility. He paired this with a dark shirt. He wore a dark cravat that he thought he might pull up over the lower part of his face if he felt the need for greater disguise. Thin, black leather gloves and a soft flat cap completed the outfit.

Rat put his lockpicks into one jacket pocket and tucked the revolver into his waistband. He considered what might lay ahead and added his pocketknife and extra bullets as an afterthought. He had brought with him a pair of old, scuffed, soft-soled leather boots that were not at all appropriate for society outings but were perfect for that evening's adventure.

Reviewing his outfit approvingly in the mirror, Rat worried about whether Melody had any clothes as practical or suitable for stealth. He continued to ponder this new worry as he made his way down the hallway to his sister's bedroom. Standing before her door, he suddenly had a new concern: what were they going to tell Mary? Mary's own delicate balancing act between companion and lady's maid meant that sometimes she maintained the kind of inscrutability one expected from servants. However, at other times, she could be quite forthright in her opinions. The latter was particularly likely if she intuited that her beloved Miss Melody might be in any danger.

Deciding that managing Mary was something Melody had far more experience with than he did, Rat knocked on the door. He had expected Mary to open it, so he was surprised when he found himself face-to-face with his sister.

Seeing the look of surprise on his face, Melody explained, "I told Mary that I had a headache and would be retiring early for the night. I suggested that she take the opportunity for an evening off." Rat smiled; he should have guessed that his ever-resourceful sister would have deftly handled this potential problem.

Rat followed Melody into the room, noting her outfit. "How on earth did you have the forethought to bring such a plain, practical, black dress to Venice?" he asked.

Laughing, Melody said, "Granny always told me to be prepared to go to a funeral. I always make sure I have something appropriate with me on any trip just in case anyone drops dead."

"Well, I am glad for her wisdom, even though she might be horrified if she knew the reason you were wearing the dress."

Melody considered his words. "Actually, I believe that if Granny knew that we were sneaking around Venice at night, planning to break into a building in order to confront a killer, her only reaction would be irritation that she was not included."

As she said these words, Melody suddenly found herself overcome with melancholy. Given her age and incapacitation, it was unlikely that the dowager would ever be included in such capers again. The thought of the formerly vibrant old woman confined to a Bath Chair for the rest of her days was profoundly depressing.

Shaking herself out of her sudden sadness, Melody said, "I am almost ready. Luckily, as part of my potential funeral garb, I have black gloves, a shawl, and a very simple black hat."

Rat closed the door behind him and informed Melody of Giovanni's willingness to help them.

"Thank goodness," she answered. "I cannot imagine how we would have done this otherwise."

Melody donned a short black jacket over her dress and slipped her revolver into one of the pockets. Rat couldn't decide if he was horrified that his little sister was carrying a gun or relieved that she had the means to defend herself.

CHAPTER 30

O nce they were seated in the gondola, Giovanni, who had also changed into dark clothes, explained the plan. He would take the gondola as far as possible, dock and then they would proceed on foot. They would make their way to the garden's Southern Gate that led onto Riva dei Sette Martiri. Giovanni assured them that it was a more isolated entrance and the surrounding area was less monitored. Again, Rat worried about whether, even if this had all been true when Giovanni was a child, it was still the case.

Finally, Giovanni told them that if they were caught by a guard while attempting entry, they should leave the talking up to him, and he would say they were late-night workers at one of the pavilions. It wasn't clear why one of those workers would be a rather well-dressed woman, but Melody and Rat just hoped they wouldn't have to put this part of the plan to the test.

Rat and Melody didn't say much during the gondola ride; both were far too preoccupied with worry to make small talk. Anyway, given the limited version of the truth that Rat had told Giovanni, there was not much they could discuss about their plan.

Eventually, Giovanni docked the gondola not far from where they had disembarked for Herr Peetz's hotel. They were near the Piazza San Marco, and, at that time of the evening, people were everywhere. Luckily, the streets were so busy that the three sombrely dressed people didn't attract much attention; there was just too much else going on. As they moved away from the piazza, the crowds began to thin, and Giovanni seemed to be trying to keep to narrow dark calles where possible.

Even though there were fewer people around, there was a constant background noise of conversations coming from terraces, music coming from restaurants, and the occasional dog barking. Rat hoped that this low-level noise would continue as they approached the garden and provide some cover for their break-in.

Melody and Rat had taken a chance that Giovanni knew the streets of Venice as well as he knew its canals. This hope was born out as the gondolier nimbly navigated the maze of streets, never pausing for a moment to wonder which way to go. He moved with such certainty and speed that Melody and Rat had to hurry to keep up with him. The last thing either one wanted was to fall behind and risk getting lost in the labyrinth of calles, canals and bridges.

As they passed under a lamp hanging next to a doorway, Rat glanced at his watch. They had been walking for at least fifteen minutes. It was at least another five, if not ten, minutes before they walked down a street with a high, red-bricked wall on one side. Giovanni beckoned for them to follow him as he walked along the wall finally arriving at a narrow doorway in the wall with a wrought-iron gate barring their way in.

Checking to ensure no one was about, Giovanni reached into his pocket, pulled out something, and went up to the gate. Seconds later, it was open. It seemed that the gondolier had lock-picking skills of his own. He indicated that if they went through the doorway, they would quickly come upon the Belgian Pavilion.

"The guards, they come round on the hour. But they are lazy, sì? They will make a quick look and then go back to their guardroom and their grappa. Keep close to the walls and the shadows of the trees. The building you are looking for is just past the first one. It is very grand, and has, how you say? I do not know the word, una bandiera." With that, he made a flapping movement with one of his hands.

"A flag?" Melody guessed. "It has an Austrian flag outside?"

"Sì. This. The flag."

They had told Giovanni that they didn't want him to accompany them, and the gondolier hadn't questioned their wishes. He told them he would wait by the gate to guide them back to the gondola. Both Melody and Rat were relieved; they couldn't imagine finding their way back the way they'd come alone. Thanking Giovanni for his help, they slipped through the doorway and into the Giardini Della Biennale.

The moon was bright that evening, which helped Melody and Rat see where they were going. However, it also increased the risk that they would be seen. Taking Giovanni's advice, they kept close to the wall. With the moonlight and the illumination from the occasional streetlamp, Melody could see how beautiful the gardens must be. Despite its charm, so much of Venice was narrow, cramped and usually quite lacking in greenery. However, the landscaped gardens were full of manicured lawns and beautifully cultivated flowerbeds. The pathways were wide and tree-lined.

Melody and Rat quickly came upon a pavilion, which, given the flag flying out in front, they assumed was the Belgian one. No sooner had they passed it than they heard voices behind them. Rat quickly scanned the area around their location; they were too exposed where they were standing, but if they moved quickly, there were some deep shadows ahead. Indicating that Melody should follow his lead and keep close to the wall and away from the glow cast by the streetlights, he moved quickly but quietly.

As Melody and Rat tried to press themselves as much as possible into the dark safety of the refuge Rat had found, the voices got louder as the security guards closed in. From what Melody could understand, one of the guards was complaining about the meal his wife had packed for him that evening, and the other was commiserating. The men were too involved with their marital complaining to notice the interlopers hiding in the shadow of the Belgian Pavilion. Soon enough, the guards had passed and, from what Rat could see, were not headed in the direction of the Austrian Pavilion, at least in what he hoped was its direction.

Just to be sure, they gave the guards a bit more time to move further away. Finally, when they could no longer hear the voices, Rat and Melody slipped out of their hiding spot. Still keeping as much to the shadows as possible, they silently began moving towards the Austrian Pavilion. It had taken them about forty minutes to get from the palazzo to the Giardini Della Biennale. They had been inside the gardens for perhaps another five minutes. By Rat's calculations, that gave them fifteen minutes to get to the Austrian Pavilion, break into it, and then find a spot to hide before nine o'clock. Of course, this was a self-imposed deadline; they had no idea when Mr X might be turning up. Nevertheless, Rat wanted to get in place as soon as possible and whispered to Melody that they should move more quickly.

From her place in the darkness, Melody looked at the beautifully landscaped grounds with their wide paths, symmetrical flower beds, and perfectly even lines of ornamental trees. Well-placed statues and water features were interspersed amongst the greenery and flowers. What a lovely place this must be to wander during the day. She should bring Mary back here one afternoon, for the grounds, if not the art.

Up ahead was a particularly grand, almost palatial building. Its neoclassical form, complete with a portico of columns holding up a very ornate pediment. From what Melody could see, the centrepiece of the decorations was a coat of arms. She didn't know enough about such things to have a clue whether it was the Austrian crest.

Rat pointed to a flagpole in front of the pavilion, but they were too far away to see the flag clearly. Moving closer while attempting to stay out of the light, Melody peered up at it.

"It is the Austrian flag, I am sure of it," she decided.

The pavilion had a pair of huge, heavy-looking, highly polished wooden doors. Rat decided to stick with the original plan and to go around the building to see if there was another door whose lock he might pick. A couple of minutes later, they had walked halfway around the pavilion and came across a narrow, unassuming-looking door. Rat took out his picks and made quick work of the lock.

"You really will have to teach me how to do that," Melody whispered.

It was neither the time nor the place for such a discussion, and Rat gave her a look that, luckily, it was too dark for Melody to see properly. Rat took his revolver out of his waistband, put his hand on the door handle and said, "Let me go in first."

Melody took her gun out of her pocket and indicated her assent. As bold as she was, even reckless on occasion, she had to acknowledge that her brother had received training in how to handle such situations, and she had not. At least, she hoped that his training had included dealing with such scenarios.

Rat slipped into the building and found himself in a dark, narrow hallway. The other item he had put in his pocket before he left the palazzo was a small, nickel-plated electric torch. This had been a gift from Lord Langley when he left London. He had not had cause to use it prior to that evening. Now, he weighed the pros and cons of turning it on. If Mr X, or indeed anyone else, was already in the pavilion, he ran the risk that the light would attract their attention. On the other hand, the hallway was pitch black, and he had no idea where he was going. Finally, he decided that the benefits of being able to see ahead outweighed any risks.

The small torch had the nifty feature of an adjustable aperture so that Rat could make the beam of light more or less widely dispersed. For the time being, he decided to make it as narrow as possible and trained the much-appreciated light down towards the floor. Looking up and down the hallway, he saw that small rooms, or perhaps large storage spaces, were off to each side. Peering in one, Rat saw what he assumed were paintings wrapped up and leaning against the walls. Up ahead, there was a staircase that he hoped led up to the main part of the pavilion.

Rat had no idea how the building was laid out. In hindsight, he wished there had been time for them to have visited during daylight hours to get the lay of the land. Still, there was no point in dwelling on what might have been. If Rat had learned anything from his years studying under Lord Langley, it was that one made the best of the information available, however limited. There was little about intelligence work that presented a complete information set. The science, or perhaps the art, underpinning the work was to piece together a jigsaw puzzle while recognising that key pieces were probably missing.

"Is the coast clear?" Melody whispered too loudly from behind him. Rat realised that, while his first impulse was to attempt to determine with certainty that it was safe to let Melody follow him, this was a futile goal; he had no idea what lay ahead or might happen over the next hour or so. Trying to guarantee his sister's safety was going to harm their mission. Instead, he whispered back that she should follow him and keep her voice down.

The hallway wasn't long, and as they climbed the rather narrow, steep steps, Rat was even more appreciative of his torch. At the top of the staircase was a door that, while opening easily, had hinges that needed oiling and creaked loudly enough to undermine their attempts at stealth. Melody, who was bringing up the rear, decided to save themselves from the risk of further creaking by not closing the door behind her.

The door opened into a medium-sized exhibition room. The room didn't have any windows, but there was a large arch at the end that led into another room that seemed to. From that room, there was enough natural light that it was possible to see something of the paintings on the walls. Despite years of being taken to exhibits by Bear, Melody didn't know much about art. However, she had a sense of what she liked. Glancing around the room at what seemed to be a lot of landscape paintings, Melody quickly decided there was nothing in that room worth coming back to see in daylight.

CHAPTER 31

With the natural light sufficient to make their way by, Rat had turned off his torch. As they began to make their way out of the room of landscapes, there was a noise ahead. Rat stopped and instinctively threw an arm out to press Melody back against the wall. Perhaps their shadowy companion was a security guard, or perhaps Herr Peetz. However, it was more likely to be Mr X lying in wait. Whoever it was, the reality of the danger he had placed his sister in suddenly overwhelmed Rat. But it was too late now to do anything about it.

Indicating that Melody should remain where she was, Rat tiptoed to the opening separating the exhibition rooms and peered around the wall. He wasn't sure what he'd been hoping for as far as possible hiding spots, but from what he could see, there was nothing in the large exhibition space ahead that would lend itself to effective concealment. There were statues; he could see their outlines clearly enough, but nothing was large enough to provide any meaningful cover.

What Rat could see was a long bench in the middle of the space. Sitting on the bench were two figures. It was too dark to be able to identify who they were, but from their voices, it was clear it was a man and a woman. It was also evident that they were speaking in German. Rat thought there was something familiar about one of the voices, but he couldn't be sure. The man's voice sounded far too young to be Herr Peetz. And anyway, it was fair to assume the woman was Fräulein Peetz. Why would her father just be sitting here if he had somehow rescued his daughter?

As he listened to the hushed tones of the conversation, what Rat realised was that whoever the man was, this was not a kidnapper and his victim. The whispered German phrases had no harshness to them; quite the opposite. While he might not understand the words, Rat was worldly enough to know when he had stumbled across lovers. The words "Meine Liebe" cemented his belief that this so-called abduction was not all they had believed it to be. As if in confirmation, the next sounds he heard were of the couple kissing, or at least that is what he thought they were.

Rat knew that Melody had learned German and had some proficiency, certainly more than he did. Stealthily returning to the spot where he had left his sister, he whispered that whoever they had come across was speaking German, and she should go and see what she could understand. It went against everything Rat believed in to send his sister ahead of him and into harm's way. If he could have thought of any other option, he would have taken it.

Melody moved as silently as possible to where Rat had been standing. The kissing had stopped, and the conversation resumed. She listened for a few minutes, increasingly in shock at what she heard – or what she thought she heard; her German was worse than her Italian.

Finally, slinking back to the relative safety of the smaller room, she pocketed her gun and indicated that Rat should follow her as she retraced their steps back to the staircase that led to the back entranceway. Rat wanted to protest at their retreat. At the very least, he wanted to understand Melody's reasons for leading them back the way they had come.

After crossing the room quietly, Melody was grateful she'd had the foresight to leave the creaking door open. As it was, she couldn't imagine how the couple hadn't heard it open before. Melody could only imagine they had been too absorbed in their lovemaking. Whatever the reason, best not to tempt fate again. What this did mean was they couldn't close the door behind them. If they'd been able to, Melody might have been tempted to explain everything to Rat as soon as they were through it. Instead, she led the way back down the narrow staircase and back into the dark hallway.

Then she stopped. Could they take the risk of going into one of the storage rooms to talk? It seemed unlikely their voices would carry. After all, the lovers didn't seem to be making a lot of effort to modulate their voices, yet Melody and Rat hadn't heard them from downstairs. Weighing this up against the risk of being discovered by security guards if they left the pavilion, Melody made a decision and walked into one of the rooms. Rat followed.

Moving as far into the room as possible, Melody turned and said, "It's a trap. Fräulein Peetz hasn't been taken against her will. I heard her saying something to the man about her father and finally getting what she wanted. Her paramour must be Mr X." Then she added, "That man, his voice sounded so familiar, but I cannot think why."

"I thought the same thing," Rat admitted. "And I couldn't even understand most of what was being said."

Suddenly, Melody was hit by the most terrible thought: was the man speaking German Alessandro? Was that why the voice was familiar even in another language? If it was, then Alessandro knew that Melody and Rat were planning to interrupt the rendezvous and must have been lying in wait for them. Perhaps it hadn't occurred to him that they would come early and break in through the back. Icy fingers of dread squeezed her heart; Alessandro and his lover were planning to ambush them. They must have been laughing at Melody's naivete in blurting out their plans that afternoon.

Melody felt hot tears well up in her eyes, and she willed herself not to let them fall; he must have been laughing at her this entire time. Was that night in the gondola nothing more than a sophisticated man of the world playing with an innocent young girl, perhaps hoping to learn what she suspected of his secrets? With growing shame, she replayed that evening and remembered Alessandro saying teasingly, "Were you asking about me?" Well, she had thought it was teasing at the time, but now she wondered if he had already been suspicious of her. More to the point, had he been suspicious of Rat? Thinking back to the day of their arrival in Venice, she reflected on the coincidence of Alessandro having been on their train. Was it merely chance, or had he been watching them? Perhaps even since London?

Rat hadn't noticed his sister's distress; it was too dark to see her unshed tears, and he was too absorbed in his thoughts to pick up on what her worries might be. Rat had experienced his own epiphany about who their mystery man was, and, for once, he wasn't consumed by Conte Foscari's likely guilt.

Instead, he said quietly, "Melody, I think the man up there may be Xander."

Melody was so surprised by Rat's words that she was shocked out of her melancholy. Having spent what felt like many minutes, but in truth could have been timed in seconds, second-guessing everything she thought she knew about and had felt with Alessandro, hearing her brother mention the name of her other suitor astonished Melody. Xander? Sweet, golden retriever-like Xander, who was courting her?

The thought was so absurd Melody laughed out loud.

"Shhh," Rat whispered.

"I am sorry," Melody whispered back. "But truly, I could not help myself. Xander? You think that Xander is in league with Fräulein Peetz?" Then, realising the implication of her words, she continued, "Wait? Do you think Xander is Mr X? That he killed Signor Graziano and Silvio Verdi?" It was all just too absurd for words. Melody tried and failed to imagine Xander, with his hair flopping over his forehead, shooting the two men in cold blood.

Then, just as she was about to laugh again, Melody thought back over the past week. She had first gone into Signor Graziano's shop when they were out with Xander, who had insisted on staying outside to smoke. To smoke! Of course, it was hardly unusual for a man to smoke, but had there been another reason he had not wanted to accompany her into the shop? Had he been trying to avoid being recognised by Signor Graziano?

Melody considered the timing of Silvio Verdi's death: Rat had taken the list to the consulate to show Mr Burrows. Xander had then spent hours in the library with Rat, helping to translate Silvio Verdi's articles. What if Xander had overheard Rat's conversation with the British Consul, and she and Rat were the reason the journalist was dead?

Rat's thoughts had followed a similar line to Melody's. He put his hand out and grasped for one of hers in the dark. "It is not our fault, Melody. We couldn't have possibly known."

Only minutes before, Melody had been heartbroken at the thought that Alessandro's interest in her might have been feigned. Now, she had to contemplate a similar possibility for her other suitor. This did not bring her to tears, but it did cause her to shake her head in confusion. Perhaps it was merely wounded pride and vanity, but Xander's esteem had seemed quite heartfelt. Was it possible it was an act to cover for something else? And if so, what?

They had lots of unanswered questions, but explanations for these things couldn't be their immediate concern. "What do we do now?"

Melody had vocalised the thought running through Rat's head. What should they do next? They had believed they were helping rescue an abducted young woman, but it seemed that wasn't the situation. Instead, if they believed what they had seen and heard upstairs, Fräulein Peetz was complicit in luring her father to the Austrian Pavilion. But why?

"We have to stop Herr Peetz," Melody announced. "We cannot let him walk into this trap."

Rat thought about what they knew. They were unsure of Herr Peetz's role in the murders. They had found a note that someone had written claiming to be holding his daughter. They had extrapolated that the kidnapper was Mr X, their murderer, but they had no real evidence to back this up. Was it possible that Xander and Fräulein Peetz were not the villains in this story and that by warning Herr Peetz, they might end up aiding the enemy?

A similar thought had occurred to Melody, but then she had realised the truth, which she now admitted to Rat. "Xander asked if he could court me. He kissed me. This afternoon." If Melody could have seen Rat's face in the dark, she would have observed his over-protective brother look come over his face. Even though it had been obvious that Xander admired his sister, Rat felt that kissing and courting her, particularly without her brother's permission, was beyond the pale.

Melody couldn't see his face, but she could guess Rat's reaction. However, they had no time for that particular conversation. Instead, she said, "The man who kissed me this afternoon is upstairs canoodling with another woman. Everything he said to me, his entire act since we met, it has all been a lie. That much is evident. But why?" Then, realising that they had overlooked the most damning piece of evidence, Melody pointed out, "And he speaks fluent German!"

Rat wasn't sure how damning a piece of evidence this really was. Britain wasn't actually at war with Germany. Moreover, learning foreign languages was a standard part of a good education for Britain's upper classes. The dowager was fluent in German, after all. Was this another piece of the jigsaw puzzle or a rogue piece they were trying to fit in where it didn't belong?

They had lost track of time, and Rat risked turning his torch on briefly to look at his watch; it was only nine-thirty. Herr Peetz had been told to arrive at ten o'clock. What should their next move be? They had the element of surprise on their side so they could go back upstairs and confront Xander and Fräulein Peetz. But to what end? There was no actual evidence that Xander was Mr X. In fact, even saying Mr X out loud sounded absurd. While Xander might be chagrined to be caught in flagrante, as it were, that was also not a crime. All they had were guesses and suppositions. They didn't even have proof that the smuggling of documents from Austria was real and not a figment of their overactive imaginations.

"Melody, is it possible this is nothing? Have we let ourselves get caught up in a story that only exists in our fancy? What would we even accuse Xander of doing? Yes, he seems to have broken into the pavilion, but so did we."

Melody could hear the uncertainty in Rat's voice, and it broke her heart. She had nothing at stake besides her vanity, but for Rat, this investigation could end his fledgling Intelligence career before it had even really begun. To accuse a member of the consulate staff of murder and perhaps treason was not an action to be taken lightly. Yet, she couldn't help saying, "Rat, we did not imagine two murders in almost as many days. Something is going on. And let us not forget that Herr Peetz was scared enough by something or someone to escape out of his window."

"Well, to be fair, it might have been us he was trying to escape from," Rat pointed out.

"I just do not think it was. I think it was receiving that note. A note that claimed his daughter was in danger. The same daughter, we believe, is sitting upstairs, letting Xander Ashby make love to her. If she escaped or was never in danger, why wait here?"

Rat didn't want to point out that Fräulein Peetz wouldn't be the first victim of kidnapping to become enthralled by her abductor. He didn't want to point it out because he didn't believe that was what had happened here. There just hadn't been enough time. They were working on the assumption that Fräulein and Herr Peetz had travelled to Venice together and were staying in the same hotel. If that was the case, then she could not have been missing for long. After all, the man had pointed out his daughter at the party just a few days before.

When Melody listed all the separate elements of the investigation, Rat had to concede that there was something there. It just didn't seem enough to accuse a man at gunpoint.

"Can we really march up there and accuse Xander Ashby of murder?" he asked, as much to himself as Melody.

"Murder now? That's what you think?" a voice said with a chuckle from deep in the shadows of the doorway.

CHAPTER 32

"**M**iss Chesterton, what kind of young lady allows a man to kiss her in the afternoon and accuses him of murder mere hours later?" Xander Ashby asked sardonically. He had turned his own torch on and used it to find the room's electric light.

When the room was illuminated, Melody's first thought was that the golden retriever seemed to have disappeared and had been replaced by a far more ferocious, snarling breed. Even the floppy hair seemed to be under tight control. Looking at the man pointing a gun at them, whose mouth was set in a nasty sneer, Melody wasn't sure how she had ever thought Xander too sweet and docile even to be considered a killer. This Xander Ashby looked more than capable of putting a bullet through someone's heart while enjoying doing so.

Rat was still holding his gun but had lowered his arm. He was a decent shot, but knew that he wasn't quick or sure enough to try to shoot at Xander before he shot back. Certainly, he wouldn't risk Melody being shot to try.

Xander saw his movement and said, "Drop your gun, Mr Sandworth. Then, without making any sudden movements, kick it over here." Rat complied, and Xander picked up the revolver and put it in his pocket.

"Meine Liebe," a female voice called out.

"Here, my dove," Xander replied.

The young woman from the party joined Xander in the doorway. When Martha Peetz had first been pointed out to Melody, she hadn't taken much time to assess the young

Austrian woman. Now, Melody realised that she was very pretty. The woman had white, blond curly hair and cornflower blue eyes framed with long, golden lashes.

Just as if they were all meeting at a society ball, Xander said, "Miss Melody Chesterton, let me introduce you to Fräulein Martha Peetz." He paused, then added with a malicious little smirk, "And the great love of my life."

Melody knew she shouldn't have taken the bait, but she just couldn't help herself: "Does the great love of your life know that mere hours ago, you asked whether you might court me?"

Martha laughed. It was a tinkling laugh that grated on Melody's nerves. "Of course I know. It was my idea, after all."

"Why?" was all that Melody could sputter.

Instead of answering, Xander looked at his watch and said, "We do not have much time. That doddering father of yours will be here shortly. We need to be ready."

Looking around the room, Martha said, "Untie the rope that is around that painting leaning against the wall and bind their hands and feet." As Xander obeyed her command, the woman continued, "I would have you shoot them now, but I am afraid that my father might be nearby and will hear the shots. We cannot afford to spook him. As soon as we have dealt with him, you can turn your gun on these two."

Returning with the rope, Xander gave Martha the gun while he tied Melody and Rat's feet together and their hands behind their back. As soon as they were somewhat incapacitated, she said, "You can finish this up alone. I want to keep an eye out for my darling papa. Do not forget to find something to gag them with. We don't need them sounding the alert." And with that, she turned and left.

With Martha gone, Melody asked, "Why are you doing this, Xander? Why have you betrayed your country?"

As Xander searched the room for some material to use as a gag, he laughed nastily and replied, "My country? My mother is Austrian. Who is to say that I'm not aiding my country?"

Melody did not realise this about Xander. Nevertheless, she

continued, "You were born in Britain. You come from an old, aristocratic family."

"And what has that done for me? Left me so poor that I had to take a job serving that snivelling toady Burrows. A man who is not fit to clean my shoes. If my dear uncle hadn't taken it upon himself to marry that chit of a girl, Burrows would be genuflecting before me and calling me milord. As it is, I have to bring him cups of tea and call him sir."

Xander stopped his search, turned and said, "You cannot even imagine the pittance the British Government pays me for kowtowing to that idiot. The Austrian government, by contrast, has paid me a lot of money for my assistance."

Addressing Rat, he said, "We had warning that the Secret Service Bureau was sending a new young operative. As soon as I met you and your charming sister at Lady Bainbridge's and you told me your name was Sandworth, I suspected that you were our man. Feigning interest in your sister was such an easy way to keep tabs on you both. I was just waiting for the right moment to unmask you for certain before reporting back to my Austrian overlords." He said this last part with renewed bitterness that made Melody believe he felt no more loyalty to Austria than he did to Britain.

The part of Xander's speech that caught Rat's ear was that his identity hadn't been exposed yet. If they could escape from the ropes and turn the tables on Xander and Martha Peetz, there was still time to save his career in the Secret Service Bureau.

Melody felt compelled to ask at least one more question before Xander gagged her; "Why is Fräulein Peetz working against her father?" To Melody, who had but the faintest memories of her parents, the idea of betraying a living one was unthinkable.

"Peetz is an old fool, and he really is a traitor. Martha is a proud Austrian who wants the empire to gain back all the Italian soil that it rightfully should have," Xander proclaimed, seemingly unaware or unconcerned about the blatant contradiction in his statement.

Melody could not let the discrepancy stand: "If it is Italian soil, then how can Austria-Hungary claim sovereignty over it?"

Xander looked at her with disdain, "Why don't you ask the people of Scotland, Wales and Ireland how that works?" It took Melody a moment to see his point. Still, even then, she refused to believe that King George's rule over the United Kingdom of Great Britain and Ireland was not completely different from Emperor Franz Joseph's imperial ambitions throughout Europe.

Whatever additional questions Melody might have liked to ask, once Xander finally found a grubby-looking rag, it was evident that her time was limited. He ripped the rag lengthwise and then moved towards them.

Melody couldn't believe that Xander was so good an actor that he felt nothing for her. Hoping to appeal to whatever affection he might feel for her, however slight, she pleaded, "Xander, please. I thought that we were friends, at least. Are you really planning to kill me?"

She had been hoping for some hesitation, for a moment of doubt, however brief. However, she heard no indecision in the meanspirited laugh he barked out. "Friends? Is that what you think we were? You believed that I was your infatuated lapdog. I will admit that your fortune was appealing, but that aside, you do not stand up to comparison with my darling Martha. You are a pathetic spoilt child, and she is a magnificent, spirited woman."

Xander's words hurt more than Melody wanted to admit. She knew that this blow to her pride should be the last thing on her mind at that moment. Nevertheless, she felt tears sting her eyes at the cruel blows her supposed suitor seemed to take great pleasure pummelling her with.

Finally, Xander took the two sections of rag and tied one around Melody's mouth and the other around Rat's. The material tasted of dust and mould, and it made Melody gag. Satisfied with his handiwork, Xander turned and left. Whether through some final prick of conscience or, more likely, forgetfulness, he did at least leave the light on overhead.

Rat had gone through a range of training in preparation

for this assignment, and one had dealt with how to handle himself in such a situation. As Xander approached him with the gag, Rat had opened his mouth slightly and tilted his head forward. Doing this prevented the gag from being tied as tightly or positioned as effectively as possible. Now, Rat listened for Xander's footsteps on the staircase, and when he was sure the other man must be sufficiently far away, Rat used his tongue to work on the slack his machinations had allowed for. Finally, the gag was out of his mouth.

In contrast to Rat's training in escaping from capture, Xander seemed like a novice when it came to restraining prisoners. He had made Melody and Rat sit on the cement floor of the storage room before tying them up but hadn't bothered to tether them to anything. Rat wiggled his way across the short distance between them until his side was positioned by Melody's tied hands.

"Melody," he whispered, "I have a knife in my jacket pocket. I'm as close to you as I can get. See if you can reach in and get it."

While Melody hadn't received the benefit of secret service training, it had been obvious to her that she should try to keep her hands as far apart as possible while Xander was binding them. Because of this foresight, she had a certain amount of flexibility in how much she could move her hands now. In addition, the rope that Xander had taken from around the painting was not a thick, sturdy one but rather more string-like. As she wiggled her hands, Melody realised she could move more than she imagined she'd be able to.

Despite a degree of mobility, her hands were tied behind her back, so she couldn't see what she was doing. Rat had a limited view but tried to guide her as best he could. As she stretched her hands into his pocket, the bindings chafed, and her wrists and shoulders ached from the strain of reaching back. After a few minutes, Melody managed to grab hold of the knife between her fore and middle finger, only to have it slip out onto the floor between her and Rat.

Exasperated at herself, Melody felt like screaming. She needn't have feared. As soon as Rat heard the knife drop, he wriggled around again until his back was almost against Melody's. Then, he felt around on the floor as best he could. Just as he was losing hope, he found the knife and managed to pick it up. He was grateful that the blade easily sprung up at the slight press of a knob on the handle.

Now that Rat had a knife in his hand, the really challenging part was ahead: he had to cut Melody's ropes without wounding her hands. A wrong move, and he might accidentally slash one of her wrists. Luckily, there was now enough slack in Melody's bindings that, with a little more effort, she was able to hold her hands somewhat apart, enabling her brother to saw at a piece of binding without her flesh in his way. Even so, neither of them could see what he was doing.

Rat merely grazed at her bindings for fear that any more drastic movement would risk him cutting his sister. It felt like an eternity of slow, almost gentle shaving at the rope when, suddenly, it fell into two pieces. Xander's knots were sufficiently ineptly tied that this was all Melody needed to free her hands. She found the knife on the floor, cut her ankles free, pulled out her gag, and then liberated Rat.

"Well, that's a start," Rat said. "Good job. But what now? He has my gun."

"But he doesn't have mine," Melody said, pulling it out of her pocket. "It must never have occurred to him that a pathetic spoilt child might be carrying a weapon." She tried and failed to keep the bitterness out of her voice.

CHAPTER 33

They were liberated from their bonds, and they had at least one gun and a knife between them, but they didn't have a plan. Now that Xander and Martha knew they were not alone in the building, they would be hyper-alert to even the slightest sound. Next time, the pair might not be so reticent about shooting.

"They believe we are tied up. Have we really lost the element of surprise?" Melody asked more hopefully than she felt.

"I heard Xander close the stairwell door behind him. With that creaking, he'll hear us open it again. It's amazing that he didn't hear it the first time. I'm sure it is only because he and Martha were otherwise amorously engaged. We cannot take that chance again."

Melody reluctantly acknowledged the wisdom of his words. "We could go out the back door and come around to the front of the building. If they hear any noise from that direction, they will assume it is Herr Peetz or perhaps a security guard."

Looking at his watch, Rat saw that it was already past ten o'clock. "We must assume that Herr Peetz is already here. I haven't heard a shot, but they may have already killed him." Melody shuddered at his words. She still could not get past the idea of a daughter murdering a parent in cold blood and for no better reason than a difference of political opinion.

Rat continued, "I do not doubt that Xander and Martha will have no qualms about shooting at a supposed security guard. Their only reason for not killing us immediately was a concern about alerting Herr Peetz. And they have an extra gun now, so

SARAH F. NOEL

more bullets. I think they would be perfectly content to shoot their way out of the gardens if necessary." As he said this, Rat turned off the overhead light. Whatever they did, they were better doing under cover of dark.

Then, they stood there, incapacitated by doubt. Rat tried to imagine what Wolf and Bear might do in a similar situation. What would Lord Langley do? What was the smart move? Rat realised that they had to make a decision of some sort; Herr Peetz's life might still depend on their intervention. If Melody hadn't been with him, Rat would have had no doubts about charging back upstairs and risking his life. However, she was there, and if he had to choose between Dieter Peetz's safety and his sister's, then he knew what he needed to do. Even as he felt a pang of frustration that Melody's company so hobbled his actions, Rat acknowledged, to himself at least, that he could never have escaped from those ropes alone. The truth was that he was glad to have a partner; he just wished that it wasn't someone with whose safety he was so consumed.

Just as he was about to agree with Melody's idea if only for want of a better one, they heard a noise above. Whatever was going on in the exhibition rooms, it was evident that Martha and Xander no longer felt the need for stealth.

"Give me your gun," Rat demanded. "Then, go into that far corner and hide."

"I am not going to let you face them alone," Melody said indignantly.

"Melody, we do not have time for this. Whatever my feelings when we each had a gun, now we do not. We have one revolver and a small knife between us. That is no match for their two guns. Worrying about you puts me at a further disadvantage. Please, just do as I ask," the young man pleaded.

It was this tone, far more than the earlier overprotective one, that convinced Melody. She realised that Rat was plagued by self-doubt about his ability to handle this situation, and he didn't need one more thing holding him back. Melody handed him her gun and moved further into the room to hide. She had barely found a box that might provide some cover when they both heard the creaking of the door again and footsteps on the stairs.

Rat pressed his back against the wall, hoping to take whoever it was by some kind of surprise when they entered the room. Of course, if it were Xander he would have already realised that the light was no longer on and have surmised that they had escaped their bonds. However, Martha didn't know he had left the room illuminated, and this was the sliver of hope onto which Rat clung.

As the footsteps moved closer, Rat held his breath and had the revolver at the ready. Suddenly, a voice called out, "Mr Sandworth, Miss Chesterton... Melody?"

Melody knew that voice and leapt out of her hiding spot, crying out happily, "Alessandro? Is that you?"

Rat didn't share his sister's immediate relief about Conte Foscari's appearance in the pavilion. While they had known that the conte was aware of their plans to come to the gardens that evening, he hadn't given any indication that he planned to follow them. Had Rat's willingness to concede Foscari's likely innocence been premature? Rat's thoughts were interrupted by Melody rushing forward and turning the light back on.

As the room was again flooded by the harsh light of the bare incandescent lightbulb, they saw Alessandro standing just outside of the doorway, a gun in his hand. The three of them stood still for a moment, looking at each other, Rat and Alessandro both with guns at the ready. Was this a rescue or another standoff?

Answering this question, at least temporarily, Alessandro lowered his gun and said, "I am so relieved to find you unharmed."

"What has happened to Ashby and Fräulein Peetz?" Rat asked.

"They are in police custody," he assured them. "I was able to intercept Herr Peetz before he entered the building, and he is safe. In shock at the perfidy of his daughter, but physically unharmed."

"You brought the police with you?" Melody asked, unsure if

she considered this an act of betrayal.

"No signorina," a voice said, appearing out of the dark hallway behind Alessandro. It was Ispettore Paolo Moretti and the young policeman, Appuntato Cavalli. The ispettore continued, "Appuntato Cavalli kept the eye on you."

Moretti then said something in rapid Italian to the appuntato, who translated, "Ispettore Moretti said to tell you that I followed you after you came to talk to him yesterday." Rat looked shocked at this admission. He wasn't sure what was more galling, that they had been followed for almost two days or that he had not realised.

The young policeman continued in a disapproving voice, "You talk too loudly in public places. When you ate lunch outside today, you talk like no one around you understands English." Both Melody and Rat looked suitably ashamed at the chastisement. It was true; they had been talking about the investigation with no regard for who might overhear. "Then, I follow you to the hotel and I wait outside. You come out in a hurry, run around to the back, and I follow you down a short way. I do not want to come too near, in case you see me. But even from where I was standing, I could hear you talk about the note you find. You need to talk more quietly."

Rat and Melody hung their heads in shameful acknowledgement of the man's words. The policeman then said in a kindly tone, "But, because you are loud, we know where to come to arrest the bad man and woman."

"So, you believed what I told you yesterday?" Melody asked hopefully.

The policeman quickly translated for his superior, who answered, "Sì E no. But we come and then the pistole."

Alessandro picked up the story, "I intercepted Herr Peetz just as he was approaching the pavilion and then was myself intercepted by Ispettore Moretti and his men." He paused, then added vaguely, "We have had some interactions over the years." Melody would have loved to hear more about those "interactions". Alessandro continued, "We quickly realised that we had a common cause and stormed the pavilion. If the ispettore had been in any doubt as to Ashby's guilt, the gunfire that greeted us was sufficient proof that there was some kind of wrongdoing afoot."

Ispettore Moretti indicated that he needed to return upstairs to deal with his prisoners. Alessandro made to follow him. Rat and Melody exchanged glances, and a silent communication passed between them; they were not ready to hand over the reins of their investigation completely and so they also followed.

The lights had been turned on in the exhibition rooms, and now Melody had a better view of the landscape paintings in the first, smaller room. She didn't like them any more for being able to see them clearly. The ispettore hadn't commented on Rat and Melody's inclusion in the group and led everyone through to the main exhibition hall, where they found Xander and Martha in handcuffs and under the stern watch of two policemen.

As soon as the group entered the hall, Martha began yelling out in a combination of German and English, "I was kidnapped by this man. He is crazy. He was going to kill my father."

The ispettore replied in his broken English, "No tedesco. Inglese." While he might not understand German, Melody wasn't convinced he understood English much better, but at least his young policeman could translate.

Martha then continued in an increasingly hysterical tone, "Ashby is a spy for der Kaiser. He killed those two men." Earlier, Melody hadn't thought Martha the brains of the partnership, but now she wasn't sure. If she was claiming to be merely a victim of an abduction, how did she explain knowing such details about Xander's nefarious activities?

It seemed that this fact had just occurred to Martha, too late. She began again, "I overheard him talking about it. He bragged about shooting those two men."

While it was evident, at least to Melody, that Moretti was very sceptical of Martha's protestations of innocence, nevertheless, the inspector said something to Cavelli, who translated, "Why did he say that he shot them?" Given the highly circumstantial evidence Melody and Rat had provided when they had visited the inspector the day before, it made sense that he was making as much use as possible of Martha's attempt to exonerate herself.

Martha paused; this was her one chance, or at least she must have believed it to be so. She had to be convincing and provide enough details to make Xander a persuasive scapegoat.

Up until that point, Xander had been surprisingly quiet, making no attempt to defend himself. Now, he used Martha's hesitation to exclaim, "Martha, my love. What are you saying?"

"Love?" the woman spat. "You really thought I loved you? Englischer Schnösel!"

From what Melody remembered of her German, Martha had just called Xander an English snob. Well, she couldn't disagree with the woman there; he was a terrible snob. She remembered how he had called Alessandro a mongrel half-breed at Lady Bainbridge's party and wondered how he rationalised his half-British, half-Austrian bloodlines as being any different from Alessandro's half-Italian one.

Now that Martha had started, the woman's voice became increasingly crazed, "I knew from the moment we met what a useful idiot you would be to der Kaiser." In her agitation, Martha seemed to have forgotten her earlier claims of innocence. "I am surrounded by idiot men," Martha sneered. "I thought that my father's delusions about what is best for das Vaterland were bad enough. But your sudden conversion to the cause of Österreich made me nauseous. No true patriot would accept money for his services."

It seemed that Ispettore Moretti had understood enough of what was being said and now exclaimed, "Enough. Finito. We go."

Turning to Melody and Rat, he said, "Grazie mille, signor et signorina. Thank you for this help you give." Then, in Italian, he told his men to take their prisoners away. With a quick bow, the ispettore followed them out, leaving Melody and Rat alone with Alessandro.

Suddenly, the situation felt very awkward; what did they all do now? There was an uncomfortable silence for a few moments until Alessandro said, "I suggest that we all return home. Do you have a way to return to Lady Bainbridge's palazzo or would you like me to take you?"

They had almost forgotten that Giovanni was waiting patiently for them by the side entrance to the gardens. Or at least they hoped he was still waiting. Rat indicated that they had no need for transportation, and Alessandro nodded. He turned to leave, then pivoted back, "I will call on you tomorrow morning if that is acceptable." Melody felt a surge of joy before Alessandro added, "Mr Sandworth. We have things to discuss." As quickly as her hopes had soared, they now came crashing down. And then Alessandro was gone.

CHAPTER 34

*D*ear Diary, Alessandro arrived after breakfast this morning and requested an audience with Rat. They have been cloistered away for more than an hour. I longed to know what they were discussing, but could not bring myself to listen at the door, however tempting it was.

Rat was quiet during breakfast. Of course, perhaps that was due to Lady Bainbridge's presence. She still has no idea what happened last night. Nevertheless, I expected Rat to be elated that we discovered the identity of Mr X. Who could have possibly imagined it would be Xander, of all people? Poor Herr Peetz. He must be devastated to find out about his daughter's betrayal. I still do not understand the full extent of his role in the scheme we uncovered, but whatever it was, I cannot imagine anything that would justify a daughter's planned murder of her father.

Will Alessandro ask to speak with me before he leaves? While I acknowledge that my willingness to be courted by Xander was little more than hurt pride at being rejected by the man I am interested in, still, it pricks my vanity to know that even his regard was not real. How did I go so quickly from believing I had two suitors to realising I had none?

There was a knock at the door. As Mary wasn't present, Melody put down her pen and went to open it. She found her brother waiting there. He looked… well, if she had to put a word to it, Melody would have said he looked bemused.

"May I speak with you?" he asked with surprising formality. Melody stood aside and let him enter. She took one of the armchairs in front of the fireplace, and he took the other.

Melody sat patiently while Rat seemed to consider what to say. Finally, he leaned forward and said, "It seems I have been very wrong about Conte Foscari."

If such an acknowledgement wasn't enough, this was one of the few times Rat had used Alessandro's title. She raised her eyebrows slightly in reply but said nothing.

Rat continued, "It seems that the conte has similar professional associations to mine." Now, Melody really raised her eyebrows. Did Alessandro work for the Secret Service Bureau? Rat continued, "He had been asked to keep an eye on me."

"By Uncle Maxi?" Melody said in shock. She couldn't believe that Lord Langley would show such little confidence in the young man he had mentored for so many years.

"No, not by Lord Langley," Rat answered with such relief in his voice that it was evident he had initially shared her horror. "By someone else in the bureau who had concerns about my readiness for this assignment. These concerns were overruled at Lord Langley's insistence. However, unbeknownst to him, they were taken seriously enough that I was assigned a secret handler, Conte Foscari. He was to monitor my activities and only intervene if absolutely necessary."

Rat made a face of grim resignation, "I suppose last night's debacle counted as absolutely necessary. Whoever had doubted my readiness was clearly prescient." Rat saw Melody about to jump to his defence and put up a hand. "Don't try and console me. I know that Xander and Martha were only apprehended because of the intervention of Foscari and Ispettore Moretti. And the ispettore was only there because we had been followed for two days by one of his men. Not only hadn't I noticed the man, but I was so indiscreet in my conversations with you that he overheard all of our plans. I do not deserve anything more than a desk job. Perhaps not even that."

"Is that what Alessandro said?" Melody asked, genuinely concerned for her brother's emotional state.

"Well, not exactly. He said that he was impressed by how we

had pieced together the parts of the investigation. But even then, I don't deserve the credit; it was mostly you." Rat buried his head in his hands as he said these words.

Melody couldn't bear to see him so disconsolate. She leapt out of her chair and went to kneel beside her brother. "Rat, do not say such things. I could not have achieved anything without your help. We were a team. A great team."

"Ha! Besides escorting you around Venice, what did I contribute?"

Trying and failing to remember a specific piece of the puzzle that Rat had come up with alone, she said, "That is not how a partnership works. Look at Wolfie and Tabby Cat. From what I have seen, she is often the one to have the important epiphanies, yet without Wolfie as a sounding board and confidante, she would never be as effective in solving cases."

Rat was not entirely sure he would characterise Wolf and Tabitha's teamwork in quite such black-and-white terms, and he was very certain that Tabitha would never take such credit for herself. Nevertheless, his sister's point has some truth to it; Wolf had been a very good thief taker before he had met Tabitha, but her penchant for puzzle-solving had elevated what he was able to achieve.

Nodding in acknowledgement of Melody's words, Rat said, "There is more."

Melody retook her seat and waited. On the way upstairs, Rat had considered how much to confide to his sister. To his surprise, Conte Foscari had left this up to him. Finally, realising that Melody deserved to know everything, he said, "When Martha was taken to the police station, it appeared that she realised her blunder in admitting what she did at the pavilion and has clammed up."

Rat smiled ruefully, "Xander on the other hand was happy to spill the beans on Martha in the hope that he can persuade the authorities that he was as much her victim as anyone. It seems the scales have fallen from his eyes regarding his lover. According to him, Martha had said that she had become suspicious in Vienna as to the extent of her father's involvement in the publication of secret government information. Initially, she had believed he did nothing more than allow, even encourage, his journalists to publish pieces that were anti-war. However, over time, she began to suspect that he had a more meaningful role. She had long despised his pacifist tendencies and reported her suspicions to the government."

"She turned her own father in as a traitor?" Melody said in horror. Though, almost as soon as she said this, she wondered why she was so surprised. After all, the woman had been willing, almost eager, to shoot her father in cold blood.

"Yes," Rat replied. "When she alerted the authorities that her father was planning to escape to Italy, she was told to accompany him and monitor his actions. Given what was being published in the Italian newspapers, there were concerns that information was being smuggled out of the country and that Herr Peetz was somehow involved. The hope was that they could uncover the source of his intelligence. Because this was the true worry: who was leaking confidential government information and papers, and how was it getting dispersed to Italian journalists?"

"And who is the informant?"

"No one knows. It seems that discovering the informant's identity is the reason that Antonio Graziano and Silvio Verdi were killed and that Herr Peetz was lured to the Austrian Pavilion. When Xander failed to get the information from the two men, Martha became convinced that her father must know and planned to force him to tell them at gunpoint before killing him as well."

Thinking back to the conversation Rat had overheard at Luisa's party, Melody asked, "Alessandro and Herr Peetz referred to their plan. How and when did they get involved?"

"Well, from what Conte Foscari told me, they only met recently when Herr Peetz arrived in Venice. However, Herr Peetz had known the conte's father many years before. The elder Conte Foscari had worked with his old friend to put this plan into action before he died last year. Alessandro Foscari merely continued what his father had started. His father had also been a member of the Risorgimento, which is how he knew Antonio Graziano."

Melody considered his words. "So, does Alessandro know who the government informant is?"

"No. It seems that the information chain had been set up in such a way that no one knew every link. Conte Foscari knew that Dieter Peetz had access to secret Austrian information and that Antonio Graziano distributed the information. However, neither Foscari nor his journalists, not even Herr Peetz, knew how the bookseller got the information from Vienna. I assume this was to keep the circle of information as tight as possible. So, it seems that Martha was correct: her father does know who the informant is."

Rat continued, "And it seems that you were correct about the medals the two men had looking alike and about the Risorgimento perhaps being the connection between them. The regular meetings Signor Graziano hosted for his former Risorgimento comrades were the perfect cover for the dissemination of materials. Silvio Verdi didn't have to know where Antonio Graziano received the information to trust his word on its veracity."

"So, Alessandro had no idea about Avraham Graziano's involvement?"

"None whatsoever. He had never met Antonio Graziano and only knew about him through his journalist, Silvio Verdi. Just before he died, Foscari's father had told him about the Risorgimento connection and that Herr Peetz was somewhere at the other end of the chain.

"Apparently, Herr Peetz began by publishing articles in his own newspapers but then felt that he could do more to promote the cause of peace if he managed to get information fed to Italians. He knew the older Conte Foscari, who, through their Risorgimento connection, knew Antonio Graziano. Somehow, a plan was hatched for Herr Peetz to receive the information and get it to Italy. It seems that Herr Peetz is still refusing to give up much information, but I believe that you were right; he must have passed it to Avraham, who hid it in the false bindings of the books he sent to Italy."

"But then, how would he justify sending books to Italy so frequently?"

"Well, I mentioned your theory to Foscari, who said that it is very common for libraries to share books either through interlibrary loans, cultural exchanges, or often academic requests. Even if they were shipping more to one library than usual, it was a common enough part of regular library operations that they would not be cause for suspicion with the Austrian authorities."

"So, they were shipped to a library in Venice and then Antonio Graziano would borrow these books and retrieve the documents?" Melody surmised.

"Foscari assumes it was something along those lines. It's quite ingenious, really. Why would anyone find anything suspicious about an elderly bookseller having regular dealings with a library? I'm sure it is common enough for the library to source certain rare books through someone like Signor Graziano, and so his visits would not be cause for comment."

"Did Martha realise that her father was the architect of this plan?" Melody asked.

Rat shook his head, "Xander didn't know, and Martha refuses to say anything at this point. Foscari believes that the Austrians wanted to learn the identity of each link in the chain and then silence them. Unfortunately, since Martha has been in custody, she has foresworn any admission of guilt she made in the pavilion and has reverted to the story that Xander was the mastermind behind it all."

"Surely no one believes her?" Melody asked in a horrified voice.

Rat sighed. "Well, Moretti doesn't. But it appears that the Austrian ambassador has become involved, and it is possible that Xander will be blamed for the entire thing. I am sure that

Mr Burrows will not be inclined to rush to Ashby's defence. Whatever happens, Herr Peetz's role in this has been exposed, and I doubt he can return to Austria. And anyway, with Antonio Graziano dead, the distribution of the documents has been brought to a standstill."

Melody added, "Given what has happened, it is hard to imagine that the remaining journalists will want to continue being involved. Few people are so wedded to their political ideals that they're prepared to risk their lives for them." Rat agreed.

It was only after Rat left that Melody considered the full implications of what he had told her; Alessandro had known who they were from the first time they had talked at the train station. He had engineered that meeting with the sole purpose of getting close to Rat to keep an eye on him. It had never had anything to do with her or any attraction, even affection, Alessandro might have felt. His attention to her had been no more genuine than Xander's.

Remembering the passionate kiss in the gondola, Melody was shamed to realise that the moonlight boat ride had been nothing more than a way to maintain a connection to her brother and that Conte Foscari had just taken advantage of a naive young woman's obvious willingness to be seduced. To see it all so clearly now was to burn with mortification and then anger; how dare he take advantage of her like that. Melody hoped that now Xander at least had been brought to justice, she never had to meet the conte again. She was deeply hurt and even more chagrined. Melody swore never to let herself be that vulnerable to a man again.

CHAPTER 35

Despite her anger at Alessandro and her declaration to her reflection in the mirror that she hoped never to see nor hear from him again, nevertheless, Melody's disappointment became more pronounced with every day that passed without any word from the conte.

When Rat had first told her the details of his revealing conversation with Alessandro, a little, ridiculously hopeful voice in Melody's head whispered that he would call later that day to apologise to her. Yes, she might have hoped that he would do so immediately after confessing his true objectives to Rat. However, she also recognised that Alessandro might want Rat to explain his role on his behalf before he followed up with his mea culpa.

When that first afternoon had passed and then another, Melody began to accept that not only would she not be receiving the expressions of regret she so longed for, but she would also not be able to vent her very justifiable anger to Alessandro at his treatment of her.

Finally, after two days of moping around at home just in case he visited or sent a note, Melody shook herself out of her doldrums. She decided that she was wasting her time in Venice mourning the loss of a man who had never been hers, not even as slightly as she had once believed.

Given her emotional state during that time, it was probably for the best that Melody had no idea that Rat had been spending most of his days during that time in Alessandro's company. Once their shared profession was revealed and Rat had managed to

SARAH F.NOEL

get somewhat over his feelings of inadequacy, or at least to tamp them down, he had been keen to spend time with the more seasoned bureau agent.

Actually, Rat wasn't entirely sure what Conte Foscari's role was. Lord Langley's involvement with the intelligence agencies of the British Government had always been somewhat nebulous. Was the conte's role similarly vague? Regardless, Rat recognised that the man had slipped into a persona and ingratiated himself with them in a manner that Rat could learn from. Of course, if he considered the nature of that ingratiating, he would have to acknowledge that it had come at his sister's expense. Perhaps if Rat had realised how far Alessandro's flirtation with his sister had gone and how hurt she was by what she saw as his betrayal, Rat might not have so reversed his initial opinion of the man.

On the morning that Melody awoke, determined to put everything about the investigation and Alessandro behind her, she received an invitation to join Luisa for lunch.

Mia cara amica, I apologise for the short notice, but I have been quite melancholy for some days and woke this morning with a determination to shake off my gloom. If you do not already have plans, please join me at one o'clock to eat only the finest delicacies and wash it down with champagne. Per sempre tua, Luisa.

Lunch with Luisa was exactly what Melody needed to raise her spirits. They would laugh and gossip, and perhaps she would muster up the courage to stroke the cheetah. Melody was determined to drink too much champagne and to put all thoughts of the handsome conte aside for good.

Melody was always conscious of Luisa's sense of style, even if it did tend towards the eccentric. That morning, she rejected dress after dress as too mundane until Mary finally said in exasperation, "Miss Melody, unless you are planning to visit the palazzo as naked as the day you were born, you must choose an outfit." Mary was not generally given to such outbursts, and this one made Melody smile. As she did so, she realised that she hadn't smiled or laughed for days.

Mary knew and loved Melody too well to have not realised

that she had not been her usual exuberant self for days, even if she didn't know its cause. She hadn't been told any of the details of the dramatic conclusion to the investigation or, indeed, that Melody had embarked on an investigation at all. Still, she was observant enough to realise that this gloom was romantic in nature. Now, happy to see her charge break into the radiant smile that she so loved, Mary said, "I believe that your pink dress, edged with white flowers, is just the thing for an informal summer lunch."

On her first pass through her wardrobe, Melody had rejected that dress because of its simplicity. Now, she held it against her and considered Mary's advice. Melody realised that the pink dress was exactly right, not despite its simplicity but because of it; one could not hope to match Luisa's outrageous outfits, and it was best not even to try.

Melody chose to wear her hair loose down her back and her least ostentatious jewellery to match the simple elegance of her dress. The day was warm and sunny, and she needed no shawl. Catching a final glimpse of herself in the mirror, Melody saw the reflection of a pretty young woman, unencumbered by worries and happy to embrace whatever joy came her way that day.

If Rat had been too caught up in his own concerns to notice his sister's melancholy, Melody had been too busy mentally rehearsing her speech of righteous indignation to notice her brother's absence for most of the past two days. Now, coming downstairs, she found him standing in the palazzo's vestibule, speaking with Rossi.

As Melody descended from the final step, Rossi nodded his head and said, "Si, Signor Sandworth. I will make all the necessary arrangements."

As the maggiordomo walked away, Melody cocked her head and asked, "What was that about?"

Rat indicated that she should follow him into the salotto. Once he had closed the door behind them, Rat answered, "I have been called away and must leave tomorrow."

"Where are you going to and what about me?"

"I have to go to Morocco. I am not sure for how long. I believe that you should stay here, in Venice, with Lady Bainbridge and Mary. I hope that I can wrap up what I need to do in a week or two. Maybe three at most."

Melody narrowed her eyes. "Is this 'work'?" she asked, putting a heavy emphasis on the last word.

Rat looked as if he didn't want to answer, but finally said, "Yes. It is. I cannot tell you more than that." Then, noticing her dress, he asked, "Where are you off to?"

"I am having luncheon with Luisa," Melody answered. "And do not change the subject. I am not going to wait around in Venice while you waltz around Europe having adventures."

"Morocco is in North Africa, not Europe," Rat answered with unusual pedantry.

"I don't care where it is; my sentiment remains unchanged. If you are going to Morocco, then I am coming with you."

Rat's first and indeed second instinct was to command Melody to respect his decision and argue for remaining safely in Venice. This next assignment was almost as vague as this first one had been, and he had no idea what dangers might lie ahead.

Melody could see various expressions flit across his face as Rat considered expressing these thoughts. Deciding to pre-empt whatever brotherly heavy-handedness he was planning to say, she continued, "Rat, I think you can agree that I played an integral role in the successful completion of your Venetian assignment." Given that just days before, he had been ready to give her all the credit, it was incredibly frustrating to find that her brother still doubted her abilities and was giving into his overprotective impulses.

Perhaps he could read her expressions and thoughts as well as she could read his because, finally, he sighed and said, "Fine. But we are leaving tomorrow. Can you be ready to go by then?"

While Melody was busy fighting for her right to be included in Rat's trip, she had not considered what she would forfeit by leaving Venice so soon. Now, she thought about her luncheon with Luisa no longer being a carefree, champagne-fuelled fun afternoon, but instead a sad farewell. She considered all the sightseeing she had been unable to do because the investigation had consumed her almost since her arrival in Venice.

And finally, just briefly, but quite painfully, she considered that, by leaving Venice now, she would lose any opportunity to bump into Alessandro casually at a dinner party or in the street. Instead, she would have to acknowledge the futility of any romantic dreams she might have, however silly they might be. Even after contemplating all this with regret, Melody knew that if she didn't join Rat now, she would be consigning herself back to the role of empty-headed debutante who flits between cities in Europe with a Baedeker in hand. Instead, this was her opportunity to continue the adventure that she had fallen into.

"Yes, I will go and tell Mary to begin packing," Melody said decisively.

Thirty minutes later, Giovanni was handing her out of the gondola at the steps of Luisa's shambolic, half-built palazzo. Yet again, her friend was waiting for her in the garden, her cheetah asleep at her feet.

If Melody had dressed to throw off her gloom, Luisa seemed to have embraced her melancholy, at least sartorially. She was dressed from head to toe in black, yet the effect was anything but funereal. Instead, the dress was made entirely of lace with some kind of chiffon shift underneath to provide a modicum of modesty. Only a modicum, given that the sheath appeared to stop above her knees. The dress was floor length with a train that Luisa had looped over one arm. She had what appeared to be a nest in her hair with a black taxidermy bird perched in it that set her fiery red hair off to even greater contrast. Her eyes were rimmed with even more kohl than usual, but her lips were bright red. The whole effect of her costume was quite dramatic, particularly for one o'clock in the afternoon.

Luisa seemed genuinely delighted to see Melody and even more genuinely downcast at the news of her departure. "So soon? You leave so soon? Why? You have only been to one of my parties, and I am throwing a very special one next month. Say you will stay for that, at least."

Melody shook her head and said sadly, "I regret I cannot stay." In fact, she realised that she couldn't even promise to return if Rat was done with his Moroccan assignment by then. If the murders in Venice showed anything, it was that tensions were coming to a boil across the continent and that war was more likely than ever. This was not the time for gallivanting across Europe, cavorting at parties with nary a care in the world. Melody didn't know what she could or should be doing instead, but she sensed that the carefree, innocent days of her girlhood were behind her.

Luisa pouted and said morosely, "Now that I have heard your tidings, I know why I was drawn to wear black today. This is the news that will send Luisa back to her bed for days."

Melody felt very guilty, but she also appreciated her friend's love of melodrama; was Luisa truly as inconsolable as she claimed? For her part, Melody found Luisa a refreshingly original alternative to the debutantes into whose company she had been forced before leaving London. The woman expressed her creativity to the fullest with no concern for the judgement of others. There was something to be learned from this, and all things being equal, Melody would have enjoyed spending longer in Venice studying her outré friend. Nevertheless, Melody knew that the work her brother was doing was of vital importance, and if she could in any way help, then it was worth whatever sacrifices she must make. Melody wished she could confide in Luisa but knew that she and Rat had already been guilty of a lack of discretion; she needed to learn from that mistake.

Two bottles of champagne later, Melody was feeling more than a little tipsy as she bid a tearful farewell to her flamboyant new friend.

EPILOGUE

L ady Bainbridge was sorry to see her young guests leave so soon after their arrival and made them promise to pass back through before they returned to England. With a final farewell, the old woman stood in the doorway to her palazzo and watched them get into the gondola for the return trip to the train station. It had not even been two weeks since they had made this same gondola ride in the opposite direction; Melody could not believe all that had happened since then.

As she took her last look at the beauty of Venice as seen from the Grand Canal, Melody reflected on how different a person she now was from the innocent, naive young woman who had dreamed of finding love in Italy. She knew that only eleven days had passed since then, yet it felt like a lifetime ago. She found her eyes welling with tears and fought to hold them back; she would not allow Rat to see that she had any regrets about leaving Venice.

All too soon, the gondola was pulling up to the steps of the train station and Rat and Giovanni were unloading their bags. Rat went to find a porter while Mary fussed around the stacked luggage, worried they had left a bag behind.

Melody stood looking at the beautiful church on the opposite side of the canal. It was an elegant, neoclassical building with light-coloured stone and a distinctive green, copper dome. Now that she had run out of time, Melody considered that she would have liked to explore the church. She hadn't even made it into the Doge's Palace.

A voice behind her said, "It is the Church of San Simeone

Piccolo. It is glorious, is it not?" That suave voice could only belong to one person.

Melody spun around. Before she could consider her words and, forgetting countless years of etiquette lessons, she spat out sharply, "What are you doing here?"

If she had been angry on hearing his voice, seeing Alessandro's self-satisfied, almost mocking smile infuriated Melody. She had practised what she wanted to say to him so many times in her head, even out loud in front of the mirror at least twice. However, now he was standing in front of her, the carefully considered speech flew out of her head, and she stood there staring at him in dumb fury.

"Ah, Foscari, good timing," Rat said, returning with a porter. "I have the tickets."

"Wait. He is coming with us?" Melody demanded of Rat. Then, not waiting for a reply, she almost snarled at Alessandro, "You are coming with us to Morocco?"

"Well, if we are being punctilious, you are coming with me to Morocco. Or at least your brother is. I was unaware that you would be joining us." At this, he glanced over somewhat disapprovingly at Rat, who merely shrugged his shoulders as if to indicate his powerlessness to control his sister.

At that moment, Melody thought seriously about whether she might not just get back in the gondola and return to Lady Bainbridge's palazzo. Then, she considered what Granny would say about such cowardice and, instead, threw back her shoulders and said in a cold, haughty voice, "Please lead the way, Conte Foscari."

* * *

Note:

Luisa Casati was a real person. From 1910 until 1924, she

lived in the building that now houses the Peggy Guggenheim Collection in Venice. She was a flamboyant character, and most of the outrageous details in this book about her are true (including having a pet cheetah and wearing live snakes in her hair.)

Many of the details I've used here I found in the book, The Unfinished Palazzo: Life, Love and Art in Venice: The Stories of Luisa Casati, Doris Castlerosse and Peggy Guggenheim by Judith Mackrell.

✳ ✳ ✳

Wolf and Bear, the duo you've grown to love, have a friendship and business partnership spanning over a decade. Curious about the beginning of their journey? Never fear. For this short story detailing their initial meet-cute, and more, **sign up for my newsletter** or find the link at **sarahfnoel.com.**

Meanwhile....

Melody Chesterton is off on her next Continental Caper.

Having left her brother, Rat, no choice but to take her with him on his next assignment for Britain's Secret Service Bureau, Melody should be excited about travelling to Morocco. However, that was before she found out that the handsome, charming Conte Alessandro Foscari would be accompanying them. Melody is still licking her wounds after her realisation that Alessandro's flirtation had been nothing more than a ploy to keep an eye on her brother. Or was it?

France and Germany continue to warmonger as they jostle for control over the strategically important Morocco. Melody and

Rat are thrown into the middle of this combustible situation as they hunt down a shadowy figure who seems determined to ignite a conflict that could plunge the entire region into chaos.

Can Melody, torn between the investigation's needs and her growing feelings for Alessandro, navigate a dangerous web of espionage, betrayal, and shifting alliances?
Pre-order the next book in the **The Continental Capers of Melody Chesterton** series, Book 2, **Mischief in Morocco** now!

Pre-order the next book in the *Tabitha & Wolf* series, Book 8, **An Intrepid Woman** now!

AFTERWORD

Thank you for reading *A Venetian Escapade.* I hope you enjoyed it. If you'd like to see what's coming next for Tabitha & Wolf, here are some ways to stay in touch:

SarahFNoel.com
Facebook
@sarahfNoelAuthor on Twitter
sfnoel on Instagram
@sarah.f.noel on TikTok
@sfnoel on Threads

If you enjoyed this book, I'd very much **appreciate a review** (but, please no spoilers).

Pre-order the next book in the **The Continental Capers of Melody Chesterton** series, Book 2, **Mischief in Morocco** now!

ACKNOWLEDGEMENT

I want to thank my wonderful editor, Kieran Devaney and the eagle-eyed Patricia Goulden for doing a final check of the manuscript.

ABOUT THE AUTHOR

Sarah F. Noel

Originally from London, Sarah F. Noel now spends most of her time in Grenada in the Caribbean. The Tabitha & Wolf Mystery Series and its spinoff, The Continental Capers of Melody Chesterton, are the kind of books I like to read on a lazy Sunday: historical mysteries with strong, intelligent, independent female characters.

BOOKS BY THIS AUTHOR

A Proud Woman

Tabitha was used to being a social pariah. Could her standing in society get any worse?

Tabitha, Lady Chesterton, the Countess of Pembroke, is newly widowed at only 22 years of age. With no son to inherit the title, it falls to a dashing, distant cousin of her husband's, Jeremy Chesterton, known as Wolf. It quickly becomes apparent that Wolf had consorted with some of London's most dangerous citizens before inheriting the title. Can he leave this world behind, or will shadowy figures from his past follow him into his new aristocratic life in Mayfair? And can Tabitha avoid being caught up in Wolf's dubious activities?

It seems it's well and truly time for Tabitha to leave her gilded cage behind for good!

A Singular Woman

Wolf had hoped he could put his thief-taking life behind him when he unexpectedly inherited an earldom.

Wolf, the new Earl of Pembroke, against his better judgment, finds himself sucked back into another investigation. He knows better than to think he can keep Tabitha out of it. Tabitha was the wife of Wolf's deceased cousin, the previous earl, but now she's running his household and finding her way into his life and, to his surprise, his heart. He respects her intelligence and insights but can't help trying to protect her.

As the investigation suddenly becomes far more complicated and dangerous, how can Wolf save an innocent man and keep Tabitha safe?

An Independent Woman

Summoned to Edinburgh by the Dowager Countess of Pembroke, Tabitha and Wolf reluctantly board a train and head north to Scotland.

The dowager's granddaughter, Lily, refuses to participate in the preparations for her first season unless Tabitha and Wolf investigate the disappearance of her friend, Peter. Initially sceptical of the need to investigate, Tabitha and Wolf quickly realise that the idealistic Peter may have stumbled upon dark secrets. How far would someone go to cover their tracks?

Tabitha is drawn into Edinburgh's seedy underbelly as she and Wolf try to solve the case while attempting to keep the dowager in the dark about Peter's true identity.

An Inexplicable Woman

Who is this mysterious woman from Wolf's past who can so easily summon him to her side?

When Lady Arlene Archibald tracks Wolf down and begs him for help, he plans to travel to Brighton alone to see her. What was he thinking? Instead, he finds himself with an unruly entourage of lords, ladies, servants, children, and even a dog. Can and will he help Arlene prove her friend's innocence? How will he manage Tabitha coming face-to-face with his first love? And how is he to dissuade the Dowager Countess of Pembroke from insinuating herself into the investigation?

Beneath its veneer of holiday, seaside fun, Brighton may be more sinister than it seems.

An Audacious Woman

The Dowager Countess of Pembroke is missing!

While Wolf is contemplating whether or not he wishes to continue taking on investigations, it seems that the dowager has taken the matter into her own hands and is investigating a case independently. But why has she gone missing from her home for two nights and what mischief has she got herself into? Tracking down the elderly woman takes Tabitha and Wolf into some of the darkest, most dangerous corners of the city.

What on earth is the exasperating dowager caught up in that she seems to have become entangled with London's prostitutes?

A Discerning Woman

It seems Christmas will be anything but peaceful this year!

Tabitha and Wolf are hoping to spend a quiet Christmas at Glanwyddan Hall, the Pembroke estate in Wales. However, before they even leave London, they receive unsettling news of disturbing pranks happening on the estate. Is this just some local youthful mischief, or is something more sinister afoot? Moreover, why is the dowager countess so determined that they not cancel their visit? With the dowager guarding a secret, Tabitha and Wolf are thrust into a desperate quest to uncover the truth. As danger looms, they must navigate treacherous paths to safeguard their loved ones.

Will Tabitha and Wolf reveal the malevolent force lurking in the shadows before it's too late?

An Intrepid Woman

Finally, Tabitha and Wolf are married and they couldn't be happier. The last thing either of them wants is to be sucked back into a murder investigation.

Tabitha and Wolf, eager to embrace their new life as a married couple, have agreed not to take on any new investigations for the time being. Instead, they want to enjoy a peaceful time as newlyweds, uninterrupted by murder and intrigue. However, their plans are abruptly disrupted when a figure from a previous investigation, Christopher "Kit" Bailey, reappears and pleads for their help. Despite their best intentions, they find themselves unable to turn him away and refuse the case.

The Dowager Countess of Pembroke typically insists on meddling in Tabitha and Wolf's murder inquiries. This time, they are relieved when her usual eagerness to be part of their investigations is replaced by an uncharacteristic reluctance to help her nemesis, Kit Bailey. However, the dowager's stance changes when she realises that this case might unearth another of her well-kept secrets, a revelation she cannot afford.

It seems that there will be no honeymoon, at least for now, as Tabitha and Wolf are caught up in the intrigue of London's West End theatres.